A Fairyta' s

Kim Archer

Title: A Fairytale of Possibilities
ID: 20983767
ISBN: 978-0-244-00980-9

K.A Books *Publishers*

www.kikiarcherbooks.com

Published by K.A Books 2017

Editors: Jayne Fereday and Diana Simmonds

Cover: Fereday Design

Author photograph: **Ian France**

ISBN: 978-0-244-00980-9

For Lisa Hallows

Friends know your stories.
Good friends help you write them.

CHAPTER ONE

I wonder if she knows?
I wonder if she knows I'm in love with her soul?

Looking towards the open fireplace, Lauren felt that familiar ache of emotion rising up inside her. It was always the same: that swell of warmth followed by that pull of attraction, her eyes drinking in as much of the moment as they could before being noticed, calling her performance to the stage once again. A nod, or a smile, often a laughing distraction, but nothing that gave evidence of the butterflies or the dreams she'd allowed to live for those few fleeting moments before falling, lurching her stomach and breaking her heart, like they always did, like they always had to do.

"You should sing," she chose to say.

"Something Mary Poppinsy?"

Lauren laughed. "I was thinking more: *I'm a firestarter, twisted firestarter.*"

Rachel snapped two more white blocks from the packet and banged them together. "*I'm a firestarter, twisted firestarter.*"

"What's with the underbite?"

"That's how he sings it."

"Please don't add them to the mix." Lauren watched as her best friend dropped to her knees and huddled back into the fireplace, adding the extra blocks to the mix.

"Toby always did the fires. These bad boys have been my salvation."

And here it came again. That painful joy of the moment, the vision in front of her, Rachel, in what could only be described as a sparkling waterfall dress, sequins of all shades of blue, cascading from neck to thigh, a fluffy white coat discarded on the hearth rug, bright tights stretched at the knee as her body worked, not wary of the soot in the chimney, or the fumes from the blocks; just Rachel, getting the job done as best she could.

"Watch your outfit," was the choice this time.

"Lauren, my lovely, stop fussing."

The sweet address gave clearance for the butterflies to soar once again. It was a constant battle between fantasy and reality, hopes, dreams, imagination... and reality. Her want and need, her hunger and desire, all trying to out-shout the truth. A truth that hadn't changed since day one: an instant connection, an instant attraction; that fairytale of love at first sight. Feelings so loud and full-bodied, never being given an actual voice because Lauren was the only party privy to this narrative, one which had been stuck on repeat for the past eleven years. Of course she'd tried to ignore it and subdue it, even confront it with her own internalised questioning, but she'd found the easiest thing was to live and let live. She was in love with her best friend and her best friend could never find out.

"Me?" she chose to say. "You're the one building a fire out of firelighters. It's May, your heating's on and let me check," Lauren uncurled her foot from the sofa and stretched down to the bobbly rug that covered the tiles, "yes, your under-floor heating's on too."

"You know I feel the cold."

"You're going out."

"Exactly, everything has to be perfect."

"I'm your chief babysitter. I have done this before."

"I haven't."

"You're dating, so I have to experience the heat too?" Lauren knew what was coming. Rachel was still face-first in the fireplace but the perfectly planned mess of curls flicked back, signalling the start of the infamous eye roll. "No come-back?" she asked once the movement subsided.

"Stop it. I'm about to ignite."

"I'm sure you are."

"The fire!"

"That's what I meant."

"No you didn't."

Lauren dropped her gaze and adjusted her words. She'd learnt not to take it too far, the banter they both seemed to enjoy. It was a silliness with no other purpose than to lighten, distract and delight. That was the only way she could describe it, a bit of nonsense that most sane people wouldn't get or even want to understand. It was their ability to not only banter back and forth with everyday chitchat, but to discuss, in great depth, issues that needed addressing. Why had the My Little Ponies become so pissy? Who the hell was that Gladiator with the louse on her tit? Had Lelli Kelly branched into any lines other than shoe? And what on earth should you call that contraceptive implant in your upper arm? I mean she'd be with you for three years; she couldn't simply go by the name 'implant' for that period of time.

It was important stuff and it needed debating, so it was, and it always led to hilarious one-upmanship until the answers were agreed upon, set in stone and added to their never ending list of in-jokes. Rainbow Dash, the pissy pony, responsible for dragging the other ones down, being ridden around by Scorpio, the Gladiator with the louse-looking creature on her tit, who, while riding said pissy pony, was parting her toes with a Lelli Kelly toe divider, because they made them, along with a whole range of Lelli Kelly nail polishes, easily storable in the bottom of your scooter, also made by Lelli Kelly. Who knew?! Well her and Rachel knew, and that knowledge had empowered them. It had united them. It had given their friendship a uniqueness that had made them inseparable for the past eleven years, even with Rachel's contraceptive implant, christened Irma, confirming she was very much into the male of the species. And it wasn't like lesbians couldn't have straight friends anyway.

Lauren smiled to herself as she met the bright eyes. She couldn't lose this. The come-down was always bearable because the butterflies always returned. "Show us your spark then," she said.

Rachel wiggled her shoulders, sending shards of light sparkling out from the sequins.

"I meant start the fire."

"I know you did."

And there was the surge. Not the usual lurch of despair but the surge of adrenaline that coursed through her body on the odd occasions when Rachel dared to flirt back. The first time it had happened, she'd experienced a huge internal turmoil. Should she address it? Should she respond? But as time passed, Lauren decided that Rachel was well within her rights to flirt back without having 'the lesbian' questioning whether she'd had a sudden change of sexuality, just as Rachel was equally allowed to enjoy the flirtations of a friend, who happened to be a lesbian, without questioning whether the banter was something more serious.

So that's where they found themselves, in a friendship brimming with fun times and frolics, their ability to see light and laughter in all situations a binding force that had helped them through the recent difficult years. And while there had been nothing funny about the sheer horror that had occurred, they'd got through it and were on the up, all of them, including Toby's doting parents.

"I can't believe Rosemary and Ken set this up." It changed the subject and calmed the internal dance party that erupted every time Rachel was cute.

"They've been so supportive it's the least I can give them."

"Your body as a thank you?" Lauren pulled an imaginary invoice from her pocket and feigned a dramatic scribble. "Just adjusting my babysitter's fee."

Rachel stifled her laughter.

4

Lauren knew what her friend's different laughs truly meant and this one, poorly held back, was the start of Rachel's wicked giggle. She'd either continue to stifle and use deep breaths and averted eyes to control herself, or she'd let rip with something equally outrageous.

"What if he wants oral sex?" Rachel's laughter was there.

Lauren knew her own humour was uninhibited and loud. She had the kind of laugh that roared out of nowhere, often shocking people around her, leading to more uncontrollable giggles. "Why would he want oral sex?"

"Why wouldn't he?"

"Rachel!"

"What? It's a thing."

"Yes, but not on a first date. A blind date. A first blind date in a posh restaurant. You did say it was a posh restaurant, didn't you?"

"I don't know, they're sending a car."

"Posh."

"Exactly, and posh people have oral sex."

"They do?"

The laugh got louder. "So I've heard."

"Rosemary and Ken? Was your room next to theirs? Paper thin walls?"

Rachel spun around on the hearth rug. "You win!"

Lauren smiled. "I'm not carrying it on, but why would your blind date want oral sex?"

"Why wouldn't he," asked Rachel, repeating the sparkling wiggle.

"Now you're carrying it on! Be serious. Are you worried?"

"About having oral sex at the posh restaurant tonight?" Rachel shrugged. "A bit."

"It won't happen tonight and it won't happen at the restaurant."

"It might. Times have changed. I've not dated for over ten years. It may be mandatory."

Lauren pulled the imaginary invoice out of her pocket once more. "Just adding that to my bill."

"What if he's called Bill or something equally crap?"

"You don't know anything about him?"

"I know the car's coming at seven." Rachel glanced down at her multi-coloured Swatch watch. "Dash!" she muttered, quickly pushing the wicker basket of kindling wood to one side in search of the matches. "Gotcha," she said, sparking up a flame and throwing it into the fireplace as she rose from her knees. The ignition behind her was immediate: A burst of fire big enough to satisfy any movie hero with an explosion as their backdrop.

Lauren jumped from her seat in an attempt to yank Rachel away from the flames. "Watch out!"

"It's fine. I do it all the time."

"Do what?" gasped Lauren, eyes on the fireplace, realising she may have over-reacted somewhat. "Sashay away from a dangerous indoor fireworks display with your sequined dress reflecting the mushroom cloud around the room?"

"Lace the fire grate with lighter fluid. I told you, Toby always did the fires. At least I got it started."

"You'll come home to find me naked and wilting on the floor. The heated floor."

"Is that a promise?"

Lauren controlled her come-back. "Yes. Next to the radiator that's on."

"Ha! Oh, Lauren, wish me luck."

"You don't need it. You look sensational, and you deserve this."

"I don't deserve this, but I know it's time to start dating, and at least the in-laws approve."

"Sorry, I didn't mean you deserved… you know, what… what happened."

"Hey, silly, I know! I was talking about a night of oral sex at a posh restaurant with a stranger recommended by my dead husband's parents."

"Rachel."

"It's fine. I'm serious. You know what to do if Parker wakes up?"

"Ye—" Lauren wasn't given chance to answer.

"And you're sure I look okay?"

"You look—" Again, no time before Rachel's lips touched her cheek.

"I'll text you throughout the evening. Don't let the house go cold."

Lauren didn't even try to respond.

"So here goes!"

Lauren simply smiled as the whirlwind of Rachel bustled out of the house looking and smelling like a firework.

CHAPTER TWO

"If Parker wakes up we have fun, like we always do," announced Lauren to the closed door. "You look more beautiful than words could ever describe," she continued. "And as if this furnace could ever drop below boiling." She laughed, her throat already scratchy from the dry air. Heading towards the kitchen she knew there'd be wine in the fridge. It was another solidifying factor of their friendship. Wine in the fridge. Always. No matter the time, no matter whose place, both could count on the fact there would be a chilled Sauvignon Blanc and a friend ready to listen, or talk, or just hang out side by side.

They were like the sisters neither of them had. Lauren moaned as she flopped herself cheek-first onto the counter's cold marble surface. Sisters who weren't actually sisters, which was a good thing because one of the sisters wanted to fuck the other sister for all she was worth. Gasping at herself, Lauren pressed her face harder on the surface to absorb more of the chill. It must be the temperature of the house talking, not the temperature of her desire. She groaned as she rolled onto the other cheek, her palms stretched out on either side like a limpet sucking onto a rock. Who was she kidding? It was her rampant lesbian desire talking. Rachel was gorgeous: bright eyes, bouncing hair, the cutest button nose that would wrinkle every time her full kissable lips rose into a smile. The most beautiful woman she'd ever had the pleasure to meet. Inside, outside, all over. Lauren groaned at herself and turned, lifting her gaze to the ceiling, her back arched over the chilly marble. Would Rachel ever push her onto this island, spread her legs and tell her she wanted her? She pulled herself up. Nope, of course she wouldn't, she was off having oral sex under the table with Bill.

"Hey ho," said Lauren, "there's wine in the fridge." Yanking on the handle, she smiled at what she saw. The inside of the over-sized American appliance was the perfect representation of Rachel herself. At first glance there appeared to be no method to the madness: stuff just shoved anywhere, bursting at the seams with bits and bobs, odds and ends, half an onion here, a container of beef stock there. Yet on closer inspection you noticed how the contents of each shelf perfectly complemented the theme: ingredients at the top, ready to heat in the middle, edible now at the bottom. Like Rachel. Lauren grunted at herself. Damn it, yes Rachel was edible now, on the counter, legs apart, head lolling back in pleasure, but that wasn't where her mind had intended to go. Her mind had intended to compare the contents of the fridge to her friend's personal appearance. She smiled. Surely even Rachel would prefer the image on the counter to the image of herself trussed up like a cauliflower.

Taking out the Sauvignon Blanc, Lauren accepted that the analogy was fair. Rachel's style at first glance was horrific: mismatched patterns with so many colours your eyes had no clue where to begin. But on closer inspection you realised the clashing of colours worked rather well. One of those styles that made no sense on paper, yet burst to life when worn by someone like Rachel.

Opening the cabinet above the fridge in search of a glass, Lauren remembered her friend's excitement when her husband of only two weeks had agreed to sell his London townhouse and buy one of the four barn conversions located in this just-out-of-town pocket of green Surrey quaintness that only money could find. It was quirky and unique, Toby's need for precision and order outlined in the sleek design of the kitchen and bedrooms. Soft-closing drawers, bespoke cabinets and wardrobes, all matching, all purpose-built, but quickly losing their elegance to Rachel's clutter that had no purpose other than to brighten, but which actually added an elegance all of its own.

The place was enchanting a bit like a National Trust shop. You knew most things were incredibly expensive, the clotted cream fudges, the hand-made wire birds, but you'd also be able to find that bargain bin at the back housing a plastic rainbow-coloured slinky or a pot of green gloop. Odds and ends of stuff that would appeal to someone. Well that someone was Rachel and she didn't so much hoard as collect. On one windowsill you could find her caboodle of cats. She didn't call it a collection of cats, she called it a caboodle of cats because there was no strict rule as to what form the trinket should take. There was a miniature cat plate, a Venetian cat wearing robe and ruffled collar, a clay cat, a Swarovski cat, a devilish looking beanie cat she'd called Chetwynd. Cats of all character and style positioned randomly for anyone inside or outside to see.

On the other windowsill were Rachel's faux Fabergé eggs, more uniform in shape and size, but bundled together in baskets and hampers and an old egg box with remnants of farm still visible. Lauren took her first sip of wine as she absorbed the warmth of the place. It was a literal warmth as well as figurative. Scratch that, it wasn't warmth, it was heat. She gulped down some more wine. It was a heat that was comforting at first as you stepped in from the cold, but quickly became stifling as you realised you had to strip off or die. Heading back to the fridge, she held the button at the front, dispensing a large amount of crushed ice into her glass. The house had become progressively hotter since Toby had passed, as if the heat had protected her friend, or cushioned her somehow.

Looking towards the beamed wall at the far end of the kitchen, Lauren noticed another picture had gone. Rachel was one of those people who snapped photos of every adventure, quickly turning the memories into picture books, collages and canvases, scattered around the barn, up the stairs, in the bathroom, in between the beams; but gradually the memories had been removed. Obviously the ones of Parker and his dad were still in position, as was the odd one of the family unit, but anything featuring Rachel and Toby in a romantic setting had slowly been taken away, one by one. They were bound to be in some wonderful memory box or attic shrine, knowing Rachel, but it seemed like her balanced nature was winning out. Like it always did; like it always would. Take tonight for instance. Lauren could see past Rachel's ditz and bustling, confident that her friend knew exactly what had to be done. Her in-laws had green-lighted her. They'd supported her need to move on by setting up her first date since the death of their son. So Rachel, being Rachel, would be gracious to whichever GP from the family firm they'd sent her tonight, before widening the net all by herself with the confidence that her in-laws approved, or at least didn't mind so much anymore. Lauren nodded, taking her wine back into the lounge. Her friend would be fine.

****

The shriek from Lauren's phone was loud. "It's weird Trevor! It's pissing weird Trevor!"

Lauren double-checked the caller display. It wasn't like Rachel to sound frantic. Giddy and dramatic perhaps, but not shouty and crass. "Trevor?"

"Weird Trevor! It's pissing weird Trevor!"

A glance towards the brightly coloured Dali-style clock above the fireplace didn't help at all. Lauren could never read the damn thing with its wonky hands and artsy numbers melting from the clock face; some ironic meaning about time slipping away from us apparently. Well the time couldn't have slipped very far as she was still on the same glass of wine and only one further chapter into her latest book. "Where are you?"

"In the toilets! I walked in and saw him in a booth."

"In where?"

"Nando's."

"What the hell are you doing in Nando's?" Lauren assumed a more upright position on the sofa. "He can't be there for you."

"He's wearing a red beret. Rosemary and Ken told me my date would be waiting in a booth wearing a red beret."

"Why a red beret and why the bloody hell Nando's?"

"Rosemary and Ken trying to appeal to my quirky side?"

"And the red beret?"

"Helping me feel at ease?"

"By setting you up with weird Trevor?! It wouldn't matter if he was wearing the most out-there outfit in the most out-there hipster café, it's still Trevor!"

"Weird Trevor!"

Lauren laughed. "What's your plan?"

"I have to go over."

"You've not been over?"

"No! It's weird Trevor in a red beret, of course I haven't."

"Right. Switch me to FaceTime."

"Why?"

"You need me. Switch me over." Lauren laughed as her friend's flushed cheeks filled the screen; it never took much. "Oh, Rachel, I'm so sorry."

"It always happens to me, doesn't it?"

"Don't worry, we'll be fine. Tap the camera the other way so I can see out."

"You're not seeing out."

"I need to see out." Watching the picture change to the toilet mirror and reflection of her friend looking into her phone, Lauren nodded. "Perfect. Right, I'm with you. I'll stay with you. I won't say a word. Prop me up against a glass or something. You can see me. I can see Trevor. I'll stay by your side so I'll be fully informed for the after-show de-brief."

"You can't date with me."

"I've wanted to date with you since the moment I met you." It was too good an opportunity to miss.

"Fine, but if you're with me you can't make a single noise."

"I'd be a screamer."

"What?"

"Nothing. Stay strong, it's one for the memory bank."

Rachel's laugh was short. "Yeah right: The time my in-laws set me up with my dead husband's brother."

"And not the hot tennis coach of a younger brother, but the forever single weird older brother whose trousers always do that thing."

The laughter continued. "Don't. I have to concentrate. I have to look pleasantly surprised."

"No, you have every right to be cross. Be natural. Be you." Lauren knew as soon as she'd said it that Rachel, being Rachel, would be lovely. She wouldn't gasp in shock at the awkwardness of the situation or the fact that weird Trevor must think his parents' plan was a go. One brother jumping into the warm bed of another. No, that was unfair. Toby's side of the bed wasn't warm. Two years had passed. People had mourned. Life had to go on. But the substitution of brothers? Well that was just wrong.

"Let's do this," said Lauren. "We'll drop our presence and go."

"I have to eat something."

"Olives?"

"I can't eat olives."

"Olives and nuts then. Something fast."

"Shush. We're walking."

Lauren watched as a ceiling lurched forwards and backwards on her screen. Poor Rachel, always finding herself in these ridiculous situations, mostly the result of her unwillingness to question or confront; a trait that had seen her joining the Women's Institute because she couldn't say no to the woman on the doorstep. She'd also endured a ten week learn-to-speak-Spanish course because a woman on the phone was 'incredibly persuasive'.

Stretching out her legs, Lauren got herself comfy. At least this time she'd be there for support. She nodded, catching a glimpse of the large gecko on the wall; it was the Nando's on the high street, the one opposite her wedding shop, smaller than most with a more intimate design: lime green leather booths, curtains of brightly-coloured beads partitioning the seating area from the drinks unit and sauce shelves. Nice for an impromptu nip over the road and quick lunch during a busy work day, but not as a first date location; unless you were fifteen, or skint maybe.

Lauren watched as the restaurant's glittering mosaic mirror flashed into view. Actually it made sense that Rosemary and Ken would think this the perfect place to send their somewhat unconventional daughter-in-law. But with Trevor their weird eldest son as her date? Of course they probably didn't think his behaviour was weird, perceiving his invasion of personal space as friendly and his inability to talk without frothing at the mouth as an indication of intelligent excitement. But the trouser thing? How could they possibly explain the trouser thing?

On hearing the muffled greeting, Lauren grabbed the cushion from the seat beside her. She'd need to stifle her laughter. This was going to be hard. Peeping over the top of the tassels she waited as the phone, now pressed up against Rachel's sequins, muffled the no-doubt-awkward hellos, and yes, there it was, the returning jolty picture accompanied by a giddy monologue about Parker and bad reception and the need to keep the phone in an upright position in case anyone called. And finally, stability, as the phone came to a rest against a glass just visible in the corner of the screen, giving an unfortunately great shot across the table of Trevor's trousers. Lauren grimaced. The bulge was on form. It was as if Trevor's crotch had been suction wrapped; no matter the trouser the bulge would be there. Lauren shuddered as she peered closer. Trevor was standing, waiting for Rachel to sort herself out. She grimaced again. Her view was of a thing so tight and full, the kind of shape you'd see on a fencer, or a dancer, just not what you'd expect on a middle-aged man wearing a tan suit in Nando's.

Lauren squinted carefully. Given that she'd never stared closely at a man's crotch before, it was the first opportunity she'd had to properly analyse the tautness of the fabric in front of her.

That's when she heard it, Rachel's laugh. It was her inappropriate one – short, unplanned – the one that slipped out when someone missed their footing, or made a faux pas. Lauren pulled back, realising her friend was laughing at her. She raised her hand to cup the imaginary crotch weight, mouthing the words: "Pig bollocks." She stopped. She couldn't see Rachel or Rachel's response and the last thing she wanted was a dismissal from the blind date. "Sorry," she mouthed, hoping the booth was positioned so no other diners would see her peeping face.

Hiding again behind the cushion, she knew she had to be good. She'd sit back and analyse, without smirking, without silliness… but what was that thing on his face? Weird Trevor had lowered himself into his seat, his bulge rising in turn like a mound of dough in a proving oven before disappearing from view, gifting her with this new and equally shocking sight: a pencil-thin beard, definitely drawn on his jaw – or at least coloured in – emerging from the usual fluffy side burns. *Don't rub it, Trevor!* she almost cried as his forefinger and thumb deliberately confirmed its sharpness. You don't need to highlight its presence, we've all seen it, mate, even though your red beret, the one you're trying to wear like a beanie hat, is doing a good job of drawing my attention. She looked closer, focusing on the face art. You've got the Beppe Di Marco and Ken Dodd mash-up down to perfection.

"Well hello there."

Lauren jumped back, pressing the phone to her chest, taking a moment to remember the greeting wasn't directed at her. She peeped again at the screen. Weird Trevor was rocking his body back and forth. What in god's name was weird Trevor doing rocking his body? It was similar to the forward and backward motion one might do at the top of a hill on a sledge. But they weren't on the top of a hill on a sledge, they were in Nando's; the small local one.

Lauren gasped as the tan suit lurched over the table.

"Or should I say *wasssssssssssup*?"

She stared. The tongue was out and it was yellow. Not like the faint remnants of a recent coffee yellow, but like the indicator of a very ill person yellow.

"That's what you youngsters say isn't it?" continued the come-on.

Rachel's voice disrupted her diagnosis.

"I'm twenty-nine, Trevor, with a seven-year-old son."

"And how is Parker the pumpkin?"

Lauren cringed, although the preparation for sledging and lolloping tongue had stopped and her gasp hadn't been heard, Trevor's attempt at being ingratiating was worse. He was forever making up nicknames and trying to sound cool and was one of those uncles no child ever liked, thinking they could impart essential knowledge and be friends, before getting irritated and paying no attention to the child for the rest of the duration.

"Parker's good."

"Says the mother with the rose-tinted glasses."

"No, he's good."

"Tint tint." Trevor was tapping a pair of imaginary spectacles.

Lauren felt awkward in the silence that followed. She knew Rachel wouldn't reply; her conflict avoidance skills were strong, enabling her to keep the peace no matter what the provocation. That's why they worked so well as best friends. Lauren would play bad cop to Rachel's good cop, and if she'd been there now, well, she'd have smashed right through that 'tint tint' with a double-pronged two finger attack. Lauren paused. Okay, she wouldn't have used violence, she'd use her quick wit instead to bring him to heel. *Tint tint? Your new shade of hair colour, Trevor?* she'd say. Or, *tint tint? You don't need the 'n' in there, mate.*

Looking carefully at the screen again, she studied his eyes; they weren't Toby's eyes, always glinting with excitement and up for adventure, they were empty, even when staring straight at you. There was no warmth or intrigue, just eyes that stared out, not eyes that called in.

"So wassssssssssup?!"

Lauren jumped back in shock once again. Trevor had opted to fill the silence with the same yellow-tongued advance over the table. Who in their right mind would think that was an appropriate first-date ice-breaker?

The voice behind the screen was nonplussed. "Shall we order?" It was Rachel in mother mode, able to ignore the naughty child and carry on without escalating the drama.

Lauren knew her friend would try her best to get through, ploughing on as she always did, another character trait she'd once classed as a fault, before accepting it was a key contributor to Rachel's easy-going take on life. The live and let live approach: Rachel never judging or condemning. And she wouldn't now. She'd simply order the plain chicken wrap with a side of halloumi and corn on the cob. Lauren took a sip of her wine and waited, nodding when the voice confirmed her prediction.

"Right. I'm going for the plain chicken wrap with a side of halloumi and a corn on the cob. You?"

"A woman guzzling a corn on the cob on a first date? What a boo-boo."

Lauren watched in horror as weird Trevor mimed an unmistakably sexual head-bob.

"I don't eat my corn on the cob like that."

Lauren snorted. God love her. And she was right; she was more of a normal, horizontal nibbler.

"Maybe I'll find out."

"Yes, if you go and order."

"They don't do table service?"

"You pre-pay at the counter."

"Ah ha. I'm a Nando's virgin. You'll be gentle, won't you?"

Lauren eased the cushion away from her face in the silence that followed, creating enough of a gap for her to drain her glass. This was unbearable. She'd have to get incredibly drunk to endure any more, and poor Rachel, she must be gasping for booze by now.

"I'll have a Cara Viva as well please."

And there it was. She'd be meaning a bottle thought Lauren as she turned her glass vertical and shook it for drips.

"Exotic."

"It's just the Portuguese white."

"Does one recommend?"

"It's okay."

"And what does one recommend for me?"

Lauren willed Rachel's response. Say: a tongue scraper, or a shave, or a castration.

"Toby would always go for the hot chicken wrap and spicy rice. Lauren was constantly challenging him to go hotter but he could never beat her taste for heat."

And that's why Rachel was a better person than she was, always able to find a positive response or a funny story. Letting the cushion drop away from her face, Lauren dramatically yanked at her collar and fanned her cheeks. "You like it hotter," she mouthed, unsure if Rachel was watching but wanting to feel part of the action. It was always the same, Rachel including her no matter the situation or circumstance, never making her feel like a third wheel, always welcoming her as a member of the gang, and they *had* been a gang, the three of them, her, Rachel and Toby. The dream team. The explorers. She felt her stomach chill, not wanting her mind to revisit.

"What's hotter than the hot chicken wrap?" Trevor's face art was looking challenged as his chin jutted.

"Lauren has the extra hot chicken wrap with extra hot sauce on the spicy rice."

"That'll be me then."

"No, it really is rather—"

"You say we order at the counter? Let me do the honours."

"That's very kind of you. Thank you, Trevor."

Lauren watched on as the tan pouch rose to fill the screen. She stared at the tautness. Why wasn't he moving?

"The counter's just behind the beads."

Rachel must be wondering the same thing.

"Yours comes to £13.65."

"Sorry?"

"You're having the large wine? I should have known. £14.65 then."

"*What a tosser*," whispered Lauren.

A zip sounded from behind the camera before an outstretched hand appeared on the screen. "Here's forty, and my Nando's card, I'll get this one."

"There'll be a next?"

"There's always a next Nando's."

Lauren waited for the pouch to push off before waving wildly at the screen with finger-twisting turn-me-round signals.

"Quietly," said Rachel through teeth that didn't part. "And I heard your snort."

Lauren smiled as her friend's waterfall torso filled the screen. It was mostly a chest shot but Rachel's blue eyes were just about visible at the top of the phone. "Get out of there!"

"I can't."

"But his trousers!"

"They're doing that thing at the back too. I see him at the counter. The jacket is too short and the pants are sucked right up his jacksie."

"The front's far worse. He's been balls first on the screen right in my face."

Rachel dropped her shoulders and crouched in closer. "Oh Lauren, how am I doing?"

"Perfectly. Now give that corn on the cob a quick blowjob and get the hell home."

"He's ordered the extra hot."

"He'll never eat the extra hot."

"I know. I should go and warn him."

"Don't. If you're lucky it might put a swift end to the date."

"This isn't a date."

"He thinks it is. And why hasn't he even addressed the fact that he's there?"

"Shhhh!"

"It's fine, there's no one's behind you. Seriously, Rachel, this is wrong on so many levels. What on earth were Rosemary and Ken thinking?"

"And for all these years I thought they liked me."

"Obviously not." Lauren corrected herself. Rosemary and Ken did like their daughter-in-law, it had been obvious from the moment their second son, the only one to follow in the family's medical footsteps, brought home the pretty young PR student. A perfect candidate for marriage and motherhood, exactly what every good doctor would need. "You know they like you. You've been a great wife to their son and a fantastic mother to their grandson. This was probably some misguided attempt to keep things that way."

"I'd never take Parker out of their lives."

"I know, and they know that too." Lauren laughed. "You're right. It must be about palming Trevor off with someone who'll love him."

"I could never love him."

"You don't have to love him! You shouldn't even feel like you have to be there, and you certainly don't need to do another Nando's in the misguided hope that tight-arse Trevor might pay."

Rachel laughed. "Quite literally."

"Come home?"

"Only if you stay."

Lauren lifted her empty wine glass. "I thought that was a given."

"Oh, why can't they do you in man?"

Lauren paused. What did she mean? What did Rachel think would change? The removal of two protrusions in exchange for one dangling one? A shorter hair style? Some face fluff? Women didn't even like beards. They were unhygienic and scratchy. You'd never get a tender embrace, only stubble rash and thigh flare-ups. Yes, she was imagining, but it had to be true. She didn't need to experience the horror of a male to see what was glaringly obvious.

They smelled, they were clumsy and they could never pleasure a woman in the way she could; that was a fact. And the idea that anyone would prefer the male version of her, well, that was plain stupid. She looked to the screen, ready to attempt some sort of reply just as the camera's direction was changed.

"Nuts."

Lauren grimaced. The pouch was back.

"Spicy nuts." The pouch was still there, jiggling.

Rachel's voice was nonplussed. "Lauren puts the extra hot sauce on those too."

"Is that because she can't handle the extra extra hot?" A black bottle with a fiery red cross slashed across the middle was placed next to the bowl.

Lauren shuddered. Don't do it, Trevor.

"Don't do it, Trevor," said Rachel. "They're spicy enough as they are. Sit down and tell me about work."

Lauren groaned. No one wanted a spicy nut death, but no one wanted a monologue about gloves either. Trevor's hobby – because it was a hobby despite yearly proclamations that a gallery show was in the pipeline – of photographing lost gloves was of absolutely no interest to anybody, including the people who'd lost the gloves in the first place. His wanderings, equipment and development costs were all funded by the family GP surgery in exchange for waiting room 'art'. It beggared belief that any poorly person would want to see a dirty old glove lost and lonely in a gutter, or penetrated by a sharp-pronged park fence, but parents did what parents had to do, and Rosemary and Ken were the only ones keeping their eldest child in paid 'work'.

"I found a red one in the sanitary bin at the surgery. At least I think it was originally red, it was hard to tell, but I fished around for another and it was definitely a solo lost soul."

Lauren baulked. What was Trevor doing in the ladies toilets at the surgery? She knew he helped with the odd fund-raising event but since when did a Macmillan coffee morning call for a rummage in the female toilets?

21

"Try the nuts, Trevor." Rachel had chosen to re-direct rather than entertain.

Lauren watched on as the sauce bottle was picked up.

"Let me just garnish."

"Honestly I wouldn't. Lauren can handle anything but even she stops at the extra hot."

"Let's see what all the fuss is about, shall we?"

Lauren winced. Trevor had scooped the sauced nuts into the palm of his hand and was nuzzling down like a pony in a feed bag. She counted. One second, two seconds, and...

"ARGHHHHH, hot hot hot hot hot hot!"

She peered, disbelieving, at the screen and saw the nuts scatter across the table, some disappearing into the lap of the tan suit. Suddenly Trevor's face filled the screen, yellow tongue out, as he fanned his gaping mouth.

"MY EYE! THE SAUCE! I CAN'T SEE!"

The dough ball rose rapidly from the proving oven, filling the screen with a sauce streaked bulge.

"DRINK! GET ME MY DRINK! I HAVE EXTRA EXTRA HOT SAUCE IN MY EYE."

"How have you got sauce in your eye?"

"EXTRA EXTRA HOT SAUCE! SHE'S BLINDED ME!"

"Sit down. Let me pass you your drink."

"NOW!"

Don't let him talk to you like that, frowned Lauren, *and who did he mean, she?*

"Is this what happened to my brother?!" Trevor was gasping between guzzles and squints. "One of her childish dares gone wrong?!"

Lauren stiffened and her hand gripped the phone, painfully.

"Who in their right mind eats stuff like this?!" Trevor tipped back his glass, throwing the water down his throat. "Mother and father have questioned it too! Saying she—"

The screen went blank. Rachel had ended the call.

Lauren stared at the phone in the silence. No, not even Trevor could possibly think that? She shook her head. Could he?

CHAPTER THREE

"How much did you hear?"

Lauren looked at the sauce-splattered sequined dress and her friend's awkward stance beside the sofa. "What do you mean?"

"You know what I mean. How much did you hear?"

Lauren hadn't planned on being sulky, but she'd stewed and agonised for the past three hours. Three hours! How could anyone spend three hours in Nando's? Discussing someone's murderous intent maybe? That or having nonstop oral sex under the table. "How much was said?"

"Only what you heard. Can I sit down, please?"

Lauren left her legs where they were, blocking both seats of the sofa. "So why hang up?"

"I didn't know what *might* have been said. Come on, lovely, shove over would you?"

"And what *might* have been said?"

"Well, nothing could have been said, could it?"

"So why hang up?"

"I didn't want to upset you."

Lauren sat up straighter. "Upset me? Aren't you upset at the suggestion I killed your husband? You know I didn't kill your husband, Rachel."

"Oh, lovely, that's why I hung up." Rachel squashed into the gap that had been created by Lauren's move. "It's just weird Trevor being weird and saying things that should never have been said."

"And Rosemary and Ken?" Lauren felt herself melting at the proximity. Rachel's aura always calmed her, or maybe it was the closeness that made her weak at the knees. Whatever the reason, she was useless when there was no space between them.

"It's nonsense."

"Is it?"

"Of course! The enquiry answered all possible questions. Not that anyone had any questions. Plus I was there. We were all there. It was an accident, Lauren. Everyone knows it was an accident. Trevor flicked extra extra hot sauce in his eye and lashed out in the worst possible way. He thought he was going blind. Can you imagine how traumatic it must have been? The realisation that you've photographed your last ever lost glove."

Lauren managed a smile. "I've been drowning my sorrows." She signalled to the second bottle of wine next to her glass on the coffee table.

"Snap." Rachel laughed. "I guzzled all four pounds forty pence worth in one go, then took myself off for another."

"Was it horrific?"

"The wine? No, rather good actually."

"You know what I mean."

"It was Trevor. He's family." The smile was kind. "But you're more than family to me, Lauren. You're you. And I don't like thinking of you sad."

"More outraged than sad."

"I've said it before: calm will carry you through."

"And real emotions let you ride that riptide called life."

Rachel was smiling. "That, my lovely, is why you and I work. You're the yin to my yang. The oars to my canoe."

"I'm a speedboat."

"Well, I'm your anchor."

"Speedboats don't have anchors."

"Yours does. It's me."

Lauren laughed. She had a mind that made everything visual, a picture displaying itself before her eyes as a sentence was formed, and the idea of Rachel somehow bound up in chains with a curving weight for feet made her chuckle. "You're the lid to my pot." And so the one-upmanship began as the atmosphere disappeared.

"We were young and at uni. We don't do that anymore."

"Ha! Good one. Fine, you're the bangers to my mash."

"You don't like bangers."

Lauren laughed. "You're on form tonight. Right, I've got this, you're the cottage to my cheese."

"Don't go there."

"The King to my Kong?"

"Better."

"The Kris to my Kross?"

Both women started their shoulder shimmy at exactly the same moment, reciting the lyrics to the *Jump* song.

"Wait!" Lauren nodded. "I have it. You're the simple to my complicated."

"Really? I think you'll find you're the blonde to my brunette, so maybe I'm the brains to your actions?"

"As long as I'm the rock to your roll, I don't care."

"I have it!" Rachel was frantically patting the arm of the sofa. "You're the Thelma to my Louise."

"I like it." Lauren paused. "But which one had Brad?"

"No clue, they both go wild at the end." The smile was genuine. "Friends?"

Lauren nodded. "Always."

"Come here then."

"I'm here."

"You're not. Stop moving away."

"I'm not moving away."

"You are. You're doing that impenetrable thing that you do."

Lauren looked at the knowing eyes, wishing she could vocalise her internal screaming of: *You can penetrate me, Rachel! You can penetrate me long and hard, or even shallow and soft, just penetrate me, penetrate me somehow, anyhow, just get in there!* But instead she opted for: "What?"

"It's that impenetrable, untouchable thing."

You can touch me, Rachel, you can touch me wherever you like, whenever you like! Fast, slow, rough, smooth. Grabbing, stroking, just place those gorgeous hands on me. "What?" she said again.

"You do it with each and every girlfriend. The minute they try to pull you in, you always get awkward."

You can watch me do it with each and every girlfriend. It would be a start. I'd be thinking of you. "Come again?"

This time it was Rachel who raised her eyebrows. "You've been with Stephanie how long now?"

Lauren could feel the depression rising. "Seven months."

"Bang on schedule. She'll gift you with something wondrous, she'll give you the chat, you'll pull back to stop her getting too close before you put her out of her misery and end it completely."

"Last Saturday. Diamond necklace. Suggested we take the plunge and move in."

"And let me guess, you've avoided her ever since? Oh, Lauren, I liked Stephanie, she was perfectly fine."

"I don't want perfectly fine."

"What do you want?"

I want you! I want all of you! I've always wanted you. You're perfection. You're my dream. You're the person no one else ever lives up to. "I don't know."

"Stop closing yourself off. You're doing it now. You get uncomfortable and you retreat. Be open to love."

I'd be open to you. Wide open. Wider than wide. Legs at an uncomfortably wide angle. Up, out, anywhere you'd put them, they'd go. "It's just my job."

"But you're such a good catch. Look at you with your perfect hair pulled into that loose bun," she reached out, "these beautiful blonde strands shaping your cherubic face."

Cherubic? Fat and puffy? "You mean my angelic sky-blue eyes, soft skin and rosebud lips?"

"More cheeky cherubic then, like one of those baby angels on a Raphael painting getting into mischief. Either way, you have the most romantic job in the world. What wedding planner doesn't love love? Your fairytale's out there, you just have to be brave enough to open that damn book."

My fairytale's right here in a sauce-stained waterfall dress. "Damn book? And can't I be a flying angel? One of the slim ones?"

"You are slim, and you're tall. You've got it all, Lauren, that's why you frustrate me."

Try eleven years of frustration. Try being the queen of frustration. Try having the perfect person by your side for so long, unable to tell them, or show them. Unable to feel them, or kiss them. Or just love them. I love you. I'm in love with you. Madly. Deeply. So totally and utterly that you render me speechless. "Frustrating," she said.

"Oh, let's just get pissed and chat shit. I want to sing the Kris Kross song with the dance moves."

Lauren jumped up. "Perfect. I'll grab us two bottles. It feels like a nursing night."

"Straight swigs?"

"Lesbian swigs, but yes, straight from the bottle, cradled in our arms without the risk of glass spillage."

"I can tell you about Trevor."

Lauren spoke over her shoulder as she walked past the now smouldering, but still very hot, fireplace. "And his taut pig bollocks?"

"Tongue action."

"What?!" Lauren stopped dead. "He kissed you?"

Rachel nodded.

"No!"

"Yep. Wine. Hurry."

Oh good god, no. Lauren scuttled out of the room, heading straight for the cold kitchen counter. She flopped chest first onto the surface and channelled limpet like she'd never channelled limpet before. Trevor *kissed* Rachel? Her Rachel? Her Rachel with her soft lips and perfect white teeth? Her Rachel with the tongue that would no doubt be timid before finding its feet and kissing the hell out of her mouth. Oh how many times had she imagined it? Pictured it? Dreamt it? And now it would be tainted by Trevor. Trevor with the taut fucking tan trousers.

Opening the fridge door, she spoke to the cauliflower. Just do the laughs. Always do the laughs. The laughs get you through. Like the time they'd almost kissed at university, a game of spin the bottle with a loo roll and rag bag crowd of people from their course. PR girls too pretty to do more than faux peck, PR boys too desperate to do less than deep throat, and her, staring across the circle at Rachel, pleading with the gods of the loo roll to spin and make her whole life worthwhile. And it did. It landed, or sort of slapped and unravelled a bit on the wine-soaked carpet, causing a frantic crawl across the circle on her part, an awkward knee raise on Rachel's part and a banging of noses that still brought stars to her eyes when she remembered it now. The clumsy crash and spillage of more drinks led to the dispersal of the circle with any planned kiss time spent assessing black eyes. And that was it. Her chance hadn't ended in marriage and kids as she'd hope, but in wet knees and fast-onset headaches.

Thinking back now, she was pleased, as she had been with the outcome of their other 'almost encounters'. And there had been a few over the years. New Year's Eve 'grab the closest person' type moments, 'my life's shit and nobody loves me' type moments and even an 'I don't mind if you try it' encouragement type moment from Toby. But each moment was riddled with booze and always egged on by others. Lauren knew she'd rather have nothing than something that wasn't all that. A DJ spraying the girl kissers with booze, a gang of friends proving Rachel *was* loved with a staged snog from the lezzie, or a husband wanting more spice in his life. No, she wasn't willing to sacrifice what should, and would, be a moment of pure awakening.

"Hurry up, lovely."

Rachel's voice halted her heart-to-heart with the cauliflower. Grabbing two bottles of fizz, she dashed back into the lounge, deciding to deal with it quickly. "I chose bubbles. I thought it would be easier to recreate the froth his mouth generated when kissing your lips."

"He kissed the area between my nose and my top lip."

"Like at school? Like fake kissing?" Lauren popped both corks and jumped back onto the sofa, handing one bottle to her friend before adjusting their legs so they were locked in together. "Weird Trevor fake kissed you?"

"I'm not quite sure what it was, but it was smoochy."

"On the skin above your top lip?"

Rachel was the first to spurt a bit of booze back into the bottle. "Mm hm," she said through the laughs.

"Why would anyone kiss the area under your nose instead of your mouth?"

"I've always liked the area under my nose."

"Yes, but not for kissing." Lauren's eyes were automatically drawn to the area under Rachel's nose and the tiny fair hairs that were dancing around as her mouth rose into a smile. "It's a nice looking area, but your mouth's just there."

"He must have missed it." Rachel nodded. "He gobbled a bit on my nose on the way down too."

Lauren spluttered. "What?!"

"He's taller than me. He was seeing me into the taxi. He bent, mouth wide, and sort of sucked and smooched me into my seat."

"What did you do?!"

"I shut the door."

"Oh god love you, Rachel. And then you screamed DRIVE?"

"I wiped my top lip first, but yes, then I screamed DRIVE."

"What took you so long?"

"To scream 'drive'? The amount of froth I had to wipe off my top lip. And there was a fair bit up my left nostril too."

Lauren was trying not to choke on the bubbles.

Rachel continued. "No, he kept taking his food back, saying it was too spicy. It took five downgrades to get him to plain."

"He had plain chicken at Nando's? He's not the right man for you."

"Of course he's not, and I told him it was nice to get out and catch up, but I'm more than happy on Tinder."

"Good one."

"I am."

"Am what?"

"Happy on Tinder."

"You're not on Tinder."

"I think I set it up wrong."

Lauren slammed her bottle down onto the coffee table. "Tinder?!"

"I keep getting matched with these gorgeous professional women and it got me thinking."

"Women?!"

"Why do you look so aghast? I set it up wrong, but it got me thinking."

"About women?!"

"Let me finish. It got me thinking about how you kiss." The smile was shy. "I think I want someone to kiss me the way you kiss your girls."

It was one of those moments that threw Lauren completely. They didn't happen very often, but when they did they rendered her utterly speechless, and then she'd realise she was mute and frozen, so she'd try to think of something to say, which she'd then remember she couldn't, so she stayed silent and frozen until she laughed. She'd always laugh, no matter how inappropriately timed, or how inappropriate a response; it was the only noise that her voice box would emit. Like the time Rachel's mum walked into their halls of residence wearing a neck brace. She should simply have said: Oh no, Margo, what's happened. But instead she was drawn to the way the neck brace pushed up Margo's skin folds and made her perm look even more frantic. So she just stared. Then laughed.

"Why are you laughing, Lauren, I'm serious. I've seen you. You're slow and romantic before getting passionate and wild. I want someone to get passionate and wild with me."

Lauren laughed again.

"But only after that long drawn out slow bit you do first. Men don't do that. They suck on your nostrils and kiss your top lip. Your kisses are like a slow burning log fire that starts to crackle before exploding into pure heat. And you know how I like my heat." Rachel took a swig of bubbles and continued. "Men have one setting: snog. And the snog's always a warm up for a grope, and the grope's always a warm up for a banging, and then you're lying there wondering why the lesbians in the corner are still on the eye-gaze."

"I've never been in the corner while you're getting banged." Her voice was back. Shaky, but back.

"You know what I mean."

"And you've never seen me kissing."

"I'm always seeing you kissing. You have your girls on their seven month cycle of constant kissing before you push them off that kissing conveyor belt into the reject bin like those poor old Raggy Dolls."

Both women couldn't help joining in with the Raggy Dolls' theme tune.

Rachel wagged her finger. "What was that one called with his head on backwards?"

Lauren was pleased for the momentary distraction. "Sadsack."

"No! He was the gingerbread one with those weird top knots. This one was called something random like Head-on-the-wrong-way."

"Back-To-Front."

"Really? What a crap name for a doll. Anyway, you treat your girlfriends just like those Raggy Dolls. But it's no wonder they try to claw their way back onto the belt if that's how you kiss them."

"I'd never kiss Back-To-Front, or Sadsack. Dotty and Hi-Fi maybe."

"And me?"

"What?"

"Would you kiss me?"

"No!" Lauren could feel her cheeks flare with colour. It was worse than St Peter's denial of The Lord. A love so deep, dismissed with one screeching: no!

"Alright! No need to sound so revolted. And I only meant the build-up. I need to make sure I'm getting top notch on Tinder. If my date doesn't start the kiss like you start your kisses I'll move away so we can stop wasting each other's time."

"Women dates?"

"Men I think. I need you to help me set it up properly, but I'll be honest, I feel a bit flattered and maybe mildly, but typically would-never-do-anything-about-it, somewhat curious."

Lauren wanted to look at Rachel's eyes. They'd tell her if she was serious, or drunk, or just messing around, but she couldn't meet them. "You wouldn't be able to handle the build-up," she said to the cushion. It was a crap response, unconvincingly cheesy, delivered with the wrong amount of flirtation.

"Try me, lady."

Now, that was the right amount of flirtation, but Lauren recognised the accent. It was the strange half-Welsh half-Australian one Rachel always did when in role play. Fine, this was role play. She looked across at her friend. This was harmless. She smiled. This could be fun. "Top secret tricks of the trade. I doubt you'll be able to replicate."

"Try me," said the accent once more.

Lauren decided to channel a weird mad-scientist of German origin. "First zee look into zee eyes. Orvays look into zee eyes."

"Do it properly, Lauren."

Lauren coughed. "Right, give me a second then." What was she expected to do? Give a tutorial like she was a teacher? A sex teacher? Fine, how would a sex teacher handle it without getting flummoxed or without accidentally ending up having sex with her instructees? Stay calm and act casual she told herself as her heart tried to smash free from her rib cage. Adjusting her legs, she positioned one foot behind her friend's back and the other between her friend's thighs. Her normal voice had to return. She was good at this. This was her thing. The breath was deep. "Even when you're moving and edging towards them, you hold their gaze. Your body knows where they are, so you don't need to look down." Using her foot she hooked the back closer. "You see, I'm still staring right at you." The smile came naturally. "And once I'm close enough, I stop. I hold my position. I feel that chemistry. I feel our hearts beating faster, our stomachs dancing with nerves. I lift my hand." Lauren raised her fingers to the back of her friend's neck. "I comb my nails up into your hair. I keep staring. I see you shiver." She broke the contact.

"What?" Rachel gasped. "Keep going."

"You shivered."

"You told me to shiver."

"Right. Okay." Lauren nodded before returning her hand to its previous position. "You shiver."

"Well I'm not shivering now because you broke the connection."

Digging her nails ever so slightly into Rachel's scalp, Lauren watched her shiver. "You shiver. I lift my other hand to your face, holding the side of your neck. Your cheek's in my palm. My fingers edge backwards. I'm drawing you closer. I'm looking into your eyes. You're parting your lips." She watched as her friend's eyes closed completely. "Then we embrace. And I'm slow, and I'm soft and your mouth's wanting more, your tongue's hoping for mine." Rachel's lips parted. Lauren watched on. What should she do? This was the end. The instruction was over. Could she move in? Should she move in? Dammit, too much time had passed. She looked again. Seconds, milliseconds left to make a decision. She saw the eyelids flutter. "It's only a demo," she chose to say quickly.

"I know!" Rachel's eyes flashed open, the sequins on her waterfall dress shaking as her bottle of fizz was grabbed and guzzled from. "Anyway, that's what I meant."

Lauren was puzzled. "You were doing your role play voice."

"Of course I was."

"Exactly."

"It's not like I wanted you to kiss me."

"Obviously."

Rachel leaned forward. "But would you kiss me?"

The laugh was the only thing to come.

"Just once. I want to know what it's like."

More laughing noises.

"Why not?"

Lauren looked around at everything and anything, finally focusing on Chetwynd the beanie cat. "We're friends."

"Even better."

"It would spoil things."

"Oh gosh, Lauren, I'm not talking about becoming old lesbian spinsters together. I just want to see what it's like."

"We wouldn't be old lesbian spinsters. We'd be a couple."

"I'm only talking about getting on-trend. Do you know how flattering it feels to get a notification from a good-looking professional woman? Scratch that, of course you do. You probably hold some notification super-matching record, but I don't, and it's flattering, and you always tell me to go with the flow. Plus you have to admit it's all got very fashionable nowadays. I just thought I could try it with you to see if I'd ever actually go there."

"I'm not a tester lipstick on the try me shelf at Tesco. You don't get to dab me on and saunter off again."

"You'd want to come home in my trolley?"

"I'd at least expect a self-scan."

Rachel laughed. "If I'm honest that intrigues me a bit too."

"Rachel! How far gone are you? Remember when you told me you'd carry my babies, like I couldn't because I was a lesbian and you'd be a surrogate? Are we at that level yet?"

"Think of it like this. Skydiving. I guess I'm open to the idea, but am I really? Would I actually ever do it if the plane and parachute were right there? Oysters too. I think I might be able to handle them, and they're apparently all the rage, but would I really? I've never been in a situation where oysters were on offer, or maybe they were but I overlooked them because I'm more of a prawn cocktail girl, but my point is I'm thinking of keeping Tinder set up as it is and I don't want to head off on a date only to stay in the plane and not eat the oyster."

"You can't!"

"You don't have the monopoly on those kisses, Lauren. I am allowed to get some of that action if I want it. I've just never had the chance to explore that side of me."

"Since when?!"

"Since I got notified."

Lauren stood up. She knew she had to get out and process. This wasn't their moment and quite frankly Rachel's blasé attitude wasn't one she wanted to hear. You couldn't just change your sexuality on a whim. A straight friend of eleven years suddenly wanting a slice of the action. She stopped herself. Maybe she should stay and hash this thing out. Wasn't it what she'd always hoped for? Always dreamt of? How was their everlasting love affair ever supposed to begin if Rachel had to stay straight simply because she'd always been straight? Lauren nodded. "I'm debriefing." The correction was quick. "I mean sleeping. Wedding tomorrow. Early start. I'll see myself to my room."

"I might be up."

"You won't be up."

"You're right. You'll come back on Monday though so I can show you my Tinder?"

"I'm not sure I want to see your Tinder."

"Yes you do."

"I know I do."

Rachel smiled. "Night, twinkle."

"Twinkle?"

"You're the twinkle to my star."

"And you're the nail to my coffin."

"Oh no, end on a nice one."

"You are! You'll be the death of me with your whimsical whims and your..." Lauren stopped herself. "Sorry, I didn't mean..."

"End on a nice one."

"Right, okay." Lauren thought carefully before turning to make her exit. She paused to look back at her friend. "You, Rachel, are the sun in my day."

Rachel smiled. "And you're the good to my night."

CHAPTER FOUR

Reaching up to fit the first of three keys into the first of three locks, Lauren's attention was taken by the red Nando's sign reflected in her shop door. She turned to look across the road, wondering where the taxi might have been that saw Trevor make his pass at her friend. She tutted and focused back on her task, catching her nail as she twisted too forcefully. "Oh, sod it," she cursed, dropping the keys into her other hand and immediately sucking the tip of her thumb. She gave it a shake before assessing the damage as if the acts of sucking and shaking would miraculously stop what had almost certainly happened. And yes, it was cracked. No one wanted a wedding planner with a cracked nail. And brides would notice these things. This bride, Jeanie, certainly would.

Spotting her neighbouring tenant sauntering up to his shop front, she shoved the key back into the lock as quickly as she could. Solicitor Sid would no doubt make a big song and dance about his all-singing all-dancing front shutters. And yes, there it was: a flick of his wrist from a good four metres away, dramatic enough to appear in her field of vision, that signalled the start of the show.

The man spoke over the buzzing and clattering. "Top of the range."

"I know, Sid, you showed me the brochure."

"Faster than those locks of yours."

"Yep." Lauren willed the notoriously stiff third lock to be un-stiff just this once. The key jammed.

"Is it the expense that stops you?"

Lauren took a deep breath. "More the aesthetics." Of course she could have shutters fitted if she wanted shutters fitted but shutters like Sid's were an eyesore, especially when positioned next to her beautiful pastel-themed shop frontage with its large arch-shaped windows inviting passing eyes into her homely yet chic office area. In fact, it looked more like a posh lounge than an office with three plush double sofas – all purple – positioned around a bottle green coffee table and one upright armchair, hers, completing the pow-wow. You could also see the large round conference table in the corner with ten additional chairs where the more in-depth planning discussions were held.

She'd originally just had the one sofa positioned on the other side of the green coffee table, naively believing the bride and groom would come to their initial consultation alone: a comfy and intimate first session before moving to the conference table at a later date for meetings with florists and entertainers and whatever else they fancied. Yet more often than not the initial consultations were attended by a whole host of people. Bridesmaids, mothers-in-law, friends of friends who the not-quite-happy-yet couple wanted involved. So the pow-wow of sofas took shape. Rachel had assured her it didn't look like a set up for the school run mums on an outing to Starbucks, and she believed her. In fact, Rachel was responsible for most of the design in the shop. It wasn't as quirky as the barn, but it certainly had character. The square footage wasn't big, it was simply her business base, and the area at the back of the shop with the desk and immaculate filing system was off limits to everyone except her. Rachel might have the style of a fashionista but her organisation skills were too random to trust.

"Speed and security always trump the aesthetics," said Sid. "And I'm in."

"I was looking at my shop." Lauren realised he hadn't heard her. He was inside, probably finalising the divorce of two of her previous customers while she was still staring through her own window waiting for this goddamn third lock to click open. It clicked. "And I'm in too," she said with a nod.

Making her way towards the cluster of sofas, she dropped her bag on the table. Sid wasn't a bad neighbour, more of a brag neighbour: *I work 168 hour weeks. I've drawn up over two million pre-nups. My divorce settlements are the highest grossing around.* Okay, so maybe he wasn't that bad but he certainly wasn't good for her business, a garish sign advertising his half-price divorce fees if the marriage didn't quite 'go to plan', written in a very similar font to the signage on the front of her shop: Lauren Hilliard – Wedding Planner. There had been a beautiful card boutique next door before it moved on, freeing up the lease for good old Sid and his soliciting. Lauren grimaced. Eww, and in fact who knew what he was up to inside those clanking shutters; it was a Sunday after all, seven a.m. on a Sunday.

At least she had a valid reason for being in so early; her own personal policy ensuring she was up and ready for the bride's potential waking, on hand for any last minute emergencies that might have plagued her bride's final night's sleep. And most did call before their big day properly began, just to double-check that she'd double-checked the caterers or the band. Those were the two major fears: a wedding without food and entertainment. Couples hired her to do these checks so they wouldn't have to, but still they did. What checks Sid could possibly be doing at seven a.m. on a Sunday morning baffled her though.

Lauren shook her head. She didn't know much about the world of law but what she did know was that she'd never get shutters like Sid's, totally garish and not at all in keeping with their high street, located in one of the posher boroughs of Surrey, with the Nando's and his stack 'em high price 'em low shop as the only slight eyesores. And it wasn't really a solicitor's shop, it was more of an office like hers, but using the word shop for their premises felt more appropriate alongside the gorgeous delicatessens, the expensive chocolatiers, the designer boutiques and the antique jewellers that were dotted among the quaint coffee shops and indulgent patisseries and the obligatory Starbucks and McDonalds out of sight at the end of the road.

Glancing back out of the large windows at the beautiful May morning, Lauren smiled as she always did at the thought of her great location. She'd made a wonderful success of the business she'd started from scratch. Three years studying PR at the University of Westminster followed by this, her dream job. And, yes, while it might have made her sceptical about love, seeing brides only there for the money and status, or grooms acting devoted whilst slipping her the eye, Lauren knew she still believed in the fairytale; you just had to wait for your happy ending. Stats showed that fifty percent of marriages ended in divorce and of those fifty percent that stayed married, half were unhappy, only a few truly able to live out the dream. She sighed. Rachel was her dream, not Stephanie, or Faye, or Jade, or any of the others, just Rachel, her Rachel; Rachel who could have partnered her in business if nothing else, but chose to get married instead.

Fellow course graduates had dispersed into all sorts of careers: marketing, accounts, advertising, event planning... or marriage and motherhood in her best friend's case. Lauren sighed. What a waste. Rachel had finished top of their year, graduating with a first class honours degree, her eye for design completely unrivalled and her sense of style something that couldn't be learnt. So much of event planning was about design. People had to get a feel for a place, or a sense of an atmosphere, and someone like Rachel was an asset to anyone in the event planning business. Lauren knew that was the major difference between them: their drive, Rachel being one of life's acceptors, just happy to go with the flow. She'd begged her on a yearly basis to join the business, but the most she ever got was help redesigning the office or second opinions on wedding locations; and while that was great, Lauren was someone who liked to know exactly where she was at all points in time. Either Rachel accepted a job description and made her presence permanent, or she was simply someone whose commitment shouldn't be counted on or assumed.

Lauren knew her cut 'em loose attitude was harsh, but ultimate control and complete organisation were the founding factors of the success she'd seen in her life to date. Folders didn't let you down, and the more folders you had the more prepared you'd be. She had folders for venues, folders for cakes, folders for flowers, folders for bands, folders for all eventualities, because as much as the bride entered the first appointment believing they knew what they wanted, Lauren would often find their vision was vague: an ivory dress, a big stately home, a band with trumpets and singers. Well, what style of ivory dress? What sort of stately home? What era of music? That's when the folders came out, giving an actual visual representation of the bride's dream, because more often than not it was just the bride's dream, the groom simply nodding in the hope that it would all miraculously happen.

Then there were the other types of brides, the ones who came with folders of their own, folders they'd worked on for years. Scrapbooks, vision charts, pictures of castles in Scotland they wanted located in London. Either way, each bride was different and Lauren loved the challenge of meeting their needs. It was a drive that was inherited from her parents who'd set her up with a start-up fund and tenancy on the shop that they still insisted on paying. As successful property developers who'd started in the 70s, they'd known which London location would work best and they'd been right. Her simply branded Lauren Hilliard – Wedding Planner business had been an overnight success.

Looking around at her empire, Lauren cursed. Damn it, she was no better than Trevor, kept by her parents. No, she corrected herself, she was making a good wage and could easily afford to take over the payments but they always said no, so she saved for the future instead. Trevor on the other hand? What would he have to offer? Nothing but photos of lost gloves. Yes, she was better than Trevor, but Trevor had kissed the love of her life. Didn't that make him the victor? Not to mention those females on Tinder who were now in the frame, described as gorgeous and professional and a possible option for Rachel. Her Rachel.

Turning away from the windows, Lauren moved to the small kitchen-style counter at the back of the shop. There wasn't much to it: a sink, a kettle and cups, but it did house her top of the range Nespresso machine. She'd quickly learnt that good coffee went a long way with her clients, quite literally being the first taste of her brand they would experience. And although they didn't know it, their assumption was that if she provided good coffee, plush seating and nice décor, the rest would also likely be good.

Popping a pod into the machine she knew she'd have time to re-debrief last night's drama. She'd already debriefed it in the spare room at Rachel's, and again on the way into work, but another hour or so to-ing and fro-ing about the pros and cons, the meanings and the undercurrents of every word, phrase and action wouldn't do any harm. She was used to analysing all aspects of their relationship, so much so that she couldn't remember a day when Rachel hadn't entered her thoughts. September 9th, 2006 maybe? The day before they'd met at uni? Pulling herself up onto the counter, she crossed her legs and leaned against the wall, re-listing the main points as the coffee machine whirred into life.

1. Rachel was open to women. Maybe. Yes, a mistake during the Tinder set-up had jolted the option into her consciousness, so did this mean she'd never viewed her own lesbian best friend as an option before?

Lauren looked across the back of the room at the mirror on the wall opposite. It was arch-shaped like the others that Rachel had insisted on hanging down one side of the shop, replicating the design of the front windows, giving the premises a much larger feel than its square footage actually allowed. She studied her own reflection. She'd been called gorgeous before, in fact she'd once been called hot. Hot and professional were the words used in a review posted by the two grooms whose wedding she'd planned last year. And, yes, while gay men were often more gushing, their assessment wasn't entirely wrong. Blonde hair – hot, tied neatly – professional. Rosebud-shaped, possibly slightly cherub lips – hot, glossed conservatively – professional. Mischievous eyes – hot, always showing interest – professional. Lauren pushed her chest forward. And boobs. She had noteworthy boobs. Plus her dress sense was on point, clothing herself in a manner that wouldn't threaten the brides, but should make them notice her style. Fitted dresses. Nice heels. She took care of herself with manicured nails, short and clear-glossed, but manicured all the same. Threaded eyebrows, never tinted or 3D embroidered, just neatly framing her eyes with a touch of less-is-more makeup finishing off the whole package. Lauren averted her gaze, blushing at her own self-congratulations, her hot professionalism clearly wasn't enough to make Rachel put on that parachute. Tutting, she moved on to point two.

2. Rachel had watched her kissing. What were the words she'd used? 'I'm always seeing you kissing?' And okay, so over the course of eleven years there had likely been that same number of girlfriends, not to mention the occasional flings, and Rachel would have met most of them, but the idea she'd been watching? Well that led on to point three.

3. Rachel had been interested in her kisses. So much so that she could describe them – point four.

4. Rachel thought the kisses looked nice. Was nice the right word? No, she'd used the words slow and romantic, then passionate and wild.

5. Then she'd asked her to kiss her. Actually asked her to kiss her.

6. And then she'd shivered. Actually shivered. Twice.

And, yes, while points five and six needed their own personal debriefing hours the point was they were points – they'd happened. And what had she done? She'd run, so far and so fast that she'd spent most of last night questioning her whole personal obsession. If she was truly in love why hadn't she grabbed the moment with two hands? Pressed her lips against the offered mouth? The mouth that was inches away, waiting for her... hoping for her... wanting her. Wasn't that the dream? She stopped as the coffee machine pinged its completion.

Lifting the mug, Lauren blew steam into the workspace. Yes, that was the dream, but the fact that she was truly in love was the reason she'd handled it badly. Everyone enjoyed a good snog, of course they did, but not when it meant more to one person than the other. What would have happened? They'd have kissed and Rachel would have nodded in confirmation that she did indeed want to check out with her Tinder trolley and go eat oysters before her skydive?

But what if they'd kept on kissing? What if she'd made her next play? She placed her mug back on the counter. She knew she needed to focus. What would she have done? Well, she'd have moved on top of Rachel in one smooth action, sliding Rachel's thighs apart with her own. She'd have pulled their waists closer, forcing their breasts together. She'd have kissed her neck, moving down the front of her dress.

Closing her eyes, Lauren tilted her head back, her legs on the counter squeezing together in a moment she'd rehearsed and dreamt about many times before. She sighed. A moment she'd now gone and fluffed the fuck up. Groaning, she left the dream where it was and refocused on the room, gasping in shock at the person standing in front of her. "Trudy! What are you doing here?"

The teasing voice piped up quickly. "You told me not to sit on that counter, boss."

"I also told you not to creep up on me, or call me boss."

"You told me to be quiet when entering and to address you more professionally. So here I am. Surprise, boss."

Jumping down, Lauren shooed away her second-in-command, a second-in-command who'd somehow managed to outlast all her other second-in-commands even though she exhibited many of the traits she hated in the world of work: spontaneity, unpredictability, impulsiveness. It possibly had something to do with the fact she loved those traits in the everyday person, and Trudy did have the ability to rein it in when necessary.

"And boss," said Trudy, stopping at the sofas, "before you tell me this shirt isn't smart enough I want to say you look *fucking* orgasmic today."

"Enough."

"Legs crossed, head back, eyes closed. Nice dress, too."

"That shirt's not smart enough and you're not needed till ten."

"Bride Jeanie news, but how about I join you in a coffee first? You can tell me more about that conundrum."

"What conundrum?"

"Your *friend*. The one who's secretly in love with *that woman*." Trudy wiggled her own shoulders.

"Trudy, that friend isn't me and that woman isn't you." Lauren tried to compose herself. She'd head to the conference table instead. She needed to regain control and the sofas weren't appropriate. Getting drunk last Sunday with her protégée was a huge mistake. Their weekend wedding had exceeded everyone's expectations and made for a very happy, very rich and very influential bride gushing her adoration and thanks, resulting in more bookings for them, hence the let loose and party incident.

Trudy continued. "I've been telling you all week she needs to just tell her."

Lauren stood in front of the table straightening the sides of her dress. "I'm not telling you anything."

"So it is me!"

"Big day. Rein it in."

"Sorry, boss, that's why I'm here." Trudy's voice was suddenly serious. "I got her the Shetland."

"You did what?!"

"Bride Jeanie. I got her the Shetland pony."

CHAPTER FIVE

"But your slogan says *your wish is my command*."

Lauren upped her pace down the narrow country lane and remained facing forward even though Trudy was trailing behind. "It doesn't! You've been with me for a year now! You should know what my slogan is!"

"What is it?"

"Lauren Hilliard – Wedding Planner."

"That's not a slogan and if you haven't got one I think you should use *your wish is my command*."

"I'm not bloody Jafar, and even if I was I wouldn't trot our brides down the aisle aboard a Shetland pony!" Stopping abruptly, Lauren stretched up onto her tiptoes, peering around at the unkempt hedges and fields. "Where is this place?" The last thing she needed on the morning of a wedding was an impromptu outing to the middle of nowhere.

"A Shetland pony was bride Jeanie's number one must have, plus Jafar was the baddy," Trudy caught up, "and this, boss, is the countryside."

Lauren ignored the remark and re-upped her pace. "She also wanted each guest to walk down the aisle to their own individual song."

"I thought we made that one happen?"

"We're doing song snippets for family and friends. Trudy, don't do this to me. You should know this, you should be able to recite the order of activities down to the minute."

"I can. Arrive at church 10.00 a.m. Check vicar, flowers, choir, string quartet, saxophonist, seating reservations, prosecco van, confetti boxes, red carpet and balloons. All of which I already re-checked last night. But I shall continue: 11.00 a.m. press play on arrival music CD, then 11.30 a.m., or circa 11.30 a.m. press play on bride's entrance CD." The pause was thoughtful. "So what's that wand doing underneath your logo?"

"It's not a wand, it's a swoosh."

"A swoosh that looks like: *your wish is my command.*"

"No, it doesn't and for goodness sake how much further?" Turning to look back down the lane, Lauren spotted their abandoned car just about visible on the grass verge. The good thing about her shop's location was that you could drive in almost any direction and find green fields within minutes, but this place was ruggedly rural.

"Just round the corner, boss. I saw it from the road last night on the way back from the church. I'll admit it's an odd place to set up a circus, but they'll no doubt open a field for parking. I spotted all sorts of animals and just thought I'd ask on the off chance."

"Can't you remember the reasons I said no to the Shetland?"

"Wasn't it a sourcing issue?"

"No, it wasn't a sourcing issue! It was a health and safety issue, not to mention an appropriateness issue."

"But it's her dream."

"To trot down the aisle and arrive at the church altar via Shetland pony? It's not happening."

"But her dad's dead."

"Well he's not been reincarnated as a Shetland pony!" Lauren tried to calm herself, lifting her head higher as she marched through the morning breeze. "Adults can't even ride them," she said, the breeze not helping at all. "And what *was* the name of that genie?"

"I don't know, but they can."

"Was it just Genie?" Lauren made a mental note to ask Rachel later. That's how it often happened, a random thought in the day immediately needing her friend's input, and if she hadn't been further out in the sticks than the back of beyond with no phone signal she'd have the answer by now. Sporadic to-ing and fro-ing was just part of who they were. Neither questioned the weirdness of certain queries, they simply understood they were facts that were essential to know. Like the time Lauren asked about disabled cats and whether any actually had wheelchairs – a picture of a wheelchair-bound, hairless Siamese having come up on her Facebook feed. Rachel had investigated thoroughly and was now a fully-fledged member of an animal disability charity group who sent her monthly reports on the one-legged dog she'd adopted; his progress reports dutifully pinned to the cork board at the barn.

"Paddy told me their height's measured in hands," Trudy was still talking, "and they can carry as many stones in weight as they are hands in height. Sally the Shetland's seven hands."

Lauren re-focused. "Well, Jeanie the bride's not seven stone!"

"She is. She said she was six thirteen on a good day."

"Maybe naked with no hair! For god's sake, Trudy, you told her!" Lauren stopped in the middle of the country lane. "She's expecting this?"

"I had to find out her weight. They had a bigger one too but if I'm honest it looked more like a donkey."

"A donkey?! She'd need a field-ploughing Shire horse with the size of her dress!" She marched on. "What is this place anyway?"

"A circus."

Rounding the narrow lane, Lauren gasped. "This isn't a bloody circus, Trudy!"

"The big top's not up yet."

"*This*," said Lauren through gritted teeth, "is a traveller camp."

"Gypsies?"

The Irish accent was thick. "Don't youse ladies be calling us gypsies."

Lauren clasped her hands in front of her, smiling broadly as her public relations skills kicked in. "Hi, I'm Lauren Hilliard, from Lauren Hilliard Wedding Planners. I believe my associate here,

Trudy Tipton, popped in last night? We're looking for Paddy. Are you Paddy? We couldn't reach him, you, on your, his, mobile." She'd learnt if you ignored the indiscretion and talked fast enough you could flummox some people into focusing on what you were saying and not what had been said. Not to mention they'd have time to appraise your smile and stance and hopefully conclude you weren't a threat.

"Right. Ha-ware-ya? Paddy'll be outta signal. Joe's me name an' oi'm only messin' witcha, traditional gypsy an' proud."

"Hello Joe. Nice to meet you. Is Paddy coming back?"

"Naw! Crossin de fields wi' Sally. De church seven mile away."

Trudy cut in. "It's only eight a.m."

"Yaw seen dem li'l legs."

Lauren took control. "Is there any way we can get a message to him?"

"Boys av de wagon an' carts. Cut him aff at de church?"

"No, no, it's fine thank you." The last thing they needed was a whip-crack-away rag-bag gang of youths whooping and hollering outside St Bartholomew's. "What time do you think he'll get there?"

Trudy cut in again. "He agreed ten-thirty, like the saxophonist and the choir and the—"

"Thank you, Trudy. Sorry to disturb you, Joe."

The man nodded. "She'll be manky from de fields. Paddy'll use de hand car wash just outside de village. You'll find 'imself dere."

"Brilliant, thank you. You've been very helpful." Lauren realised her smile had morphed into that customer services one you see stuck onto those women who don't really want to help, but she realised if she moved her face her poise would disintegrate completely. Turning on her heels, she hissed through her teeth. "Trudy..."

"I know what you're going to say, boss," came the quiet reply as the escaping pace of both women quickened.

"Trust me, you don't."

"You're going to ask me how they're going to clean a Shetland pony in a hand car wash, but don't worry, he said she'd have gold ribbons through her hair."

"Gold was on the banned list!"

"Only for guests because that's Jeanie's accessorising colour."

"Sally the Shetland is not, shall not and will never be an accessory at this wedding!"

"Did you spot the donkey? It was lying down by that first wagon."

"That was a collection of bin bags."

"No. That was the donkey."

"Oh Trudy, why do you do this?!"

"You're smiling."

"I'm not."

"How about Jeanie just walks in holding it?"

"What, under her arm?!"

"On a leash? By her side? Whichever, her dream will come true."

Lauren stopped their walk. "She falls off it, I'm sued. It poops on her dress, I'm sued. It drinks from the font and trashes the church treasures, I'm sued. It kicks a small infant, I'm sued."

"Sally the Shetland's got an awful lot of activities planned."

"I'm serious. It's not happening."

"Two minutes down the aisle. Think of the photos."

"And then what? Paddy the gypsy comes shuffling in to walk her away? Or maybe we could get the men from the hand car wash to carry her out like a coffin?"

"I thought you took risks? You're always talking about your live hard, live fast life philosophy."

"This is work."

"You're right. I'm sorry. I'll sort it."

Lauren looked up at the blue sky dotted with a scattering of wispy clouds. She sucked the cool air into her nostrils and breathed deeply. "Good."

"Am I fired?"

"For goodness sake, Trudy, you're like one of those wind-up toys; in fact you're that monkey with the cymbals."

"Everyone likes that monkey with the cymbals."

"Exactly, even though it's annoying and not something you'd ever choose, you can't help being drawn to it."

"I knew you wanted to play with me."

"Just go and start the car, would you? I need to think this thing through."

"Righto, boss. I've got some shoe polish in the boot and my posh shirt's in the back, plus I have those head-sets I was talking about."

"We're not wearing head-sets! This isn't America and we're not J-Lo. Her representation of the wedding planning business in that film was utterly ridiculous. We're British. We blend into the background. We work *before* the big day, not *on* the big day."

"Look at us now though, boss." Trudy gestured expansively to the unexpected scenery surrounding them. "We're right in the thick of it, and if I had that headset you'd struggle to tell me and J-Lo apart."

Lauren looked at her Janette Krankie-type second-in-command. "Oh Trudy, you really are something."

The smile was wide. "I goddamn knew it was me!"

"It's not you."

"It is me!"

"It's not you, now go back to the car. And it's not me either," added Lauren quickly.

The melody that sang out caught on the breeze as Trudy danced her way down the lane. "*Tell me lies, tell me sweet little lies.*"

****

Standing outside the front of St Bartholomew's church with David the vicar, Paddy the gypsy and Sally the very beautiful gold-ribboned Shetland pony, Lauren couldn't quite believe what she was about to say. "So if Jeanie wants Sally to walk her down the aisle that's okay with everyone here?" The chorus of agreement encouraged her to continue. "And if something happens to Sally, or Sally causes any damage, that's your liability, Paddy?"

"Naw problem. She's gran' is me Sally."

"But you'll take responsibility?"

"I'm a man av me ward. An look at 'er, what's she gonna do?"

Lauren couldn't help but glance again at the cuteness of the little legs and small, alert ears. "She really is rather splendid."

"They've done a great job at the hand car wash," said Trudy, joining the gathering.

Lauren ignored her and looked hard at the vicar. "And David, you're sure the parishioners won't have an issue with a Shetland pony being in the actual building."

The voice was long and slow. "Jesus… was born… in a stable."

Lauren waited for more, but when it didn't come she continued. "And if there's mess on the floor? Obviously we'll clean it up, but that won't be an issue?"

"Jesus… rode in… on a donkey."

"And if the news spreads amongst the normal congregation? They won't write an open letter of complaint about me, or start a petition against my business?"

"The parishioners of St Bartholomew's… were more than happy… to have this Sunday morning's services… cancelled. St Mary's church… kindly opened… their arms."

"Even de church likes de nicker," said Paddy with a wicked laugh.

"The donation… was very gladly… received."

"We're al' as bent as each udder!" laughed Paddy once more.

"Jesus surrounded himself… with beggars… and thieves."

Paddy slapped the man on the back. "An' prostitutes! You're a gran' man, Vicar David, a gran' man."

"I shall be… in the vestry."

Lauren watched the man walk away, thankful that she'd followed up on bride Jeanie's request for a celebrity vicar to perform the service. Vicar David wouldn't have been able to get past the welcome before the saxophonist interlude began and the prosecco was handed around. "Paddy, you're okay staying over there near that bench with Sally? Guests might come and give her a pet when they arrive."

"Can I charge de kids for de rides?"

"No, you're more of a showpiece, like these fire-breathing girls. Hi girls, bang on schedule. If you'd like to get yourself ready Jeanie would like you either side of the church porch." Lauren took a deep breath as the adrenaline began to pump. It was always the same on the build-up to arrival, nerves easing as the months of planning fell into place, anxiety making way for excitement. She smiled. This was going to be one of those garishly awful weddings she knew she'd thoroughly enjoy.

She always tried her best not to judge her brides or insist they be classy, simply working instead to give them the day of their dreams; and for bride Jeanie, with Sally the Shetland now in place, this was sure to be it. Yes, Jeanie's wedding invitation demand that: *All women must stay away from lace and any colours of the blush, champagne, gold, or taupe family* had been bordering on rude, but Lauren had learnt that most wedding guests were of the same social standing as the couple and they'd no doubt view this request as intriguing, just as they'd view the scantily-clad fire breathing girls as spectacular and the three-wheeled prosecco van parked in front of the stained-glass window as incredibly posh.

"The first guests have arrived," said Trudy, nodding towards the pebbled path that led up to the church.

"Crikey, that's early. Is Derek here yet?"

"Who's Derek?"

"The groom!"

"Yes, sorry, the groom's name always passes under my radar," said Trudy. "He's here, with his fourteen ushers. The string quartet's already warming up, ready to start properly in a minute, so as you say to me: this, my lady, is our cue to step back."

"I've never called you my lady."

"Oh, I must have imagined it."

"Confetti boxes in place?"

"Yes."

"That vicar from *Gogglebox*?"

"In the vestry with David."

"Any word from Jeanie?"

"We don't contact them, unless they contact us."

"Did I call you my lady when I imparted that bit of knowledge too?"

Trudy laughed. "In your mind you did, I'm sure."

"Oh go sit with Sally the Shetland."

"You're on back pew duty?"

"No one even knows I'm there."

"If we put those headsets on I could alert you to Jeanie's arrival. You could come out and help me discuss her entrance options."

"The last thing any bride wants, or any photographer needs, are two women flapping around the bride as she makes her grand arrival."

"But Paddy the gypsy's okay?"

"Be discreet, show her the Shetland, advise her to save it for photos, but if she must she can walk in leading her with the leash."

"And if she wants to get on it?"

"You don't let *anyone* straddle that Shetland."

CHAPTER SIX

"She straddled the Shetland!"

The gasp from Rachel was loud. "No!"

"Well, she side-saddled it. Trotted straight down the aisle like Lady Godiva!"

"You said her dress was huge?"

"Huge see-through bits! No wonder she didn't let anyone wear lace, she'd got it all wrapped round her chest."

"Was it awful?"

"The wedding? No, it was perfect – perfect for her." Lauren tilted her head back against the sofa. She was sitting, legs stretched out on the bobbly rug that covered part of the heated floor, her friend on the sofa, rubbing her shoulders from behind. "And Trudy was right: the Shetland trotted in, then Paddy came down the side aisle and took her out. It was over in seconds but the gasps and the photos were so totally worth my outrage and anxiety."

The fingers stopped working. "You know you smile every time you talk about her."

"Sally the Shetland?"

"Trudy the PA."

"She's not my PA, she's my assistant."

"It's the same thing and the fact she's lasted so long tells me a lot."

Lauren turned around. "It doesn't tell you anything. She's like a little Janette Krankie with ADHD."

"You're smiling."

"At myself!"

"She gets on your bus."

"So?"

"I know you. It'll happen sooner or later. You're a lady magnet. You're the Barbie to all of those Kens."

Attempting to position herself back under the fingers, Lauren jiggled her shoulders to get the soothing started again. The heat from the crackling fire, roaring radiators and under-floor heating meant she was already down to her vest top, but it was nothing compared to the close contact from her very hot friend. The first time she'd been massaged by Rachel, she'd almost fainted because she'd forgotten to breathe; Rachel's fingers on her flesh had been too much to handle. They'd been in her small room at uni, her back jarred from a fall on a night out; Rachel had offered to sort it. Lauren remembered how she'd pictured Rachel's lips joining in on the action, her fingers moving round to the front, tweaks and twists starting the come-on, but none of it ever happened, and over the years it continued to not happen, so she'd learnt that even though the massages were incredible, they were always of the standard variety and she should just breathe instead of imagine.

"Trudy's not butch," she chose to say, "she's just a bit boyish, in a pretty way. But she's far too short for me and I'd never mix business with pleasure."

"Defensive and defending. Interesting."

"Oh, take away the spotlight and pass me your Tinder. I'll set it up properly so *you* don't end up with a Janette Krankie all of your own." The shoulders wiggled once more. "Keep going though. It's lovely."

"Lovely? I'm trying to be forceful." The soothing stopped completely. "Is that why you always go for tall lesbians? Big hands?"

"You know what they say about big hands."

"Wide fingers?"

Lauren laughed. "First you heat your house so I have to strip off, then you offer me one of your massages, then you start talking about wide fingers. What's with you tonight?"

"What is it then? Big gloves?"

"Hard fucks actually."

"Lauren, you dirty bitch!"

"You started the vulgarity!"

"I mentioned wide fingers."

"Women with big hands don't have wide fingers, they have long fingers. Long, nimble, skilful, dancing fingers."

"Mine dance."

Lauren couldn't help but laugh as the fingertips started to quick-step over her shoulders. "Now make them cha-cha."

"Always so demanding."

"It's the only way to get what you want."

The pause was notable. "Is it?"

Tilting her head over her shoulder, Lauren caught Rachel's gaze move towards the fireplace. "You okay?"

"Yep, come on." The focus was back. "You need to sort out my Tinder. Just delete it and start again. Ooo, hang on." Rachel lifted her phone. "I've got a notification."

Craning her neck, Lauren tried to look at the screen. "Show me?"

"I should ignore it."

"Show me!"

"Wait."

Pulling herself onto the sofa, Lauren saw a red flame in a white box congratulating Rachel, telling her she had a new match. "You should click it. This might be Mr Right."

"You think?"

"Definitely."

"Fine." Rachel clicked. "Mr Right's called Jenny."

Lauren studied the small round picture. "How have you been matched with a woman called Jenny? She's absolutely gorgeous."

"I told you. Maybe *I'm* the lady magnet?"

"No. You must have swiped her first."

"I haven't swiped anyone first. And why is it so hard for you to believe a gorgeous woman like Jenny might like me? Fair enough, I'm not your cup of tea, but I seem to be Jenny's drink of choice."

Lauren paused for a second. Rachel was more than her cup of tea, she was her shot of tequila, her elixir, her antidote, the one taste she wanted lingering on her tongue. "I'd drink you," she said without thinking.

"Like a child being force-fed cod liver oil."

"More like a connoisseur tasting fine wine."

"That's right, you'd judge me, wouldn't you? And I wouldn't want that with all your experience and whatnot."

"I'd tipple your fancy."

"My fancy's not fancy."

"I fancy it."

"What are we talking about?"

"I don't know." Lauren stopped. Rachel didn't want to hear how she'd obsessed about sipping from her sweet cup of love, how she'd dreamt of parting her waves and throwing herself deep into her ocean to lap up as much of her tide as she possibly could. "You must have swiped her." She thought it best to get back on topic. "Tell me what you did when you joined."

"I logged in with my Facebook, obviously clicked some wrong boxes and this woman's face just appeared, a weird one, more of a nostril shot, so I scrolled to get rid of it and another face popped up. There were men, women, couples, even some animals."

"So you kept scrolling left?"

Rachel's thumb twitched left. "Like you do with photos, yes. But then I flicked past this one rather handsome man and I tried to get him back."

"So you swiped right?"

Rachel's first finger was now twitching right. "I was trying to find him."

"Then what happened?"

"Well, I kept looking until a screen flashed up saying I was out of likes. It said I'd get more in twelve hours so I just left it. I've been getting these matches ever since."

"No wonder! You get a hundred likes on Tinder! You must have swiped right on a hundred people! If any of those then go on to right-swipe you, you get a notification like this. And FYI there aren't actual animals on there, it simply uses a person's Facebook profile picture."

"How do you know so much about Tinder?"

"Everyone knows you right-swipe if you like someone."

Rachel squinted at the small image on the screen. "I'm clicking her."

"Don't!"

"Too late. Oh yes, I do remember seeing her now. Look, she's given me some information."

"She hasn't given you information, that's general information."

"She says she's a thirty-year-old lawyer looking for the love of her life. That's sweet."

"That's general."

"And there, she's asking me to insert a compliment below."

"No, Tinder's asking you to insert a compliment below."

"I'm inserting a compliment below."

"Don't you dare."

"Why not?"

Lauren didn't know what to say. *Because I'd rather you insert your compliment into me? Because I'd rather you swiped your finger over me?* Left, right, up, down, multi-directional swiping, soft swiping, slow swiping— "Because I like her."

"You do not."

"I do, she's gorgeous, and now Stephanie's off the scene I might just start swiping myself."

Rachel's eyebrows raised slowly.

Lauren got it. They both always got it. "Don't tell me you're not a self-swiper."

"I'm not saying anything."

"Everyone self-swipes. Especially straight women. It's the only pleasure they get."

Rachel laughed. "Toby wasn't that bad."

"And there we go, straight women thinking it's okay to have 'not that bad', gushing about that one occasion on their honeymoon when he really took his time and she actually had one without having to force it."

"And here we go. Lesbians announcing they're such great lovers."

"We are."

"I guess I'll compliment Jenny and find out then."

Lauren shook her head. "Not all women are good in bed."

"Aren't they?"

She paused, actually they were. Women knew what felt right and they weren't in a rush. Two things that the male of the species couldn't lay claim to. Again, total speculation given the fact she'd never actually sampled the salami, but she'd heard enough rantings from straight friends and frustrated brides to know the facts: men found the giving of orgasms chore-like and difficult. In fact, they probably enjoyed emptying the filter on the tumble dryer more and did so with greater frequency and success. "All women are good in bed. Apart from the ones called Jenny," she said. "They're shit."

"Just Jenny?"

"Yes. And I've heard she's got a big bush."

Rachel laughed. "Good, I can make use of those secateurs Rosemary and Ken bought me last Christmas."

"You really want to compliment her?"

"She's got nice eyes."

I've got nice eyes, screamed Lauren. And they're looking at you. They're always looking at you. They see you on your good days and your bad days and they shine. They're shining now. Look at them shining! "Can't we go back to my shoulder massage?"

"I bet Jenny's not as demanding as you. Seriously, Lauren, have you ever seen eyes quite like these?"

Lauren looked carefully then nodded, satisfied she was about to deliver the appropriate level of vengeance. "Is that a stye?"

Rachel laughed again. "Fine. You win. I won't message her."

"Why not?"

"She's all yours."

"I don't want her."

"Make your mind up, would you?"

It's made up. I'll marry you. I do. We will. Forever and always, till death us do part. "I'm not on Tinder."

"No, but you'll do your reverse image search, hunt her down and make her yours until you dispose of her and move on to your next victim."

"They're not victims, they're just not, not..." *Not you!* she silently screamed.

"It's fine. Look. Boom. Another notification. You take Jenny, I'll take this bitch."

Lauren laughed. "A few days on Tinder and look at you, you call girl."

"I'm not a prostitute."

"Yet."

"Oh, Lauren, I wasn't serious about your next victim."

"I'm not serious either. I'm just not used to you getting all the attention, that's all."

"Because it's always on you?"

"It's not. I'm sorry. Maybe I'm a bit jealous."

"That the attention's not on you?"

"No, that it's not me..." Lauren's gaze shifted to the wonky Dali clock above the fireplace. Why did time always seem to stand still when she was struggling to find her words?

"Exactly."

Giving you the attention, she was about to say.

"I'm clicking on this new notification and messaging whoever it is. Here goes."

Lauren gasped as the image filled the screen. "Holy mother of hell, who's that?!"

Rachel spoke through her grimaced squint. "That's Stacy, 34, unemployed. She says she's looking for fun girls to get dolled up, wined up and dressed up so we can have our wicked ways with

each other… Ballet dancers, nurses, underwear models, teachers—
"

"She doesn't want much."

"It carries on. Teenagers, hippy chicks, goth whores and anything else your deepest darkest fantasies desire."

"Not goth whores."

"Let me finish. It says: let's kiss, nibble, stroke and caress each other's bodies and minds all night long."

Lauren nodded. "Sounds perfect for you."

"Don't."

"What are you waiting for?"

Rachel's pause silenced the room. The voice that finally emerged was quiet. "You," she whispered.

"I'm not messaging her."

"Oh damn it, Lauren." Rachel's volume was resumed. "Always there with the jokes, aren't you?"

"You love my jokes." It was her knee jerk reaction. It always had been. Laugh it off whenever she thought she heard tone or meaning. She wouldn't let herself believe. She couldn't let herself believe.

"There are lots of things I love about you."

"My big hands?"

"Yes, Lauren, your big hands." Rachel shook her head and moved her feet down to the bobbly rug. "Seriously, I can't do this anymore."

"Do what? Come back. Sit down."

"I can't do this and I certainly can't start off again with someone new. I don't want to sift through all the goth whores in the hope I might find someone special when—"

"Jenny's a start."

"I'm not messaging Jenny."

"Wise. She's got a big bush."

"Let me finish." The smile arrived on Rachel's lips. "But that was funny."

Lauren spoke quickly. "So let's keep things light. It's what we're good at."

"What if we're good at more?"

Lauren didn't know where to look. She laughed nervously instead. "You're not going to ask me to kiss you again, are you?"

"I was thinking about it."

"So you can practice for Jenny?"

"No, so I can... will you *please* just look at me?"

"I can't."

"Why can't you look at me, Lauren?"

Lauren knew the line. She'd prepared it years ago. It was dramatic, but it was the truth. *I'm afraid my eyes will betray what my heart wants to say.* Connecting their gaze, she took a deep breath, jumping instead as the noisy door latch clicked open.

"Mummy! I had that bad dream again."

Parker was standing behind them, clutching on to his cuddly. It was the last remaining intact piece of yellow cot blanket she'd bought as a gift seven years ago when he'd been born. "Hey, Parker, my favourite ever godson."

"Hey, Aunty Lauren."

Rachel got up and reached out her hands. "It's okay, champ, I'll come in for a cuddle."

The young boy ran around to Lauren. "Can't I stay with Aunty Lauren for a bit?"

Lauren loved the way she'd always been 'aunty.' Her younger brother was nowhere near ready to settle down and her older sister had married into a ready-made family with older children who already had aunties of their own. "Shall I tell you a story?"

"It's too late for stories," said Rachel, reaching out for her son once again.

"Please, Mummy?"

"No, it's too late for stories."

"One of Aunty Lauren's funny songs then?"

"Certainly not one of Aunty Lauren's funny songs."

The young boy snuffled into his cuddly. "But my bad dream was about Daddy."

"Oh, Parker, come here." Rachel finally managed to pull the boy in to her side. "Just one verse then."

"And you'll come to bed with me?"

"I'm not ready for bed yet. Aunty Lauren's here and we've got some business to attend to."

"Business?" said Lauren with a whisper. "That we're attending to?" she added, with a deliberate gulp.

The young boy continued. "But my bad dream was about Daddy and you got taken away too and I want you to sleep with me so I know you won't go away like he did."

Lauren reached out and ruffled the curly hair. It was Rachel's hair, wild and full of life. "I was heading home in a minute, so how about I give you one verse and then you try to be a brave boy and go back to bed by yourself?"

"I want Mummy."

"Two verses and back to bed by yourself?"

Rachel cut in. "It's fine. You're going."

The young boy threw down his cuddly and broke free of the arms, bouncing onto the sofa. "Yay! Can it be about me?"

Lauren tried to catch Rachel's eye. Parker was fine. He'd been fine for the past two years. And, yes, while losing his father at age five couldn't have been easy, he'd coped well and would only have sudden bouts of remembering at times like these. Both she and Rachel, and Rosemary and Ken, had done their own individual research on grief and how it might affect a child. Rachel's expat parents, Margo and John, had returned briefly from Spain to offer their condolences but had dashed back as soon as was politely possible. Their advice had centred around a dose of soothing sun on everyone's skin – a week or so, nothing permanent obviously – but Rachel had declined and the doctors and counselling route was taken instead. Thankfully, Parker was young and strong and more often than not these 'memories' were testing rather than poignant: Daddy used to play football with me every night for five hours, you need to keep playing. Daddy always let me have pick and mix and popcorn at the cinema, I remember. Daddy would let me stay up late and watch films. Toby would in fact do none of those things, but no one wanted to tell a bereaved seven year old the truth: his father was a good but busy man.

"A funny song about you?" said Lauren with a smile. "Okay then." It was one of her party tricks. She could pen a verse about anyone or anything immediately and on the spot, always sung to the tune of Twinkle Twinkle Little Star.

"*Parker Parker you're so cool, but it's Monday and there's school. If you don't go straight to bed, you'll turn in to a blockhead. So Parker Parker close your eyes, or you'll always be pint-sized.*"

"What's pint-sized."

"Small. You need sleep to grow."

"He doesn't know what a blockhead is either," added Rachel.

"Yes I do. It's someone like Uncle Trevor."

"Parker!"

"What? Aunty Lauren taught me. Do the one about Uncle Trevor."

Lauren coughed. "No."

"Please!"

"Okay. *Uncle Trevor's head is big, and I think he wears a wig.*"

"I think we'll stop there," said Rachel. "Bedtime."

"No!" squealed Lauren and Parker in unison as the singing continued. "*He kisses like he needs a cloth, as there is a lot of froth.*"

Rachel let out a laugh. "Stop it."

Lauren finished off. "*Uncle Trevor is alright, shame his trousers are so tight.*"

"See," said Rachel, finally managing to lift her son into her arms before whispering over his shoulder to Lauren, "there are so many reasons to love you."

CHAPTER SEVEN

"What's the difference between saying you love someone and saying you're in love with someone?" Lauren was sitting at her desk at the back of the shop, loudly directing her question towards the round conference table where Trudy was surrounded by two hundred Velcro name tags and one humongous seating plan. Lauren knew she didn't have to shout, the distance between them wasn't great, but she wanted her voice to sound firm and thoughtful rather than weak and uneasy.

Trudy kicked back on her chair and interlocked her fingers, pretending to crack out her knuckles. "Trust Trudy time again, is it?"

"I'm just asking."

"For that friend?"

"Forget it."

"No, no, pull up a chair, I'll guide you through it."

"You haven't got time to guide me through it."

"Camilla and her party of groupies? Actually, I'm using the word *party* loosely there, aren't I? Who has a dry wedding with no children on the anniversary of their mother's death?"

"Camilla does and we respect her wishes, and apparently it's just her and Ian today."

"Who's Ian?"

"The groom! Trudy, the wedding's in two weeks, you should know this by now!"

Trudy lifted the Velcro name tag. "Ian – groom. You're so easy to wind up, boss, but in all seriousness everyone knows you need alcohol and kids to make a good wedding." The fingers were flexed once again. "And of course love. Not the kind of love you have for a brother or sister, or a mother or father, but the kind of love you have for someone who arouses you, who stimulates you. Someone who piques your desire with their loaded questions and sexy work outfits. Nice dress by the way, boss."

Lauren raised her eyebrows. "We both know you don't need that for marriage. We've seen enough couples come through here for the status or the money, or quite simply the lack of better options, and my original question wasn't loaded, and please, for the umpteenth time, don't be inappropriate."

"You get flummoxed too easily."

"You take it too far."

Trudy stood up and walked to the back of the shop. "I just blur the line between boss and best friend."

"We're not best friends."

"You *can* have more than one you know. And it's important to have someone to go to when you need to talk about her."

"Who?"

"Rachel. I can be that person. We can go for coffees and gossips; we'll grow close and you'll realise it's actually me you want."

"I don't want Rachel."

"So you *do* want me?"

"Just go back to your plan, would you?"

"Camilla will only change it when she arrives. This is more important. I feel like we're nearing a breakthrough." Trudy nodded her head and spoke gravely. "I know," she said.

"You don't know anything."

"I know that being in love is physical, not just emotional. Okay, here goes."

Lauren watched as Trudy stole the ruler from the perfectly organised pot of stationery on her desk. "Put that back."

"No. I've lost mine." Trudy lifted it like a lecturer instructing a class. "I'll ease you in gently. Think of something non-human that you say you're in love with."

Lauren smiled. Despite being an irritant, Trudy was annoyingly entertaining: always full of energy and enthusiasm no matter how many times she was chastised. "They'll be here at ten."

"You asked me the original question, so now I'm answering it. Tell me something you're in love with."

"Fine." Lauren rolled backwards on her chair, crossing her legs to the side of her desk. "Chocolate." It was the obvious choice.

The slow pacing began. "Because of the way it makes you physically feel. The taste on your tongue, the way it melts in your mouth."

"Fine, I'm in love with my friend's ice-making machine."

"On a fridge freezer?"

Lauren nodded.

"Crushed ice?"

Lauren nodded again.

"Nice. You're in love with it because you anticipate what it can do, how it can satisfyingly crunch the ice, the sound it makes is pleasing to your ears, the waft of cool air feels great on your skin, the shudder and prickles you experience when you finally take a piece inside your mouth…"

"You do talk some bollocks, Trudy."

"Listen, if you're in love with someone, your body reacts. If you love someone you have a very strong liking for them but they don't do anything to you physically."

"My heart swells when I look at my godson."

"But it doesn't flutter and it doesn't race, and I bet it only swells occasionally during a proud moment or a time where he says something cute or has learnt something new. You're fond of him, there's a friendship and a respect, a certain devotion I guess, but there's not desire."

"Of course not."

"Think of the chocolate again. You're infatuated. There's a lust and a passion. A yearning and a greed for its flavour, for its taste, for the way it makes you feel. Your godson makes you feel happy, but that piece of chocolate turns you on."

"Chocolate doesn't turn me on."

"You've never used chocolate to turn you on? I lost four Maltesers once."

"Too much, Trudy."

"You're turned on, aren't you?"

"I'm not turned on."

"Someone like Rachel will enjoy Maltesers."

"Why do you keep mentioning Rachel?"

Trudy slapped the ruler onto the desk. "Because I know!"

"Steady!"

"You don't have to cover your ears, boss. I've known since the first time I met her." The cough was regretful. "And I apologise for the noise, but I'm making a point. Listen, you didn't fire me for sending Sally the Shetland down the aisle, so you won't fire me now, even as I dare to say the unsaid." The intake of breath was dramatic. "You're in love." Trudy paused before nodding and resuming her pace. "And how do I know this? Well, apart from your glaringly obvious drunken gushings about a curly-haired free spirit, you become a completely different person when you're with her."

"I do not!"

"You do. In fact, it's gorgeously cute and endearing. You become unsure of yourself and you're quieter."

"I'm not quiet around Rachel."

"Well you're certainly not the bolshy, power-dressing ball-buster I see at work. You become giggly and doe-eyed."

"She's my best friend of eleven years. I don't get doe-eyed. And I'm not entertaining this, I'm just waiting to see how far you take it."

"I'm taking it all the way, boss. Fine, maybe quieter's not the word. You become attuned, more so than usual. All of your senses are in overdrive so there's more thought to your processing and reactions."

Lauren paused. Trudy had hit the nail on the head. She wasn't a toned-down version of herself with Rachel, but a more receptive and aware version of herself: sometimes funnier, often more sensitive, but definitely more mindful... of everything. That's why so much debriefing had to be done. She sighed. She'd been up half the night trying to figure out what Rachel had been saying before Parker woke up. The bottom line was she'd honestly never once entertained the idea her best friend might like her... that way. She was straight. Straighter than straight. Straighter than any other straight woman who'd found their man at nineteen and been happy. Yet there'd been a tone to the way Rachel had said 'you.' *What are you waiting for?* was the joking question. *'You'* was the serious answer. Lauren heard the ping of the coffee machine and refocused. Trudy was carrying two steaming mugs towards the purple sofas.

"I thought I'd give you a moment. Now come. Sit. I used the hot chocolate pods. Appropriate, don't you think?"

Lauren's laugh gave way to the deeper emotion evoked by the unfolding scene as Trudy carefully placed the mugs on the bottle green table with a plate of her favourite biscuits. Now Trudy was sitting with one arm across the top of the sofa, the other sweeping the purple velvet, as if to say: squeeze in, I'm ready, I'm here for you.

"You okay, boss?"

Lauren knew she wasn't okay. This simple gesture was more than a cheeky colleague wanting the gossip, it was a friend offering her hand, a hand she'd never accepted in the past... from anyone. She had friends and acquaintances, of course she did, but no one she'd ever open up to, apart from Rachel, and she couldn't talk to Rachel about Rachel so her thoughts were always kept in check.

"You don't have to say anything. We can just sit together and take five if you like."

The emotion rose up once again. Trudy, for all her faults, was a genuinely nice person; in fact she'd make a great friend, but she'd never had the courage to let anyone in. Rachel was in and that was all she needed… wasn't it? Coughing at the lump forming in her throat, Lauren tried to stop herself by biting her lip, her fingers quickly moving to halt an escaping tear. Why was she upset? This was ridiculous. She was a strong woman. She didn't need anyone; she'd never needed anyone… but maybe because no one had ever really been there. Not like this anyway.

Turning on her chair, Lauren tried to regain her composure, finding the wall easier to face than her fears. It was a fear of saying it out loud. This secret she'd kept for so long. This irrational, unstoppable attraction that was affecting all parts of her life: sleepless nights, half-hearted relationships, a basic inability to grasp any sort of conscious control.

"Oh my lovely, it can't be that bad. Turn round and come here."

"Don't call me lovely. Rachel calls me that." Lauren shook her head. Being guarded was the easiest option, it always had been. She swallowed. But having no one to talk to had hurt her the most.

"Just sit. Come and sit. Snuffle if you like."

"I'm not a snuffler."

"They say the minute you say it out loud it's no longer such an issue."

Lauren dared to turn around. "I want it to be an issue, or I thought I wanted it to be an issue," she picked up the discarded ruler and flicked it gently between her fingers, "until it appears it might be an issue and I'm no longer quite sure."

"Are we talking about snuffling?"

The laugh came all by itself. "Oh, Trudy. Look at you sitting there all sweet."

"And look at you sitting there all alone."

Lauren knew the comment wasn't meant with malice and Trudy was right, she was alone; one of those popular people who appear to have the world at their feet, able to take what they want and live how they please, when really they just want to be found. She took a deep breath. "Can I trust you?"

"You're in love with your best friend. I already know that. It's glaringly obvious every time she's here."

"She doesn't know."

"Of course she knows. They always know."

"She's not just any old straight girl."

"No, Rachel's a really smart woman. Crikey, she'd be such an asset to the business."

"You don't think I've tried?"

"And she always says no. She's said no because she *knows* she's your world and she doesn't want to encroach on every aspect of your life."

"She can encroach all she likes. She's there already; in my thoughts, my dreams, my plans."

"And your cross-legged, on-the-counter, head-tilted-back fantasy daydreams."

"Oh, stop it!"

"That's it, you're smiling. Now come over and sit down."

"That hot chocolate better be worth it."

Trudy took a sip from her mug. Her groan was long. "It's orgasmic."

"Fine." Lauren made her way to the sofas. She needed to do this; in fact, she wanted to do this. "Where do I start?"

"Let the froth brush against your top lip as you let the chocolate pour over your tongue."

"I was talking about talking."

"Oh god, you do know I'm not qualified, don't you? And Camilla's coming at ten."

Lauren laughed. "You're such a little shit, Trudy."

"But I got you sat down and smiling and you've even chosen the seat next to me, not your upright armchair, so that's a start."

"I don't want to talk too loudly."

"Solicitor Sid can't hear."

"You never know with that man." Lauren took a sip of her drink and smiled. "Ooo, this really is good."

"Talking's good too, so are friendships, and letting people in, and I added sugar."

"You added sugar to hot chocolate? Who does that?" Lauren let it lie. "Fine. I guess I've not wanted to feel vulnerable and the fact I'm your boss doesn't help."

"We're not the ones having the affair and you have to admit our working relationship's more about teamwork than me answering to you."

"I don't think you've ever answered to me, Trudy, and the Rachel thing's not an affair."

"So what *is* the Rachel thing?"

Sinking back into the purple cushions, Lauren knew it was time to let it all out. Taking another slow sip, she enjoyed the sweetness of the drink and its heavenly aroma before the words slipped from her mouth. "I love her." She spoke softly. "I'm in love with her. I've always been in love with her from the moment I met her. It's so clichéd but I knew. Straight away she had this hold on me, as if I lost a part of myself to her the very first time we talked, and it's been pulling me back ever since. Whether that's to give her more of me or to reclaim what I lost I don't know but there's been this indescribable, indestructible pull from day one."

"Boss, *this* is the real you and you're lovely."

"But I want to be sexy and attractive and I want her to feel that pull too."

Trudy sloshed her mug back onto the table. "Get on your goddamn feet and look in that goddamn mirror would you, woman! You're like Sharon Stone on a good day."

"But she's never shown any interest."

"Straight women tend not to."

"Exactly! So what am I even doing talking about it?"

"Because something's happened. Something's happened that's made you start to ask questions. Tell me what's happened. Even if it's something tiny like a positive comment about another woman maybe, or a glance your way that you couldn't quite place."

"Well she's joined Tinder and listed 'interested in women'. Plus she asked me to kiss her and said she was *waiting* for me."

Trudy's mouth made a perfect circle. "No!"

Lauren shrugged.

"No!"

"She said she wanted to explore that side of her."

Trudy squealed as she jumped knees-first onto the opposite sofa. "My lady's getting a lady!"

"Watch the table, would you, and I'm not your lady, nor am I getting a lady, especially not Rachel."

"Oh wake up and smell the coffee, boss! She asked you to kiss her? What more do you want?"

"I don't want to be her test-case for any subsequent Tinder trysts."

"Why in hot heavens not? Get in there! Show her your stuff. Plus she won't want any Tinder trysts after she samples your snogs. The lesbian world's small. Trust me, I've heard you've got skills."

"Trudy, don't." Lauren smiled. "But I do appreciate your enthusiasm and I have to admit this hot chocolate's rather good." She took another sip. "But I can't get carried away. Don't let me get carried away." She nodded with force. "Rachel's made a couple of confusing comments, that's all. She's had a tough time. She's probably just a bit lost and I offer her a memory of part of what she once had."

"Philosophical bollocks. She's free, single and finally ready to mingle."

"With me?"

"What better person than her best friend?"

Lauren patted the sofa. "Come back. There's this woman called Jenny."

"This is about you, not some woman called Jenny." Trudy stayed where she was, pointing fiercely over the coffee table. "*You* can do this. *You* can tell her. *You* can make this happen."

"The straight girl has to make the first move, every lesbian knows this."

"In case we're tarred with that lesbian predator brush?"

"Exactly."

"It's been eleven years, boss. If you were after one thing you'd have had it by now. Seriously, you've got nothing to lose."

"I've got everything to lose. My best friend, my godson, my home from home, my—"

"Alright alright, don't worry, we'll plan it out to perfection. This is so incredibly exciting. I'll get a mood board and a dream chart and we can start a new folder; I know how you love your folders." Trudy stood up and spoke louder. "And we'll plan it out to perfection."

"You said that already."

"Yes, we'll plan it out to perfection." A louder voice still. "Camilla's seating arrangements, planned to perfection. Camilla, hi, we were just talking about—"

The voice was sharp. "Lauren, there's been a disaster."

Lauren got up as a woman in a long coat swept into the shop. "Camilla, how lovely to see you. No Ian today?"

"Am I not enough?"

"Yes, yes, of course you are." She remembered not to stare at the hair. "I just thought we were finalising the seating arrangements."

"Exactly the issue. I rushed ahead. He's parking my Jag. I want his mother in the main crowd. She's taken a fall. She's in a wheelchair. I'm not having a wheelchair at my top table. We'd need ramps and all sorts."

Trudy smiled. "It's do-able."

The fifty-something Cruella de Vil lookalike continued to focus on Lauren. "She's in the main crowd. You have to tell him."

"We really can accommodate a wheelchair at the top table." Trudy tried once more.

"Main crowd. Here he comes now. Daaaarling," the long coat swirled around and swept back to the door, "Lauren's got something to tell you. Not good news about poor ma'mar I'm afraid."

Trudy turned and whispered to Lauren. "I bet telling Rachel seems easy right now."

CHAPTER EIGHT

Seated around the conference table with air kisses, Camilla's latest self-indulgent anecdote and Ian's first toilet trip out of the way, Lauren lifted the Velcro name tag: Ma'mar – *Mother-in-law*. She'd been instructed to print off the list of names exactly as detailed in Camilla's email, hyphens and descriptions included; and while that was fine for these initial workings and re-workings, the idea that Jemima – *Alopecia*, or Kim – *Derek's Thai bride*, might ever see these draft name tags was horrifying. Usually they'd make the final seating plan 'in-house' in line with the theme of the wedding, but Camilla had chosen to outsource the end production to an old-fashioned window frame company who'd promised her a concertina of French windows with guest names and table numbers painted on the glass in delicate white calligraphy. The idea being that nothing would block the view of the bride, which was, in effect, the whole theme of the wedding.

In the same vein, the table decorations were to be made of one clear vase holding one *Lunaria annua* plant, sometimes known as annual honesty or silver dollar but universally recognised in its seed case form as the world's most translucent flower. Not to mention the top table that was to be raised by a full metre to ensure all eyes were facing front.

Camilla had chosen the historic Farnley Castle on the western border of Surrey as her venue and as accommodating as they'd been it had taken the commitment of a local theatre company to source a stage that would lift the 25ft-long top table to the required height. Block steps to access the seating had been selected but a ramp had also been mentioned as an option so, realistically, Ma'mar – *Mother-in-law* could still keep her place, but Camilla had been clear and the discussion had to be had.

"So," said Lauren, flicking the name tag between her fingers, "I hear your mother's in a wheelchair, Ian."

Camilla waved away her elderly fiancé's attempted reply. "I called ahead. Informed Lauren of the drama. Health and safety means we'll have to park her up here." The name tag was snatched and slapped onto table nineteen near the fire escape. "Isn't that right, Lauren?"

Trudy cut in. "Your last email said Sandra – *Bridesmaid (poor)* can't make it so that should free up a space on table one."

Lauren watched Camilla's eyes narrowing as Trudy relocated Ma'mar once again. "Is Sandra a definite no?" she chose to say.

"Couldn't afford the weekend at Claridge's."

"You had your hen do at Claridge's?" Trudy was wide eyed.

"I'm paying for Lauren Hilliard, not, not..."

"Trudy Tipton, my lady. This is the fifth time we've met."

The face softened somewhat at the polite address. "Well busy yourself elsewhere, please. It's essential my fiancé and I listen to Lauren." Camilla leant over and ripped Ma'mar from her upfront position and stuck her back near the fire escape. "Lauren thinks the wheelchair will be better off out of sight at the back, isn't that what you said? Plus Jacquie's resuming her role on table one as fifth bridesmaid. She lost the baby."

Trudy quietly pushed herself away from the table and stood up. "Boss, I'll go and make headway with Rachel's big day."

Lauren knew exactly what Trudy was thinking. There'd been a big kerfuffle three months ago when Camilla and her entourage of bridesmaids had attended a previous meeting. Jacquie, the very lovely daughter-in-law of Ian from a previous marriage, had announced with great joy her first pregnancy, only to be kicked out of her role with immediate effect. The dress designer who'd been hosting the meeting had assured Camilla she could take new measurements and make alterations without the design losing too much of its flair, but the idea of a baby bump stealing Camilla's thunder had been the final nail in the coffin of an already half-hearted attempt to allow some of Ian's relatives a part in the day.

Hey ho, one miscarriage and a chance to replace Sandra the pauper and all's well with the world, thought Lauren, trying to keep her disgust from showing. She nodded at Trudy, thanking her for holding her tongue.

If only Camilla had indeed phoned ahead with news of Ma'mar, at least she'd have options and some force to her voice. "I think—"

"I'm sorry, Miss Hilliard, but I'm not having my eighty-two-year-old mother seated in front of a draughty fire escape."

Lauren felt her insides dance with relief; she wouldn't need her voice, old Ian had finally found his. "We could—"

"Farnley Castle isn't draughty," interrupted Camilla. "Fine, we'll put her here, shall we?" The Velcro name tag was ripped off and slapped in the middle of the top table. "Not only will your mother's wheelchair become centre of attention, it'll roll right over my mother's memory in the process."

"Ma'mar was sitting here." Ian moved the name tag to the end of the top table. "Your mother will still have her place."

Lauren looked at the name tag to the right of the bride: Mother – *RIP*. Neither Camilla nor Ian had opted for the traditional top table seating format that ran: chief bridesmaid, groom's father, bride's mother, groom, bride, bride's father, groom's mother, best man, because the chief bridesmaid was too pretty, Ian's father was dead, Ian didn't want an empty space next to him, yet Camilla had insisted a seat must be held for her own mother who would have passed away a year ago to the wedding date, so Camilla had Ian on one side, a place fully laid for her dead mother on the other, her father towards the end with her two previous ex-husbands and a selection of faux but notable friends filling in the other places.

Lauren pointed to an open area to the right of the 25ft long structure. "Why don't we have a mini sweetheart table down here for Ma'mar?"

"Regular height?" asked Camilla.

"Probably wise given the wheel chair."

Camilla nodded. "Wiser if we drop the table height further. Wheelchair seats are notoriously low."

Ian sighed. "Just as long as she's not at the back in a draught."

"She's lucky she's coming at all. This latest fall was gin induced no doubt."

Ian clarified to no one in particular. "Sunday morning at church. On the way to the altar. Loose floor tile."

"Alcoholics always defend each other." Camilla turned to Lauren as she fingered her fluffy two-tone hair. "Did my fiancé tell you about his episode? Ever so lairy." She nodded. "Dry wedding. Neither of them tempted."

The elderly man's voice tailed off as he weakly retorted, "I had three Champagne cocktails that once."

"Sorry, what was that? Exactly, and now our two hundred guests are paying the price."

"They could drink."

"And give all-inclusive wrist bands to the ones who haven't got hyphen-alcoholic next to their name?" Camilla pointed at the table plan. "Or hyphen likes karaoke, or hyphen loud talker. No, Ian, it's not happening. It's a dry wedding so you won't be getting all silly."

Lauren looked at the hen-pecked husband-to-be imagining what all silly might look like. He was a portrait artist and widower of five years, seemingly good-natured with friends and family aplenty, most of whom had been refused roles in the wedding, but were there all the same. So what could have drawn him to Camilla and kept him sucked in was hard to comprehend. There didn't seem to be a love or even a slight fondness shared between the pair but Lauren knew all too well that some couples simply needed that other half just to be there… even if only to bicker.

Lauren had learnt that Camilla's first marriage was for stature, a husband better known as Town Mayor, never losing his seat on the council, earning him access to the top table alongside her second husband, the money man, well known for his radio work and also enough of a celebrity to be raised in front of the crowd, any potential awkwardness giving way because he had value. But Ian? What was Ian's value? He had his own gallery and was often featured in the local paper. Could this be the marriage of culture? Or maybe Camilla wasn't that bad? In fact she must have something to be on such great terms with her ex-husbands and she did have a certain flair with her style. Maybe the quiet artist needed the brash wife to do the talking when he didn't want to. She could perform the hosting and the schmoozing, the publicising and the posing while he did what he did, which at the moment, with Velcro name tags being snatched out of his hands, was to keep his head down and stay silent.

"Boss, can I just check this, please?" Trudy was crouching next to the round table, opening a folder for Lauren's eyes only.

Lauren smiled. The title read: *Make Rachel Mine* and was surrounded by delightful winged hearts fluttering in and out of the letters. Point one said: 'Send her a message, a sweet, unique, slightly puzzling one that announces your intended arrival.' Point two said: 'Arrive.' Point three said: 'Tell her.'

Lauren nodded. "Good plan. Do we have a time frame?"

Trudy tapped point three. "Tonight. Shall I lay the groundwork?"

"How do you propose you'll lay the groundwork?"

"I'll Google unique messaging services."

Camilla sniffed. "Ghastly. Some bride wanting a stripper no doubt."

Trudy stood back up. "Now there's an idea. Sid?"

Lauren hissed. "Don't be ridiculous."

"Sid," said Trudy again. "How can I help?"

Lauren spotted her neighbour, smiling at the front of her shop. "We're in the middle of a meeting, sorry."

But the solicitor maintained his gaze as he lifted his hands to his heart. "I apologise at this unorthodox entry but I've been next door for the past half hour umm-ing and arr-ing and the arr-ing finally won out."

"Sidney Enbrook? Is that you?" Camilla was rising from her seat, clasping her heart, mirroring Sid's stance.

Sid stepped forward. "Camilla Riggins, it is indeed."

"Camilla Riggins, I haven't been called that since I became Camilla Hollop, then Camilla DeLacy."

"And she's soon to be Camilla Brennan," said Ian, pushing himself up from the table.

"My Camilla Riggins." Sid ignored the man completely. "Sid and Rig, reunited at last." He banged his fist against his chest. "If you could feel my heartbeat right now. I thought it was you. I knew it was you. I just needed the nerve to come in."

Camilla threw her arms around the solicitor. "My heart's racing like yours. I still have it you know."

"Your cherry?"

"My cherry."

"I still practise. Every Sunday morning I come in at seven and flick and fold until my fingers are raw."

Camilla turned to the astonished group. "Origami. Sid was the star of the school. He used to make me little animals and pieces of fruit."

"I've progressed to skyscrapers and aeroplanes now. Would you like to come round and see?"

"Your skyscraper?"

"It's impressive." He waved his index finger in the general direction of next door.

"You own a shop on the high street?" Camilla's nostrils visibly widened with respect.

"The solicitors' office next door. Do you have someone doing your pre-nup?"

"Ian's got nothing to lose."

"And you?"

"He wouldn't dare take it, would you, Ian?"

Sid cut in. "You never can be too sure. Let me do this one on the house. You could pop in after your meeting?"

"I think we're finished here already," said Camilla. "There's not much more I can do until Natalie confirms whether or not she's willing to wear a pashmina." She nodded at Sid. "Large arms. If she's not willing to cover up she'll be at the back."

"Bride's day, bride's way," Sid said.

"Oh I love that! Lauren, you should use that." Camilla slung on her coat. "Come come, Ian, let's make this thing legal."

Ian frowned. "I thought we already were."

"Don't be smart with me. Here, put your coat on." She paused. "Sid, do your premises have a restroom?"

"That they do, with origami birds hanging from the ceiling. I've been told it relaxes one."

"Ian, you can use the bathroom in there. Lauren, I'll keep you informed of the movements." She laughed at herself. "Seating plan movements, not Ian's bowel movements."

Sid laughed raucously. "Camilla Riggins, you sure haven't changed."

"Her name has, three times," announced Trudy.

"I don't know who this woman is," said Camilla, lifting her nose as she waltzed from the shop.

Lauren waited for the door to close behind the group before turning to Trudy. "At least we know what he gets up to at seven o' clock on a Sunday morning."

"Poor Ian."

"I bet Sid made her that cherry as a symbol of something he wanted to pop."

"Too late now. Hers has been popped more often than a packet of party balloons."

"Trudy!"

"What? She's horrible and mean—"

"And employing us. We don't judge, we provide."

"We provide a crappy dry wedding with a seating plan that clearly hosts all the fat and ugly people at the back."

"Who's on back of the room duty that day?"

"Ha, I think it's you. Let me get you a biscuit, you'll need feeding up."

"Ooo, and another one of those hot chocolates please." Lauren smiled. "We've got planning to do."

"She'll only be back with more changes when someone gets a sudden face rash."

"I was talking about Mission Make Rachel Mine."

"Oh, boss, you're really getting into this, aren't you?"

"If couples like those aren't a wake-up call then I don't know what is. Plus you've excited me."

Trudy raised her eyebrows. "It's happening already, we're getting closer; you'll shift gears by the end of the week."

"I won't be driving up your alley, Trudy."

"Good one, boss, but you will."

"I won't, now go make the hot chocolates. I've got an idea. I'll send her a gif message on Facebook. Rachel loves gif messages."

"You two are total weirdos."

"I know, but she does. I thought I could send a whole message using only gifs."

"You mean like *I Love You* using a picture of an eye then a heart then a ewe like a sheep?"

"We're much more advanced than that."

"Show me."

"Make the drinks and I will."

"I like this. You never mess around on a work day."

"Camilla was booked in for another hour. Plus you made a Rachel folder, so it's like an official job." Walking back to her desk, Lauren picked up her iPad and opened her Facebook Messenger tab. She'd often chat with Rachel with gifs or emoji, but this would have to be something special. This would have to be novel length and difficult to decipher. Rachel loved a challenge and wouldn't rest until it was solved and by then she'd hopefully be eager to know what it all meant.

Getting herself comfy on the purple sofas, Lauren patted the velvet seat next to her. "Right, come and give me your input."

"Where do you like it?"

"Stop it, Trudy, this is serious."

"No it's not, it's fun and you're smiling and when you sip this hot chocolate you'll be gagging for it too."

Lauren shuddered. Maybe she *should* be sexy, or at least a little bit provocative. She took a deep breath and began by sending a gif of a man with a spliff.

"What's that?" Trudy was peering closely at the moving picture of a man sucking on a joint.

"It's hi. High? Get it?"

"Hardly an appropriate way to start the first conversation of the rest of your life."

"You don't get it. She will."

"High?"

"It's been known. Let me carry on. I'm an artist at work."

"Maybe Ian will display you." Trudy pointed at the third gif that flashed onto the screen. "But not with that image! I get the second one, the swimming ray fish, but the burning effigy of the devil?"

"Hell."

"High Ray Hell?"

"Exactly."

"She's called Rachel."

"You read between the lines."

"And she reads that you're a devil worshipping spliff head? Honestly, Lauren, this isn't quite what I imagined. I was thinking more of a Boomph delivery, you know, those marshmallows that have your photos printed on them? You could send her a batch of your face and put: I've always wanted you to eat me."

"And that's not weird or gross at all?"

"Okay then, flowers, with a nice message attached?"

"Clichéd and awkward. Nope, these gifs are the way to go."

"At least change the hell one to a shell. A nice pretty shell floating in the ocean. High Ray Shell. Sounds better too."

"You can't un-send a gif, the devil's already out there."

Trudy was peering at the screen. "And so is that sheep and that flashing letter R."

"Ewe R. You're."

"Why have you just written: the?"

"There isn't a gif for the. But there is for sun, and to, and shine."

"Oh I get it, that's lovely, but does it have to be someone polishing a car window?"

"They're shining it. It's gone already and she'll get it. We both always get it."

"Well clearly you don't otherwise you wouldn't be doing this now." Trudy paused. "What if she reads: Sheep are the hottest double polished?"

"Oh no, I missed out my! You're the sun to my shine." Lauren shook her head. "She'll understand. I'll do another. Stay quiet, you're putting me off."

"Sheep, R, the, House, Double, my – well done for writing it this time, Heart."

"You're the home to my heart."

"Oh I see it now! That's so sweet."

"I am sweet and I'm funny and she'll find this endearing and we'll chat and laugh and hopefully have the courage to be honest with each another."

"That's my lady."

"You need to stop that. It doesn't work."

"Camilla liked it."

"She didn't. How's this: Hi Rachel. You're the sun to my shine, the home to my heart, if you want a nice woman, then I'm a great start."

"That dancing stripper on that gif isn't a nice woman."

"That Nice biscuit gif's the nice, that's just a woman."

"She might think you're offering her a cup of tea and a tit show."

"Wait!" Lauren gasped. "She's just come online!" Clicking back to her timeline she scrolled through the feed. "Let's just wait here all casual."

"She can't see you loitering in the messenger."

"She can if she replies and I'm right there waiting like some loser."

"So we'll just wait here like some loser, shall we? You need to know if she's read it."

"Trust me, she'll read it."

"What's that?" Trudy pointed to the new notification.

"Rachel's just shared a competition to win a May meat deal. She always shares competitions."

"What's a May meat deal? Some sort of straight woman's thing?"

Lauren peered in closer. "It's from the butchers in town. You have to like and share the competition to win. You'll get 450 grams of minced beef, four pork chops, two shoulder steaks, 500 grams of back bacon, four gammon steaks, six—"

"Wait. Rachel shared the butcher's May meat deal before reading and replying?"

"She's probably just catching up with everything. Yep, look." Lauren pointed at another notification. "She's just tagged herself in that photo. The WI cake sale from the weekend. The photos have just gone live."

"Why are you getting notified?"

"She's on my close friends list. I see whatever she does on Facebook."

"Stalkerish."

"It's not. I have so many brides adding me and guests from weddings that I need to make sure I see who's important."

"Is that the list there?" Trudy was pointing to the top of the Facebook page and the cluster and starred profile pictures. "Why aren't I on it?"

"Stop it. Look, she's done something else." Lauren paused.

Trudy read loudly. "Rachel Moore became friends with Jenny Leonard. Who's Jenny Leonard? Dammit she's gorgeous."

Clicking on the image, Lauren felt the nausea rising as the incredible eyes appeared on the screen.

CHAPTER NINE

Pulling onto the gravel driveway of Rachel's barn conversion, Lauren checked her phone for the hundredth time, hoping something had changed. It hadn't. Seen 11:02. Rachel had seen the gif messages but not replied. Rachel always replied, mostly instantly, but always eventually, and never nine hours after the fact. Checking the time on the phone screen, Lauren panicked. It was just gone eight p.m. Nine hours had passed. Both she and Trudy had been on the edge of their seats once they realised the message had been read, checking in every ten minutes to see if there'd been a reply, growing more anxious that the addition of new friend Jenny Leonard could be the cause of the silence. Lauren bit her lip, her initial nervousness had quickly turned into fully fledged dread. What had Rachel been doing adding this woman on Facebook? Yes, Jenny could have requested her but it meant some contact must have been made. Did they stay up late last night messaging each other on Tinder? Did they want to share photos so moved over to Facebook? Were they sexting already? Trudy had thought so, especially given the magnificence of Jenny's incredible eyes. Come to bed and let me fuck you eyes was how she'd described them. Eyes you couldn't resist.

Lauren looked back at her phone. It wasn't her gif story. It couldn't have been her gif story. Yes, she was putting herself out there as a possible option, but it was jokey and funny and in line with their theme of paying compliments. She re-opened the thread and smiled at the Tony the Tiger gif. He was swishing his spoon through the Frosties and giving a thumbs up. Everyone knew that meant: great. G-g-g-g-g-reat. And before that was the gif of a start line, runners starting their race. She paused. It should say great start, I'm a great start, not start great. Scrolling quickly, she noticed a couple of other gifs playing out of order. How ridiculous that she hadn't spotted it already, obviously too focused on the message seen time and anticipated reply. "That's it!" she said, slamming her palm on the steering wheel. "They've been delivered out of order!" Popping her belt quickly, she jumped out of the car. Rachel obviously couldn't make head nor tail of it. Maybe the connection was slow in the shop? Or maybe... oh it didn't matter, Rachel wasn't not replying, Rachel was just waiting for clarification.

Tapping on the large wooden door, Lauren lifted the latch and let herself in. Parker would already be in bed so they could laugh about her random message and she could gently bring up the dangers of adding people you didn't really know on Facebook, without sounding jealous or judgmental but having her say all the same.

"Lauren? Is that you, dear?"

Looking across the beamed hallway, Lauren stared into the lounge. Rachel's in-laws were standing in front of the fire. "Rosemary? Ken? Hi."

"I'm here too," said Trevor, popping up from his prone position on the sofa.

Shifting squeakily on the wooden floor, Lauren was quite tempted to turn and leave the way she'd arrived except faster, but she couldn't, so she entered the warm lounge and smiled. "Is Rachel around?" It wasn't very polite, but she hadn't expected to see them. Yes, they popped in relatively frequently, assuming, no doubt, they were providing a service that Rachel's absent-by-choice parents could not, but Rachel nearly always told her about an impending visit or last minute drop-in, often asking her to call round to diffuse any atmosphere, an atmosphere her own arrival could sometimes accentuate rather than diminish. Rosemary and Ken weren't too bad, in fact they were fine; it was their inaction regarding their weird son, Trevor, that got on her nerves. Like now, for instance, throwing himself back onto the sofa, lying with his feet up on the armrest, pig bollocks poking up like a sunrise. "Take your shoes off, Trev," she chose to say.

"Tile floor. Rachel says shoes are fine."

"It's not a tile armrest though is it? And that bobbly rug's a magnet for dirt."

Rosemary cut in. "Cup of tea? I'll put the kettle on. Is she outside? Change of plan?"

"Who?"

"Rachel."

Lauren paused. "I thought she was here."

"She's with you," continued Rosemary. "We're babysitting."

Trevor made a strange clucking noise as he pulled himself up. "I see what this is," he said, as he fingered his pencil thin goatee. "She's got a date. She didn't want to upset me so she used you as an excuse." He nodded and continued to half-pace, half-preen. "Which is good news because it shows she *does* have feelings for me and she didn't want to hurt mine."

"Good point, son," said Ken, reaching out to pat the fully-grown man on the back.

Lauren tried to perform her best false gasp. "Oh shoot! I thought we were meeting here, not there! I've got to dash; how stupid of me!"

Trevor stopped his strutting. "You are part of her plans?"

"Of course I am."

"Even better," said Ken, giving his son a thumbs-up.

Trevor nodded. "No date means no competition, as yet."

"You're awfully late," said Rosemary.

"I had a bride crisis. Right, I'm off. Bye everyone. Sorry for the confusion!" Darting from the lounge, Lauren scooted through the hallway and out of the barn, closing the heavy wooden door as quickly, but as quietly, as she could. The evening air was warm but exactly what she needed in response to the heat of the house and flush of embarrassment on her cheeks. Crunching across the gravel back to her car, she cursed herself for not noticing the black estate in place of Rachel's black hatchback. She'd been too busy flapping about stupid gifs. There was no way Rachel was thinking about stupid gifs. Rachel was off out with someone she didn't want her to know about. Jenny. It had to be Jenny. Jumping into the car, Lauren dialled Trudy's number. "That's the last time I'm listening to you," she snapped.

"Boss?"

"Rachel's gone out with Jenny. Not only did she not bother to reply to my gif messages, which, even if they were delivered out of order, was rude, she got the in-laws to babysit. I babysit. I'm the babysitter. I'm the one she calls, not them."

"She's not going to call you if she's going on a hot date with Jenny though is she, boss? I wonder what she wore. Something gorgeous to get those amazing eyes looking at her no doubt."

"Trudy!"

"What? Come down to The Shaker."

"The what?"

"The Shaker. Ooo, you're not as with it as you think! Cocktail bar, lesbian chic, all the cool girls are here."

"And you're there?"

"Err, of course I am."

"Where is it?"

"Just off King's Street, next to the Pizza Express. I'll get you a Sweet Tight Pussy."

"I can find one myself, thank you very much."

"It's a cocktail. Pineapple juice, peach schnapps."

"I knew that."

"No, you didn't."

"I'll see you in twenty." Lauren hung up and slammed the car into reverse. She was the cool one. She knew all the cool places and cool drinks. She was the one women wanted, not Jenny, but Jenny was out, and so was Trudy, and so was goddamn Rachel! Clicking the car into drive, she sped past the other barns towards the main road. Well, she was coming out too.

****

Glancing around The Shaker, Lauren suddenly felt old. Groups of identical-looking girls with tight body-con dresses, big hair and black pointy eyebrows were posing through plumped-up lips and fake eyelashes; faux friends fanning each other with praise as they pushed and shoved for their angle, all awkwardly uncomfortable as they stood round the tall tables. The bar wasn't much better: sterile and uninviting. In fact, Lauren couldn't see any seating in the whole of the venue.

"Seating's last season," said the voice behind her.

"Trudy? What *is* this place?"

"I told you, it's where all the cool girls hang out."

"And what are you wearing?" She didn't mean to sound rude but Trudy, trussed up in a body-con like the rest of these clones, was a sight to behold.

"It's my evening attire. You don't think I wear those shirts off the job, do you?"

"You shouldn't wear those shirts on the job."

"Ai ai, let me get you a drink before you rip my kit off."

Lauren ignored her. "Who are you here with?"

"Myself."

"Why?"

"How many times! It's where the cool girls hang out."

"And you pick them up, do you?"

"Over here," said Trudy, signalling to an empty corner.

Lauren reluctantly followed on, moving around the ultra-modern white pillars and past the minimalistic décor to a tall table at the back. "I thought we were getting drinks?"

"Smart tables, like smart glass, and I have been known to get girls." Trudy reached out to swipe the surface. "Here's the menu and there, click on two Sweet Tight Pussys."

"I don't want two Sweet Tight Pussys."

"Steady, boss. One's mine."

Lauren raised her eyebrows. "Really?"

"It's been said, and I *was* with someone but they've left."

"Because of me?"

"It's fine, you seemed stressed. Here, just show your card to the corner of the table. Contactless payment."

"My card?"

"Yes, boss, your card."

Lauren finally smiled. "Fine. It's the least I can do if I've ruined your date night, even though your ridiculous excitement and encouragement has ruined my self-respect and led me down a merry path of total nonsense."

"It wasn't nonsense."

"That folder gets shredded tomorrow."

"She might just be using Jenny as a warm-up for you."

"As if!"

"She sees your gif messages, panics, knows it's going to happen so dips her toe in the water before she takes the full plunge."

"That's like saying you go and listen to a Cheeky Girls concert before booking your Beyoncé tickets."

"Boss, I'm not being funny, but you're not Beyoncé and Jenny's much hotter than both Cheeky Girls put together."

"They look the same!"

"Plus, Beyoncé doesn't dress like she's off to the library. Honestly, boss, this is a real disappointment. You're a total sex siren at work, but this," Trudy made waving hands in Lauren's general direction, "this lets you down."

"I was going to Rachel's to chill out. These are my chill out clothes."

"No wonder she went out with Jenny."

"We always—"

"Boom, and here are our drinks."

Lauren turned to the waitress, also trussed up in a body-con dress. "Do I look like I'm going to the library?"

"Are you?"

"No! I'm here!" She stopped and smiled. "Sorry, I'm having a bad day. What do I owe you?"

"You've already paid. But you can leave a tip by swiping the heart if you like. We have your card details."

"Of course you do," said Lauren, swiping the heart, then swiping again. "It's not working."

"You have to put in an amount, boss."

Lauren looked up at the waitress who tutted before walking back to the bar, obviously used to people claiming technological incompetence or faulty connections as the reason for not leaving a tip. She groaned. "I'm so out of touch."

"It's only been a week since Stephanie."

"Oh, Trudy, will you be serious for once! And there, I've done it."

"Wow, that's generous."

"I didn't mean to put that much." She shrugged. "Anyway. Cheers." Lifting her glass, Lauren took a huge sip of the cocktail. "I can't just be casual with her. I can't just casually say: oh, I noticed you befriended Jenny with the hot eyes, or: I found out you chose Rosemary and Ken over me."

"The waitress?"

Ignoring the comment, Lauren took another huge sip before ploughing on. "I can't casually say: oh, sorry for the barrage of gifs where I offered myself up on a plate that you may or may not have realised was food, but it is food and it's tasty." She drank again. "I'm tasty. Why's Rachel not hungry?"

"Take it easy on the Sweet Tight Pussy, boss."

Lauren raised her voice. "I know how to handle a Sweet Tight Pussy."

"Did that come out louder than you expected?"

She nodded. "It did."

"Shall we just have a slow, steady, sophisticated night?"

Looking around, Lauren grimaced. "That's what they do here, isn't it?" She groaned. "Even the fake body-con queens have more style than I do."

"I don't mind if you want to swap outfits in the toilets."

Lauren actually laughed. "You're tiny!"

"So are you."

"I meant short."

"It stretches down."

"Bless you, Trudy, but no." She smiled. "Thank you though."

"I never like that tone. It comes with that look. That: aren't you so cute and adorable, Trudy."

"You are, and you're kind."

"I don't want to be kind, I want to be a mean-arsed kinky mistress who's kissable and bedable and desired."

"So that's why you come here?"

"Ha, who's the joker now?"

"You're a lovely catch."

Stepping away from the table, Trudy threw her hands onto her waist and pushed out her hips. "Lovely?"

The cough came all by itself. "You're very... it's very... fetching?"

"I've got a hot little body and you know it, boss."

"And a Sweet Tight Pussy to match," said Lauren, lifting the discarded cocktail. "Drink up."

"Tastes good, doesn't it."

Swiping the table, Lauren nodded. "I'm going for a Corn-Fed Country Pussy next."

"Did I tell you I grew up on a farm?"

"With peppermint schnapps, grenadine syrup and orange juice?"

"Fields of the stuff."

"Oh, Trudy, you're funny."

The wiggle was resumed. "With a hot little body."

Appraising the flaunted figure, Lauren tilted her head from side to side as she finished her drink. "Some might say."

"And I can do sultry," came the announcement and pout.

"Some might say."

"You're a tough nut to crack, boss."

"I feel like a flaked almond when Rachel's around."

Trudy huffed back to her position at the table. "Rachel's sprinkling herself on top of someone else's tart tonight so get over it or go home, Dumbfuck."

"*What* did you call me?"

Trudy swiped the table. "Cinnamon schnapps and whiskey."

Lauren sighed. "Right. Sorry. And maybe I am." She smiled. "I'll try one too. And you do look great. You look really great, Trudy."

"And that library's lucky to have you."

"That library might be my only option."

Trudy winked. "It's not your only option, boss."

"Trudy…"

"You've got that Corn Fed Country Pussy on order." She laughed. "You don't think I was offering myself up, do you?"

"Were you?"

The pouting and hip thrusting began again. "We both know it's happening tonight."

****

"We both know it's happening tonight," said the smooth voice.

Rachel looked across the table at the confident woman whose eyes were twinkling with mischief. "Do we?"

"You came for a meal after a few flirty messages. Imagine how you'll be coming after an evening together."

Rachel managed to maintain the connection. This woman was curiously fascinating: arrogantly presumptuous in the most unassuming of ways. If a man had been so bold and full on it would have sounded sleazy and sordid, but this woman had a tone to her voice and a look in her eye that made everything sound naturally likely. And the fact was, she *was* here, sitting in a quiet corner booth, eating thin-crust pizza and drinking Peroni with someone she'd known less than a day. This wasn't like her, none of this was like her, but she'd been flattered when last night's message came in. 'Your picture made me smile,' it had read. Simple, sweet and honest. It didn't ask for a reply, it wasn't a warm-up for more; it was just a statement that made her smile in return. And it was true, her picture *was* good. It was colourful with her big curls on show and a glimpse of her cat collection in the background. Jenny had obviously seen something she liked, smiled and passed on the message. In the same vein, Rachel reasoned she should reply with an honest reaction to Jenny's photo. 'And your picture's stunning,' she had said.

Lauren would have no doubt told her not to reply, or at least to reply with something more subtle, but Lauren hadn't been there; she'd left, singing her funny little limericks, just as one day she'd leave her for good. Yes, Lauren had been a tower of strength before and after Toby's passing, filling in the gaps he left even when he was present. Her rock, her person to turn to, the one who brought real joy and laughter into her life, but one day her best friend would find the girl of her dreams and pull back on her presence, a presence that had always been so welcomed. Rachel looked up. That's why she was here, eating pizza, with Jenny.

Jenny smiled. "Tell me about you. So far, you've come across as charmingly shy, deeply layered and incredibly thoughtful, and I do have to mention your obvious external beauty. I can tell you're a radiant person, Rachel. You're one of those people who glow."

Rachel swallowed. It was probably just the embarrassment in her cheeks and lack of confidence in her conversation that had led to the thoughtful and glowing part of the assessment, plus they'd only been here an hour so the deeply layered label was quite a stretch. This woman didn't know her, no matter how perceptive her wide eyes appeared, not to mention the fact that her 'compliment someone to put them at ease' strategy had been visible a mile off.

"I'm a bit boring really. I'm twenty-nine, I have a son called Parker—"

"You said that in the messages last night. I mean *you*."

"That is me. He's my life."

"Do you work?"

"No."

"Hobbies?"

"I'm in the WI." Rachel spotted the smile. "What? It's interesting."

"I knew you looked different to those other women. You hardly ever see someone smiling on Tinder and you certainly don't see them with unruly hair and a mish-mash of ornaments in the background."

"That's my carefully selected cat collection and my hair's not unruly, it's free."

Jenny nodded. "Exactly the right word. You're like a free spirit."

"Now I know you don't know me." Rachel half-laughed. "I'm predictable and boring and—"

"Let me stop you right there." The hands reached across the table. "You're on a date with a woman and from what you've been saying that's far from predictable." Jenny's eyes glinted. "Who knows where this evening might take us."

Pulling back from the contact, Rachel glanced around the restaurant. It was exactly the same as all the other franchised branches: a predominant black and white theme with secluded booths and tables far enough apart to feel private, but she lowered her voice all the same. "Are you after one thing, Jenny?"

Her dinner guest maintained her volume. "Yes. And that one thing might lead to another one thing and then there'll be two things and before you know it we'll have our own thing going on."

Continuing to look around at the diners, all occupied with pizzas, laughter and chat, Rachel let out a small chuckle of her own. "Are all women like this?" she asked, her eyes back on her companion.

"I'm honestly your first?"

"I'm new to this." Rachel turned her attention to her food. "Dating. Women. Chit-chat."

"We don't have to chit-chat, we can just stare."

"What do you mean?"

"Stop cutting your pizza and put your hands down. That's it, come on, hands on your lap. Let's just look at each other. We don't have to talk, we can just look. Who cares what we do, or say, let's just see how we feel."

Rachel knew her eye rolls were infamous; whether they were the result of having a young son who could sometimes try it on, or a brother-in-law who tested the boundaries, or a best friend who could be so outrageous that only an eye-rolling reply would suffice, she wasn't sure, but she knew she'd just done one. This woman really did have all the tricks in the book. She looked carefully. Jenny was smiling in a provocative, slightly intimidating, but incredibly good-looking fashion. She tried not to blush. Her tutting must have been noticed. Taking a deep breath, she decided to play along, studying the incredible eyes with interest. They reminded her of the hot springs she'd visited in Iceland: pale blue with a cool warmth, and so inviting you found yourself jumping straight in. She smiled. She'd jump in again if she could.

Her date spoke softly. "See?"

Rachel nodded. "I see."

"Now let's go with the flow. Just two women appreciating each other."

CHAPTER TEN

"You do appreciate me, don't you, boss?" Trudy was sipping on her third Rotten Pussy, one arm clinging on to the tall table for support. "I mean really appreciate me, boss?"

Lauren looked around the venue. Surely there'd be some seating somewhere? "You're going to slide right off that surface in a minute."

"I'm good at the worm. It could be my slinky start to the ripples."

"How are you not slurring? There must be four spirits in that one."

"Five actually: melon liqueur, almond liqueur, peach liqueur, coconut rum and sours." Trudy sipped again. "Plus a shot of apple juice."

"Where do you put it? You're only a tiny dot."

"Would you like to see?"

"Trudy, that doesn't work on any level."

"What about: would you like to see my tiny dot?"

"No."

"Right. Sorry, boss." Trudy stood up straighter. "Rotten Pussy?" She held out her drink.

"I'm quite happy with my Virgin Pussy thank you very much."

"No, you're not."

"I am. Watermelon schnapps, cinnamon—"

"We're talking about Rachel."

"Are we?"

"Yes, we are, and you're miserable. You're on a sophisticated night out with a little hotty in a body-con dress who's got a stomach of steel and who can turn any fall into the worm dance move, yet you're prickly and glancing around and you haven't let yourself go."

"I was looking for somewhere to sit."

"Dear god you *are* old."

"I'm not, I'm just…"

"Pining for something you'll never have?"

"I don't want a seat that badly."

"Ha! That's my boss."

Lauren sighed. "I'm sorry, I'm just…" She thought carefully. She'd pined for eleven years and been fine and now all of a sudden, with Rachel as a potential possibility, everything had turned on its head. Her dreams were no longer pure fantasy and any visualisation of a romantic awakening between them brought complications instead of the fairytale of possibilities she'd so often imagined. "Okay, it's like winning the lottery," she finally said.

"I'd love to."

"Exactly, but would you really?"

"Yes."

"See, that's what we all think. But imagine a really big win."

"Even better."

"You'd have to decide if you wanted to remain anonymous or go public."

"Anonymous."

"But the press would find out. You'd be outed."

"I'd move away."

"And leave all your friends and family? Your home?"

"I live in a flat and all my family are up north."

"Trudy, just listen. You'd have begging letters and people turning up at your house. You'd be a sudden kidnap risk. Any potential children you had wouldn't be safe. You'd have to live in some gated estate with a load of snobs. You'd probably buy a really fast car and be at risk of dying. You'd go on more planes and be at greater risk of dying. You'd probably order loads of takeaways and get fat."

"And be at risk of dying."

"I'm serious. Your friends wouldn't be able to afford the things you could. They'd get jealous or use you for money. Nothing would have any value. You'd turn into a greedy pretentious prick."

"Who dies."

"Listen, you win big on the lottery, you're probably going to get murdered."

"You've thought this thing through, haven't you, boss?"

"Of course I have and the dream is always so much better than the reality. I've dreamt of Rachel for so long now, that actually—"

"She'd murder you in your sleep the first time you fucked her?"

"What if she did?"

"Crikey, boss, we need to lighten this up." Trudy reached for her bag and unclasped the catch, pulling out two yellow dice.

"Why do you have two yellow dare dice in your bag?"

"I was with someone."

"Playing dare dice?"

"We didn't get that far. Come on, boss, we need to yank ourselves out of this dark pit."

"So I'm an old cripple who needs a chair and depresses you? I might as well go home."

"No, roll the dice. I'll do it for you. There you go, sing here comes the bride or boogie on a table at the bar." Trudy shrugged at Lauren's raised eyebrow. "What? They're from a hen party."

Lauren took a deep breathe. *Here comes the bride, all dressed in white, la da da da da da da da da da dar.* Ha! What are the words?"

"I told you this would be fun. My turn. Ooo, dance dirty, or what does that one say? Let the group give you a new hairstyle."

"I'm not sure I could do much with that bowl."

"It's a pob! A posh-bob! That one Posh Spice invented."

"In the nineties?"

"Oh come here, boss, I'm about to dance sexy."

****

Looking around at the other enamoured diners chatting away, Rachel tried to pinpoint the atmosphere on her own table. She wouldn't describe it as stilted but there was a definite something missing.

Jenny nodded. "I'm sorry, I can be a bit serious on a first date."

"No, I wasn't..."

"You were." The woman pushed her knife and fork together on her plate and lifted her bottle of Peroni. "I've just had lots of time wasters and bad matches and I like to get straight in there with a person's potential."

"Potential for one thing?"

"I was being blasé. I wanted to see how you'd react."

"Really? Gosh, I think I seemed quite open to it."

"If I'm honest, I'm not sure you seem open to any of this."

Rachel smiled. "You make a lot of statements. You've done it all evening."

"I'm a lawyer. I have to analyse, decide and cut to the chase."

Rachel lifted her own bottle and drank. Did this feel surreal because she was with another woman, or because the main source of excitement in her daily routine was usually just the three-for-two offers at Tesco or the arguments between the mothers on the school PTA. Either way, she should go with the flow. This was freedom. This was what she'd craved. Wasn't it? She met Jenny's eyes. "Jenny, I am interested. You're beautiful, articulate, intriguing..."

"But there's no spark?"

"There might be."

"It's either there or it's not."

Her thoughts immediately turned to Lauren, always so sparky and fantastic at banter. She stopped herself. Lauren was like that with everyone. The person you had to have at your party. The one who'd always make sure there was fun.

"You have someone, don't you?"

"I don't."

"You want someone though."

"There go those statements again."

Jenny smiled. "Right, decided; there's a wonderfully modern cocktail bar next door. We've eaten, now we should drink and get merry so you can open up about the love of your life."

"That wouldn't be good date etiquette, surely?"

"Which bit?"

"Any of it."

"One drink then? To bid each other farewell?"

Rachel laughed. "Are all women this simple?"

"We're realists most of the time."

"I like that," she said, smiling. "Maybe you could teach me some more?"

Jenny's eyes glinted. "And there's our first spark."

****

"Lauren! The rules are the rules! You can go and get yourself a pair of boxer shorts or you can finish your drink." Trudy was squinting at the two yellow dice.

Lauren hiccupped. "This is my second Virgin Pussy. I can't down it."

"Go get a pair of boxer shorts then; there are two men over there. And regarding the Virgin Pussy, you might have your third tonight if you play your cards right, boss."

"Rachel's not an option. We decided that, remember?" Lauren held on to the table for support. "Lottery, murder, stabbed after sex."

"I wasn't talking about Rachel, boss, and you're wobbling."

"Who were you talking about?"

The shimmy came again, albeit this time more shaky.

"Give over. You, a Virgin Mary? As if!"

"I am and you are."

"I'm not."

"Wobbling, I mean."

"Stop it. I'm downing my drink. Swipe me for a Hard Fuck, would you?"

"I thought you'd never ask."

"The Blue Curacao one."

"I am, you know," said Trudy as she tapped in their next order. "Sod off!"

"Boss! I'm your employee, you can't speak to me like that."

"Sorry, I'm getting lairy, I need to slow down." Lauren tried to whisper. "But sod off, would you?"

"My hymen's intact."

"Is that the name of the cocktail you're having?"

"Boss, look into my eyes. I'm levelling with you. I still have it. I check in the mirror like they taught us at school."

Lauren flopped her head onto the table as she snorted with laughter. "Stop it!"

"I let women lick but not poke."

"Face fucking's more intimate than finger fucking!"

"I quite like it."

"But it doesn't make you a virgin, Trudy!"

"I don't like the idea of penetration."

"Still not a virgin."

"I'd let you penetrate."

"I don't want to penetrate!"

"More of a face fucker?"

Lauren laughed loudly. "Oh, Trudy, I needed this. Your roll. Make it a good one."

****

Walking down the steps into the modern venue, Rachel looked around curiously. There were lots of women, lots of dresses and lots of posing, which did seem in tune with the sharp, sterile look of the place, but was definitely out of tune with what she'd expected. The lesbian bars she remembered from her jaunts out with Lauren at uni were dark and dank. This was new age. This was a representation of all the hot women who'd matched her on Tinder: gorgeous, posing, well-kempt.

"It's not a lesbian bar," said Jenny, following Rachel's gaze, "but the cocktail names seem to bring a lot of lesbians to the bar."

"*My milkshake brings...*" She stopped. Jenny wasn't Lauren and probably wouldn't dive straight into a yard song mash-up in the middle of a posh bar like Lauren would. "Can I get you a drink?"

"You order at the tables. Are you okay to find one? I just need to nip to the bathroom."

Rachel nodded. It would give her time to acclimatise. "Of course," she said, walking away from the stairs and heading towards the tall tables at the back. She'd have to tell Lauren about this place. It had been years since they'd gone anywhere 'lesbian' together, mostly choosing the regular high street haunts, cinema showings or spa days instead. In fact, Lauren had stopped asking her to be her wingman almost as soon as Toby came on the scene.

Walking around the modern white pillars, she wondered if that had been her doing or Lauren's. Finding an empty table, she assessed the doing must have been Lauren's; whether that was because Lauren didn't want to rub the young free and single life in her face once she'd committed to Toby, or whether she just wanted to keep that world away from her straight friend, she didn't know. What she did know was it didn't seem fair. She might have married a man but that didn't mean she couldn't have questions, questions that had become nigglingly re-ignited by Tinder.

She sighed. Why was she even here? Because she'd been flattered by Jenny? Because Lauren's only response to last night's intrigue was a weird splurge of gifs? Or because she did actually want to try skydiving? Looking towards the kissing couple on the table two rows from hers, Rachel nodded. It was this world. This world where hot ladies kissed each other. It was intriguing and enticing and… she froze.

The kissing couple were Trudy and Lauren.

CHAPTER ELEVEN

Following the white pillars, Rachel dashed back up the stairs as she held on to her breath. They hadn't seen her but Jenny had seen her and Jenny was catching her up.

"Rachel, wait!"

Racing out onto the street, she squinted at the bright overhead lamps, taking a moment to assess her direction. She'd driven here and only had one Peroni so she'd have no problem getting herself home.

"Wait!"

Turning on the pavement, Rachel looked at her date. "I'm sorry, I'm not sure I can do this."

"Do what?"

She gasped, confusion swirling around her in a mixture of anger and envy. To hell with it, she thought, stepping forward as she lifted her hands to the face. "This," she said, planting her lips onto Jenny's.

****

"Too far, Trudy!" snapped Lauren, stepping back from the table.

"They both said kiss, boss!"

"That dice said tell a joke!"

"Did it?"

"Yes! Right. I'm going. I'll see you tomorrow and don't you dare mention this again."

"What? All the fun we've had?"

"No, that, that, that... whatever that lunge and suction thing was."

"I might have latched on a bit too long. Apologies, boss."

"Get yourself home."

"I need to finish my Blowjob."

"Finish it and get yourself home." Lauren turned to leave. "And make sure it's a registered taxi."

"You do care."

"I don't care." Lauren nodded. "But stay safe."

"Of course I will, boss."

"Text me when you get home."

"Shall we sext?"

"No, we shall not sext! I'll see you tomorrow."

"With a big smile on your face."

Lauren stalked away from the table, past the white pillars and up the stairs, unable to stop her lips from turning at the corners. Trudy was a little shit, but an incredibly funny, really rather quite likeable little shit. Stepping onto the street she glanced at the kissing couple. If only Trudy was tall like those women. She froze.

One of those women was Rachel.

CHAPTER TWELVE

Closing the door on her in-laws, Rachel bolted the lock. She'd tried to hurry them out of the house as quickly but as politely as she could, a difficult task given that Rosemary and Ken had disappeared into the kitchen as soon as she walked in, leaving Trevor alone in front of the log fire, two brandy glasses hanging from one hand, the bottle in the other, offering up a night-cap like he'd lived there for years. It was clearly all pre-planned but what on earth did Rosemary and Ken think would happen? Their son would woo his woman while they waited in the kitchen? And then what? He'd nod to say when he was ready to go home, like some sixteen-year-old boy collected from a house party? No, she'd politely declined and asked him to put the brandy back where he'd found it. Likewise, she'd asked Rosemary to stop boiling the kettle. One last round of tea wasn't needed as she'd really rather just jump straight into bed. Trevor had attempted a smart remark that was thankfully ignored by everybody before Ken actually manned-up and gathered the troops. And now, Rachel sighed, they'd gone.

Turning around, she leaned back against the wooden door, opening her mouth in a huge silent scream. What had just happened? She'd kissed a woman! She'd openly kissed a woman! On the street of all places! What would Rosemary and Ken think of her openly kissing a woman on the street? She gasped. What did she think of herself openly kissing a woman on the street? It had all happened so quickly, that desire to just give it a go, driven on mostly by the vision of Lauren giving it a good old go with Trudy. How long had that been going on? The two of them? Sneaking off to cool venues she knew nothing about? Lauren was meant to be her best friend who told her everything and, yes, admittedly she hadn't told her about Jenny but she was going to. This Trudy thing, however, must have been brewing for ages and it was a shock; a shock that had driven her onto the lips of her date.

And, yes, she had made the initial lunge and connection but it was Jenny who'd turned the somewhat awkward meeting of mouths into a hot mess of tongues and moans and searching for more, and if they hadn't been on the street more would probably have happened. Shaking her head, Rachel went into the kitchen and took a glass from the cupboard and a wine bottle from the fridge and poured a lot of wine into the glass. Why would more probably have happened? She didn't fancy Jenny. Okay, she was intensely hot and nice to look at but she hadn't been drawn to her until that actual physical connection; yet with Lauren she'd often found herself looking and wondering. She paused. How much hotter might that connection be because of the emotional investment as well?

Walking into the lounge, Rachel dropped onto the sofa, unable to stop her sigh from sounding loud. Lauren wasn't interested in her. Even though she could be ridiculously flirtatious with over-the-top innuendos and provocative play-talk, when push came to shove she'd never tried it on once. And she'd had lots of opportunities; crikey, Toby had even drunkenly suggested a threesome one time. Plus Lauren was a sexual person, always dating between her non-stop rotation of girlfriends. Surely if there'd been any attraction on Lauren's side she'd have made a move by now. Lauren could have done it at uni, or with Toby's permission, or now that she'd heard her direct, not so subtle, hints about wanting a kiss. Rachel cringed at herself. Where had this all come from? There'd always been that intrigue, but most straight women would confess to that, wouldn't they? Yet this thing was more than re-ignited, it was somehow super-charged.

Taking a gulp of wine, she ran her fingers through her hair. She was confused. And it was okay to be confused, and maybe it did have something to do with Toby. Rachel got up off the sofa and started to pace. No, she wasn't going there. This wasn't about Toby. This was... this was... She stopped herself. Was this just something to do? What was the saying? There's nothing more dangerous than a bored housewife? Or was that a saying Lauren had made up when teasing her about joining the WI? Either way, there she was again, back in her thoughts, always in her thoughts. She shook her head. Of course she was going to be in her thoughts; her best friend had played such a big part in her life for the past eleven years that she'd inevitably pop into her mind every so often.

Sitting back down, Rachel put her feet up on the armrest. But why had it turned physical as well as emotional? Why had she actually asked for a kiss? Rachel laughed at herself. Even at uni when she'd drunkenly tried to initiate some action she'd never dared ask her friend outright and, anyway, how ridiculous to assume the lesbian would want it. Lauren could kiss whomever she chose whenever she chose. Crossing her legs, Rachel squeezed her thighs together. She'd been celibate for over two years now. Maybe she was just incredibly horny?

I'm not just incredibly horny, she cursed, swinging her feet back down to the bobbly rug, beautifully warm from the heated floor. If she was just incredibly horny she'd have accepted Jenny's invitation of a lift home. She could have parked them up in the lane before the barns came into view and quenched her horniness before walking that final bit home. Jumping up again to resume pacing, she knew it was ridiculous. She needed someone to talk to. She couldn't just dart around her lounge all night questioning her confusion; she needed a sounding board, someone who wouldn't sugar the pill. Lauren wouldn't sugar the pill. Lauren would set her straight. Lifting her phone, she stopped as she pictured the kiss in the bar. Lauren wouldn't be setting anyone straight, she'd be with Trudy, doing the most un-straight things.

Dropping back onto the arm of the sofa, she imagined what those un-straight things might be. Lauren would occasionally go into detail about her sex life but a certain shyness would always stop her from being too graphic. Rachel gulped down more wine. Why on earth did she want graphic? She was straight, wasn't she? She'd always been straight. This was all just a natural bit of girl-on-girl inquisitiveness, wasn't it?

The beep of her phone took her attention.

Reading the message slowly, Rachel realised she might have a chance to find out.

****

Hiding out in the Pizza Express, Lauren ran through her plan once again. She'd consumed far too many cocktails and didn't want to act rashly or do something she'd later regret, but she knew some action was needed. Food and water was step one. A corner booth in the fast-emptying restaurant had provided a change from the cocktail bar's low-lit stairwell, her previous place of hiding after spotting the kiss. She had thought about going back down to tell Trudy, but that would have caused a whole other interference that she didn't want to deal with, especially considering the seriousness of what she'd just seen. Trudy would try to make it funny when it wasn't funny at all. It was heartbreakingly horrifying. Her best friend had done this all by herself and Rachel never did anything all by herself.

Lauren bit into the pizza. Plus, this was her area of expertise. She was the lesbian. She should be offering the guidance, but Rachel had frozen her out. Jenny however, well she had the all-access pass, didn't she? Lauren tapped the table. She'd go round. She had to go round. It wasn't too late and she had a key. She'd just wander in, acting like she'd been in the area and see what was said. She stopped herself. She'd have to get a taxi. But why would she be getting a taxi to Rachel's at half-ten at night? And without a text? She'd always text first, not necessarily to ask permission, but at least to announce her arrival.

She took another bite. What if she said she'd lost her phone and her house keys? Her whole bag in fact. And maybe whoever she'd been with had ordered and paid for her Uber. But who had she been with? She couldn't say Trudy because she was bad at lying and when asked how Trudy had been she wouldn't be able to reply without cringing, or laughing, or going red. No. She'd been with a bride, testing the drinks on offer from a mobile cocktail bar they were thinking of using at a reception. But what reception venue wouldn't be able to make their own cocktails? A marquee? And who was having a marquee? Rachel knew details of all the weddings she was planning, plus she'd have to throw her bag and phone into the bushes at the barn because she couldn't leave them here and she couldn't arrive with them either. Dropping the pizza back onto her plate, Lauren rubbed at her temples. She was too drunk for all this, plus she couldn't lie on a good day, so maybe she should just text and turn up. What was the worst that could possibly happen?

****

Sliding her phone under a cushion, Rachel knew she had to ignore it. She didn't know Jenny well enough to have her in her home at ten-thirty at night while her seven-year-old son slept in his bedroom. What if he came downstairs? She glanced back at the old-fashioned latches on the heavy wooden doors. They made such a racket whenever Parker reached up to open them that she'd have plenty of warning of his imminent arrival. She lifted the cushion and found her phone. No. She couldn't. What if Jenny was actually a murderer? Yes, she had spent the afternoon carefully assessing Jenny's LinkedIn profile and lawyer details on her firm's website, and everything appeared to be in order, but what if she wasn't who she said she was? Rachel stopped herself. She was. She'd met her. And other people had seen her meeting her too. So it was fine.

She tapped on her phone. But this was her home and it was late. What did the message say again? She read it once more. **I live ten minutes from the barn conversions. We never did have that drink.** Again, like Jenny's initial contact it was factual and to the point. It didn't ask for a reply but it would be rude not to give one; plus the way she'd rushed off after their kiss was abrupt and uncivilised and she hadn't properly thanked Jenny for getting the bill at the restaurant. But what could she say? **Do you want a quick coffee? I'm the barn at the end.** Or: **Maybe another day. Thanks for the meal.** Or: **Are you after one thing, Miss hot-shot, hot-eyed lawyer?** Of course she was after one thing. Coffee at ten thirty at night almost always led to one thing. But Parker was here so that wouldn't happen. Not that she even wanted it to happen. Or did she? And why couldn't she? Having a child shouldn't make you a saint. And when was the last time she did something for herself? Something daring and rash? She refreshed the screen ready to type before pausing; but she *was* a saint and she'd *never* been daring or rash. Taking a deep breath, Rachel closed her eyes, only opening them when her phone buzzed once again. Reading the new message, she smiled. And that was her mind made up for her.

****

Great. It had gone. Shoving her phone into her pocket, Lauren shuffled her way out of her booth and double-checked the cash she'd left on the table. People deserved to be treated properly. The service was good, so she left a nice tip. Her best friend was Rachel, so she was on her way round.

****

Pacing the hallway, Rachel questioned why she was nervous. She knew why she was nervous. She was nervous because she knew what was happening. She was opening that door, literally as well as figuratively.

The tap was quiet.

And there she was, in her space, lips on her lips, pushing her up against the beamed wall. 'I saw you drive off,' read the message. 'There are only four barns. I'm sure I can find you. Up to you if you open the door.' Upon which, Rachel had turned off her phone, thrown it under the cushion and started to pace, not knowing if she'd hide there in silence or open the door to all this. Well, she had opened the door, and it was happening, and it was—

"I'm sorry, I just came round for a coffee."

Rachel tried to recover from the full-on encounter. "I—"

"It's not nice being left hoping for more, is it?"

Rachel looked at the woman standing in front of her. "You've come round to teach me a lesson?"

"Do you want me to teach you a lesson?" The smile was wide. "See, we do have that spark."

"I shouldn't have run off."

"Let's just finish the night properly."

"Coffee?"

"In that gorgeous kitchen through there?" Jenny was craning her neck.

"Is that where you want it?"

The pause was deliberate once more. "So many sparks."

Rachel smiled. "Follow me."

CHAPTER THIRTEEN

Standing in front of her built-in coffee machine, Rachel spotted Jenny's approaching reflection in the chrome fascia before feeling her hands on her neck. The woman had stepped up behind her and was gently moving her curls to one side. Toby would often do that too, throwing his arms round her waist, before reaching up or down for a squeeze or a grab to signal that he wanted some action… and as much as she was quite happy to let him do what he needed to do, it was more of a 'get on with it' routine as opposed to this current tender, lighter-than-light touch on her neck that was sending goosebumps down her spine and shivers up her arms. Reaching out to steady herself, Rachel pushed her palm against the cold metal for support. Jenny's mouth was tasting her neck, the soft and supple lips were moving gently so the tongue could trace the fine hairs on her skin. Rachel moaned.

"I've not done anything yet," whispered Jenny.

Rachel moaned again. She knew from Lauren's discussions that lesbian sex lasted forever, pitched as a guaranteed succession of orgasms where you'd feel more than you'd ever felt before and question why you'd not got involved sooner. Well, she knew why she'd not got involved sooner: she'd been staying loyal to Toby, plus Lauren had never made any moves. She coughed. Why was she thinking about Toby and Lauren? Fair enough, this was the first time anyone had touched her since Toby had passed, but there was certainly no need for Lauren to pop into her mind.

"Everything okay?"

Rachel nodded as she picked up the two mugs from under the steaming spouts. "The coffee's ready."

"You liked that though?"

"I did like that."

"You're distracted."

Rachel turned around. "I was making the coffee. Here." She passed over a mug. "Shall we sit in the lounge?"

"Oh-kay."

"What?" Rachel glanced over her shoulder as she led the way. "Everything alright with you?"

"Usually when this happens we don't actually have the coffee."

"Don't we?"

"No, we go back into that kitchen and take each other on that counter of yours."

"*We* meaning the other women on Tinder?" She sat down on the sofa. "I'm new to this, remember?"

Jenny joined her, placing her mug on the table. "If it's happening it happens. It doesn't matter if a woman's never touched a tit in her life. If she wants to touch that tit she'll touch that tit. It's a myth that straight girls get nervous."

Rachel glanced down at Jenny's ample chest. Tits? Is that what they call them? Is that what they said? Touch my tits? Maybe she needed to be more forceful with Lauren. "I thought lesbians were meant to take it slowly with straight girls?"

"Another myth. It's the lesbians having to slow down the straight girls because they're so excited about touching that tit that they miss out the foreplay."

Rachel took a sip of her coffee. "I thought tit touching was foreplay?"

"Why are you smiling?"

Rachel tried not to laugh as she swallowed. Lauren would find this conversation hilarious. "Sorry, nothing."

"You don't want to touch my tits?"

Rachel looked again at the chest. "I might do."

"You don't. If you did they'd be in your mouth by now. We'd be up on that counter, my tits in your mouth, me trying to calm you down by scratching your back."

"Ooo."

"You like that?"

"I might."

"Can I be honest with you?"

"Of course."

"You're straight. You're sitting there all huddled up, clutching onto the coffee that you're actually drinking while I'm open to you, tits on display, coffee on the table, hands free and ready for action."

"Does this directness usually work?"

"It doesn't have to work. It's already happening, we're already on that counter—"

"With tits in our mouths. I get it."

"But you don't want it?"

Rachel shrugged. "I opened the door, didn't I?"

"So maybe you're interested in the idea, but not the execution."

"That kissing was hot."

"So let's kiss. Put your coffee down, I want you closer to me."

Rachel put down her mug. This was ridiculous, she felt all giggly and childish. "So I don't go for your tits first?"

"You stop talking and let your emotions take over."

"I'm not sure I've got any emotions yet."

"Your physical desires then."

"I liked that kiss."

"So close your eyes and just kiss me."

"Why do I have to close my eyes?"

"Because you obviously want somebody else."

"Do I?"

"I think you do."

"And you don't mind me using you?"

"I'm a lesbian. You're cute. It's no biggy."

Rachel laughed. "Like my test flight."

"What?"

"Nothing." She closed her eyes. "I'm leaning over to kiss you."

****

Lauren walked the final bit down the lane because she hadn't wanted the taxi to draw attention to her arrival. Rachel's non-reply to her text had awoken a ridiculous paranoia in part of her brain that she couldn't switch off. What if Jenny was there? No, it was the concoction of cocktails talking. There was no way Rachel would have invited that woman back to her home. Rachel was sensible, and the in-laws were there, and weird Trevor and so was Parker. So why was she walking the last leg of the route?

Looking towards the communal parking bay, Lauren noticed the black Jag. Usually, the area was only occupied when one of the residents of the four barn conversions held a party or gathering, but there were no other cars in the spaces. She walked up to it slowly. Surely Jenny didn't own a black Jag? If she did she'd have parked it on Rachel's drive. But what if she didn't know which barn was Rachel's? What if she was an unexpected guest? An unwelcome guest? Everyone knew of the new barn conversions on the Langley Road, not that they were that new anymore, but people knew them, and Rachel was friendly, she was bound to have mentioned where she lived.

Looking towards the barn at the end, Lauren decided to run. What if something bad was happening right now? What if Jenny was having her wicked way with her Rachel? She slowed her pace. The in-laws' car had gone and Rachel's hatchback was in front of the barn. Maybe she should look first? A quick peep through the window wouldn't do any harm.

****

Pushing Jenny's arms above her head, Rachel straddled the woman on the sofa. She held onto her wrists and moved back to her neck.

"See, I'll be asking you to slow down in a minute."

"Shhh," said Rachel, "I thought we weren't meant to be talking."

****

Lifting her hands to the window, Lauren cupped her fingers together. She was crouched in the flowerbed in front of the lounge, peeping just high enough to see over Chetwynd the beanie cat on the windowsill.

She gasped. Who the hell was in there?

CHAPTER FOURTEEN

"It was like some full-on professional lesbian show!" Lauren was pacing around the purple sofas in the middle of her shop. "There was bondage and hair flicks and all-sorts."

Trudy frowned. "Whose hair flicks and what bondage?"

"Wrist holding bondage and Rachel's big curls flicking around everywhere. She was acting like a total dominatrix, holding and flicking, before she moved in for some full-on porn star snogging."

"What's the difference between porn star snogging and normal snogging?"

"The bondage and the hair flicks! Plus it was all grindy and their tits were pushing together."

"I thought they had their clothes on?"

"They did, but you could still see their bodies all intertwined."

"So it was just a kiss then, boss."

"It wasn't just a kiss, it was a wrists-held, bondagey hair flicks, porn star type snog." Not once in her multitude of first encounter scenarios with Rachel had she pictured anything so graphic. She'd imagined her best friend looking angelic in soft lighting with smooth music and the gentle lifting of hands to cheeks, not some full on onslaught of degradation.

"How long did you watch for?"

"Trudy!"

"What?"

"Seconds! Milliseconds! I fell backwards into the plant pots and crawled down the drive on my knees. Then I ran down the lane and phoned another taxi like I was the murderous freak with dirty plant pot legs and a post-traumatic shocked white face."

"You can't have been that shocked by it though, boss? If you saw them kissing on the street the logical assumption would be that the kissing carried on at home."

"Not on a first date!"

"You, my lady, get down before you've even had a proper first date. The scene's small, I've heard the gossip."

"I'm seasoned!"

"So? Good for her, I say. It's about time she let loose and had fun. She's been through a lot, Lauren."

"So have I!"

"He wasn't your husband."

"What are you talking about?"

"She's been through a lot. She's finding her feet."

"I'm her feet. I'm her backbone. I'm the skin to her skeleton."

"That's gross."

"It's our thing!"

"Just talk to her; this is getting boring and I've got a bride in at ten."

"We've both got a bride in at ten. This is my company, remember?"

"Just calm down, would you? Let me make you one of my hot chocolates."

"It's your bloody hot chocolates that got us here in the first place! And I hope you've shredded that ridiculous folder."

"I've adapted it. Please, just sit down and listen."

"I haven't got time."

"You have. It's Deloris at ten. Deloris is always late."

"What is this? Role reversal? If I sit down it's because I decide to sit down, because I'm the boss."

"You are, boss."

"Right. Well I'm sitting down."

Trudy picked up the Rachel folder that had been nestled next to the sofas. "I'll rip this page out. See, boss, it's ripped, it's screwed, it's gone."

Lauren watched the ball of paper roll to rest under her desk. "You need to pick that up."

"I will, just wait." Trudy started to scribble. "Plan B." She underlined the next word three times. "Jealousy. You make her jealous."

"Of what?"

"Of me."

Lauren laughed. "Trudy, bless you. I know I've come in all of a flap and rattled on about my own personal dilemma, but we will, at some point, have to address our little tête-à-tête from last night."

"No, we won't, but what we can do is use our natural spark and banter to launch Plan B."

"There is no Plan B."

"What are you going to do then, boss? She hasn't replied to your gif messages, she hasn't replied to your text message last night. You need a plan."

"I'll talk to her."

"You won't. You'll make her jealous. You'll say we're dating."

"She's seen me dating for the past eleven years and never been jealous."

"And how many of those women have you gushed over? How many of those women has she actually believed you'll end up with?" Trudy lifted her fingers into zeros. "None. Exactly. No one's ever threatened her role before. She's your number one and she's got comfortable in that position. If she sees you actually happy for once it might nudge her into action."

"What action?"

"Her declaration of attraction."

"She's not attracted."

"She will be when she sees you wanting me and me wanting you, and it'll be hard, boss, but I can take one for the team."

"A face not a finger?"

Trudy laughed. "Very witty, boss, but I'm serious, sometimes people don't know what they want until they can't have it anymore, then they realise they actually want it."

Lauren stood up and walked to the front of the shop. "Trudy, I like the simple life and I had that simple life before you started your folder and led me to believe I could have something I couldn't. Rachel always has been out of bounds and she always will be out of bounds. If I hadn't listened to you I wouldn't have gone out last night, I wouldn't have seen them kissing and I wouldn't be feeling like I'm feeling right now."

"And how are you feeling?"

"I feel hurt. Deeply hurt. And stupid. I feel like a fool who's trespassed somewhere they shouldn't. Rachel obviously has her own life – which she's fully entitled to have – and I have my own life that's simple and predictable where I know what I'm doing and where I'm going."

"Your social life's far from predictable. You're an adventurer, boss."

"Fine. I mean my relationship with Rachel. It's been predictable. I've secretly lusted, she's stayed my friend."

"You're scared, aren't you? This has thrown you." Trudy joined her at the shop window. "Fantasies are safe because they're just that – fantasies. The minute there's a chance reality might creep in, you have to assess whether or not you really want that fantasy after all."

"See, too confusing, too deep. I like simple. I never play games. I'm someone who says what they mean and means what they say."

Trudy's pitch was high. "You are not, boss!"

"I'm not talking about Rachel."

"Everything's always about Rachel."

"I just want things back to how they were."

"But she's moving on. From what you've said you had it easy with Toby. He liked you, you were part of their gang and you had your own little place in their setup. You're starting to realise now that you might lose her when someone else comes along."

"I'd never lose her, she's my best friend."

"Who's moving on, and you need to move on too."

"With you?"

"To gee her into action."

"Games! I'm not playing them!" Lauren looked out onto the street. "And what's Camilla doing crossing the road? I thought it was Deloris at ten?"

"It is."

"So why's Camilla..." She stopped as the woman surreptitiously slipped into the shop next door.

"Ooooo," said Trudy.

"It'll be her pre-nup."

"Without Ian? No. They'll be having an origami session in his back room."

"I really hope not."

"Why? It'll give Ian an easy out."

"And if Ian doesn't know? It's more games and more lying." Lauren shook her head. That's what was hurting the most.

"What?"

"Nothing."

"I get it. You feel like Rachel's cheated on you with Jenny. Boss, just get rid of this downcast, deadbeat mindset. It hasn't even been twenty-four hours since that Facebook friend request. She'll tell you. You're best friends of eleven years, of course she's going to tell you, and if she doesn't then I spring into action."

"With your offer of a face fuck?"

"I'd like to be wined and dined first."

Lauren smiled. Trudy, bless her, was trying her best. The least she could do was play along for a second. "And where would you like me to take you, my lady?"

"I'd like you to throw your arm around my shoulder. That's it. Like that. And walk me over to the coffee machine. You can start by feeding me biscuits and hot chocolate before we head over to Nando's for lunch."

Lauren guided them away from the window. "You're a cheap date, I'll give you that."

"Fine, I'd like us to go to that grotesquely expensive posh restaurant in the centre of town."

"Skyward?"

"Yes, take me to Skyward, and isn't this cute the way I fit under your arm?"

The cough interrupted their role play. Lauren turned first, gasping as she saw Rachel standing in the doorway. "We're not going to Skyward," she said, trying to prise Trudy away.

Rachel nodded at the door frame. "How many times have I told you to get a bell on this thing?"

"There was nothing to see." Lauren tried to shift sideways. "Trudy, will you please let me go?"

Rachel shrugged. "It's fine. I know about you two anyway."

Lauren freed herself and walked to her friend. "There's nothing to know! We're just messing around!"

"Lauren, my lovely, you can do that with your other girlfriends, but don't do it with Trudy." Rachel moved to the coffee machine and selected her usual skinny latte. "I'm happy for you both. Honestly I am. A bit gutted you didn't tell me, but—"

"You didn't tell me about Jenny!"

"What about Jenny?"

Lauren shifted her weight; she couldn't say she'd been knee-deep in plant pot last night. "You became friends on Facebook."

"That happened yesterday."

"So did this! Not that this was anything, it was just…"

Trudy sidled up to the pair. "All a bit awkward isn't it? All of us moving on with our lives, I guess." She clapped her hands. "I know, let's make it a double date at Skyward on Saturday."

Lauren ignored the suggestion. "So you're just friends with her on Facebook?"

"I…" Rachel lifted her latte and blew on the froth. "I was coming round to talk to you, but now's obviously a bad time. I shouldn't assume I can just pop in and you'll free up whatever you're doing for me."

Trudy nodded. "She was finger feeding me hot chocolate and biscuits."

Lauren ignored her again. "Like I'm wrong to assume I can just message you and pop in?"

"I only saw your message this morning, but I think it's quite obvious now what you wanted to come round and say." She looked at Trudy. "Saturday at Skyward sounds lovely. I'll see if I can find someone to join me."

"Jenny?"

"Boss," Trudy was shaking her head, "that sounded too pointed."

"You still call her boss?" Rachel was frowning.

"She loves it, don't you, boss." Trudy reached out and squeezed Lauren's bottom.

Lauren jumped at the contact, as a loud "Uh!" sounded out.

Trudy laughed. "Steady on, it wasn't that good."

"Uh."

"I'm not even touching you now."

Rachel pointed to the wall. "And how many times have I told you to sound proof?"

"That's Sid's side. There's never usually any noise from Sid's side."

"Either side, it's off-putting. What even is that?"

Trudy shrugged. "I like the low hum of the delicatessen next door."

"That's not the low hum of the delicatessen." Rachel set her mug back down. "I wasn't even thirsty." She nodded. "Trudy, I'll see you on Saturday. Lauren, will I see you at four?"

"It's Wednesday, of course you'll see me at four. Why are you asking? Don't you want to see me at four?"

Rachel nodded. "I'll see you at four."

"Of course you will; it's Wednesday!"

Trudy waited for the shop door to close before spinning on her heels. "And Plan B gets fired into action!" She stopped spinning. "Are partners allowed to this thing at four?"

CHAPTER FIFTEEN

Walking into the community centre, Lauren felt more anxious than she'd felt for a long time. She'd spent the last two years coming here with Rachel and Parker, working with a couple of other families whose young children had also suffered bereavement; and while it had been incredibly tough at the start, that wasn't the reason for her current nerves. Parker loved this place; he'd made great friends with the boy who was there after the loss of his mother, and the girl who'd lost her sister, both accompanied to each session by one or two family members, as Parker was; because she *was* family. She was his godmother and she'd never let any personal anxieties get in the way of her duty.

She looked around for the Positive Purpose sign. It was one of those portable swinging ones with the PP bereavement charity logo in the centre and an arrow pointing her in the direction of whichever room had been allocated for the session. Parker had quickly found it very funny that on a Wednesday they'd always 'go pee-pees'. He had no clue what the sessions were ultimately about, apart from being fun with his friends… a sign their intended purpose was working.

Some days, the sessions would be in the big hall with the tumble gym equipment, other days they'd be in the media suite with interactive activities. Days like today they'd be in the small classroom with arts and crafts, guest speakers, or story time. Parker's favourite sessions, however, were the ones that took them outside: the adventure playground, the trampoline park, the swimming pool; he even quite liked the museum.

Opening the door to the classroom, Lauren knew he'd miss this when the two years of allocated funding ran out. The group had talked about continuing the meetings themselves, but if and when that happened was anyone's guess. She knew from her line of work that it was a lot harder to plan events than people first thought. Either way, next week's final session would be bitter sweet. Time had passed and healing had happened, but there would be a certain sadness when it all ended. Focusing, she smiled around at the group, not wanting to add maudlin to her already anxious mood.

"Parker," she said, instantly brightening as she saw him sitting on a table at the back of the room.

"Aunty Lauren! Where are your wellies?!" The young boy laughed as he jumped from his seat, racing into her arms.

"Wellies?"

"We're at the farm, remember! I told Mummy she had to go to your shop and remind you!"

Rachel made her way over to them. "I was a bit flustered, sorry."

"You didn't remind her, Mummy? You had all day to remind her!"

"I did remind her, just not about the wellies."

Lauren looked down at her white chinos and sandals. She always brought a change of clothes to work on a Wednesday so she could fully participate in whatever activities the session involved, and this afternoon was meant to be classroom-based. "The farm trip's today? I thought that was next week?"

Rachel nodded. "Sorry. They changed the plans. I... It genuinely wasn't deliberate. I was a bit..." She dropped her gaze and fiddled with the tassels on her hoodie rolling them between her fingers.

Parker wrinkled his nose. "Why are you two being weird?"

"We're not!" said Lauren too quickly, false laughing as she smiled down at the boy who'd been watching with obvious interest. "My stripy t-shirt and white trousers make me look just like a zebra, which is perfect for the farm."

Parker performed his best mini-me eye roll. "You don't get zebras on a farm!"

"The text only came in this morning," said Rachel, her fascination with the tassels continuing. "I did come round but..."

"It's fine!" Lauren ruffled Parker's hair. "How many times have we done that barefoot walk at Bishley Gardens?"

"Loads!"

"Exactly! A bit of mud won't hurt your Aunty Lauren."

Rachel smiled and pointed at Lauren's sandals. "Aren't those your designer sandals?"

"It's fine, honestly, your Aunty Lauren never lets anything stop her!"

"Why aren't you talking to Mummy?"

"I am!" said Lauren, false laughing again. "We're all here and we're all going to have fun!" She nodded. "At the farm." She nodded again. "With my white chinos and sandals."

****

Sitting on the minibus, Lauren tried her best to sing *'chick chick chick chick chicken, lay a little egg for me,'* as enthusiastically as she could, but Rachel's distant gazes and occasional shy glances were getting to her. How could Rachel feel hurt or upset? Rachel was the one with the secret. Obviously it can't have looked good walking in on Trudy nestled under her arm as they planned a posh meal at Skyward, not to mention Trudy's initiation of Plan B, but it was nothing compared to the bondage porn snog she'd had to witness. "Join in, everyone," she said sharply, pointedly directing it at Rachel whose humming hadn't even been half-hearted.

Rachel's volume increased, but her gaze didn't move from the window. *"I haven't had an egg since breakfast, and now it's half past three."*

Lauren couldn't help it. "What did you have for breakfast?" she asked.

"What do you mean?"

"Breakfast. Was it eggs?"

"I'm not sure."

"You're not sure what you had for breakfast?" Lauren hummed the chorus. "Must have been a busy morning." She knew she was being testy. There was no way Rachel would have risked her son walking into her bedroom at night or finding a strange guest downstairs at breakfast.

"You two are definitely being weird," said Parker, turning in his seat with his nose back in its wrinkled position. "Is it because Mummy forgot to tell you about the farm and now you're going to get poop on your sandals?"

"I didn't forget," said Rachel, "and don't be rude, I just..." She turned to Lauren and lowered her voice. "You must really like her to keep it from me."

Parker spun round completely. "Ewww! Do you have a new girlfriend, Aunty Lauren? Uncle Trevor was saying last night that someone who has lots of girlfriends is dirty; that's why he hasn't had any yet because he likes to be clean."

Lauren knew a trademark twinkle twinkle was the only appropriate response, albeit a quiet one. "*Uncle Trevor talks such twonk, because he is a great big plonk. He lives alone with no girlfriend, because he is a big bell—*"

"Lauren!"

"What? You can't have Trevor telling him things that aren't true. The reason he doesn't have a girlfriend is because of his weird pig bol—"

"Farm!" said Rachel, pointing her finger at an opportune sign that had appeared up ahead. "Isn't this going to be fun!"

Lauren spoke under her breath. "*Bollocks.*"

****

"So," said the messy-haired lady who was hosting the session at the front of the farm building, "we'll start with a few warm up activities before we move on to the reason we're here." She smiled widely. "Hippotherapy."

Parker and his two friends laughed, their voices echoing under the corrugated iron roof. The space they'd been led to had clearly been used to house animals, machinery and crops at various points over the years as there was a scattering of hay, straw and fodder on the floor with rusty contraptions not-quite-hidden under tarpaulins in the corner and a lingering smell of manure.

"Hippotherapy?" Parker repeated. "Aunty Lauren watch out, hippos eat zebras!"

"They do not!"

"They do! I saw it on YouTube."

The woman continued. "Hippotherapy comes from the Greek word hippo, which means horse."

The three children whined. "Oww."

"And horses are very good at reading human emotions. Your horse will be able to tell if you're disappointed that it's not a hippo."

Parker spoke up again from his seated position in the circle of hay bales. "My aunty Lauren won't be disappointed because she's dressed like a zebra."

Lauren nodded at all the eyes that turned her way, nodding again as they came to a rest on her hugely inappropriate sandals. Everyone else in the group was kitted out in dark trousers and wellies, in keeping with their relaxed, if slightly prickly, seated positions. She, on the other hand, was perched on the edge of her bale, white chinos tucked together at the knee, sandals at tiptoe angle so they touched as little of the floor as possible. "It's fine," she said, "it's an old outfit." She placed her feet down properly to demonstrate, immediately feeling the soft surface of the barn floor squelch under her expensive soles.

The woman in command of the circle smiled. "Horses are also inherently honest."

"It's old stuff! It really doesn't matter." Lauren shoved up on her hay bale to make the point.

"They have an innate ability to mirror the thoughts and behaviours of others. They will read your body language and respond instantly. If you enter the horse's space with a negative attitude and defensive body language, chances are the horse won't want to interact with you. But if you enter their space with a sense of calm, confidence and openness you will see the horse respond positively." The woman clapped her hands together. "So today's hippotherapy, or less scarily for the zebra over there, *horse therapy*, should help us relax, think positive thoughts and forget all our negative emotions."

Parker put his hand up. "What do we actually do with our horse?"

"Whatever you want. Just try to interact. Talk to the horse, stroke the horse, some of you might even be able to lead the horse."

Lauren turned to Rachel and whispered, "I'm riding it," before remembering things were meant to be weird.

Rachel's reply was quick. "I'm going for the canter."

Turning properly on her bale, Lauren smiled at her friend. The fact Rachel was sitting there, all cute in her hoodie with wide eyes and a little lost soul look on her face, overwhelmed her with an urge to forget about everything. When you were best friends of eleven years there was nothing a good laugh couldn't solve. "I'm sorry," she whispered.

"For wearing sandals?"

"Ha. Good one."

"It's fine. Jenny's agreed to come out on Saturday."

Lauren shifted suddenly on the sharp straw. "Oh. Right."

"As my date."

She looked at the eyes. They weren't narrowed with malice, instead they appeared wide and wounded. "I was actually saying sorry for Trudy's make-believe relationship, but hey ho."

"Don't do that."

"Mummy, shhh, they're bring out the chicks!"

Lauren twisted back around. "Chicks. Yay." She lowered her voice. "We all know how I, with my never-ending rotation of girlfriends, love the chicks."

Rachel nodded. "Facts are facts."

The woman spoke loudly. "Aunty Lauren, you're very chatty, why don't you have a go first."

"I thought we were talking to horses?"

Parker tutted. "Weren't you listening, Aunty Lauren? We're warming up with some other animals first."

"That's right." The woman reached into the basket. "Come and sit on this bale at the front. I want you to show everyone how gentle you have to be. Let the chick sit on your knee, hold it in your hands. Just let it get to know you. Tell it what you're feeling."

Lauren stood up and muttered. "Trust me, it doesn't want to know."

"Eugh! Poo-ee!" Parker was giggling.

The little girl giggled too. "Your Aunty Lauren's done a poo poo."

The other little boy screamed and pointed: "Poo bum!"

Lauren glanced down at the back of her white chinos. "It's just a bit of dust from the bale." She tried to wipe, making the mess even worse.

"Accident, accident, accident!" Zoe, the youngest of the group, was revelling in the misfortune.

"It's just dirt from the bale."

"Accident, accident, poo, poo, poo!"

The little girl's mother stepped in. "That's enough, Zoe."

Lauren stood still waiting for the onslaught to end. "Right, where do you want me?"

"Accident!"

She turned again and stared at the girl. "Quite finished?" Zoe might have lost her sister two years ago, but that didn't give her an excuse to be such a little savage.

Parker giggled as he nudged his friend. "Do it, Zoe."

The mother's tone was warning. "Zoe..."

"ACCIDENT!" squealed the girl.

"I haven't had an accident! There was dirt on my hay bale!" Lauren coughed as she tried to regain her composure. These kids were all fine. If anyone needed therapy right now it was her. "Right. This bale?" she asked.

The woman nodded. "We need to show all the animals how calm we are, how open we are, how at ease we are with ourselves and our lives."

Lauren reached out to wipe the hay bale before sitting. "Damn it!" she gasped, stabbing herself with a stray piece of straw. "Sorry! But oww!" She looked up at the group. "Sorry, I'm sitting."

"On your poo bum," whispered Zoe.

Lauren stared at the girl. "I'm ready for my chick."

"You have to be calm."

"I'm calm."

"Look this way then please."

Lauren gave up eyeballing the six-year-old and looked at the woman with the messy hair. "Holding this chick will relax me?"

"No, this chick is a prey animal. It will read your body language and respond instinctively." She placed the fluffy yellow bird on Lauren's knees. "Let's see what it does."

Cupping her arms either side of her legs, Lauren started to coo. "Here we go, chick chick, you want me to lift you up? You want me to hold you?" She watched on as the yellow bird emptied its tiny bowels all over her white trousers.

Zoe screamed. "The chick's done a poo poo!"

Parker jumped up to get a closer look. "Eugh, it's all brown and watery."

Rachel cut in. "It's probably just more dust from the bale."

The woman with the messy hair spoke seriously. "No, that's definitely faeces."

Lauren nodded. "Of course it is."

"Surely that's just happened by chance?" said Rachel.

"No, that's a nervous bowel movement and that's what today's all about. Animals are known for their ability to foster change.

Once you become comfortable with yourself, the animal will become comfortable with you."

"I'm sitting in white chinos and sandals in a muddy barn," Lauren lowered her voice, "being shat on from all angles," she spoke again so people could hear, "of course I'm not comfortable."

The woman ignored her, instead working around the group to hand a chick to each member of the circle.

Lauren continued. "Or maybe it was so relaxed that it thought, hey, I don't care that everyone's watching, this lady's cool with it, so I'm just going to drop my load and go."

"What's with you today?" asked Rachel, having received her own chick and moved to the bale next to Lauren's. "Look, mine's nestled into my hoodie."

Lauren glanced down briefly before nodding at the coo-ing group. "Everyone looks like they're in a cute Easter advert while I'm over here with the one rogue baby chicken who's got the squits."

"It can feel that you're tense."

"Aren't you tense?"

Rachel shrugged. "I am as I always am."

"What's that meant to mean?"

"I never judge you, Lauren, I never have, I just—"

"*You* judge *me*?! What about—"

Rachel gasped. "Your chick!"

"What?"

"You dropped it!"

Lauren looked down at the muddy barn floor, her chick was lying on its back by her sandal, its stick legs pointing into the air. She scooped it back up between her palms and tried to rock it under her arm.

"Everything okay over there?" asked the woman.

Lauren rocked higher. "Yes lovely, thank you, we're getting on well."

"Don't be too vigorous, they're only a week old."

She waited for the woman to walk away, slowing her roller-coaster version of rock-a-bye-baby before looking down at the prone animal. "I've killed a one week old baby chick! Where can I put it?!"

"It's not dead and you can't put it in your handbag."

"I left my handbag on the minibus and it is, look." She placed the chick back on her knee only for it to keel over. "Swap, please Rachel, she'll think my dark persona killed it."

"It did."

"It didn't. I dropped it by accident."

"Because you weren't loving and caring enough. Because you were being defensive with a negative attitude."

"I wasn't, but please, if you love me you'll swap."

Rachel picked up the chick. "You know I love you. Here, look after mine."

Lauren cupped her hands around her knees as Rachel placed the new ball of yellow fluff onto her lap. "See, this one likes me. Here chicky chicky chicky." She tried to stroke it. "Dammit, now this one's gone and dropped its timber as well!"

"You've dropped it?"

"No, it's just jettisoned all of its sadness, which is no doubt my sadness, from its colon."

"Lauren, that's too much, but look, this one's tweeting again!" Rachel lifted the previously dead chick to the light. "This one's fine, come here you little cutie."

Lauren looked on as the bird's beady eyes squashed into the cheek that she'd never be squashed in to, being coo-ed over by the voice that would never coo over her. She sneered. "That chick was faking it."

"You're jealous of this chick?"

"Of course not."

"Just jealous that I became friends with Jenny on Facebook? Honestly, Lauren, it all happened so fast and I was going to tell you but when I came round today it was obvious you've got stuff of your own going on."

"Trudy was playing!"

"Lauren, that's the third time now. Please don't make me angry."

"You never get angry."

"Exactly, but I will. I know what I saw."

"You saw her messing around."

"Why deny her? You seem happy."

"I'm not happy! Look at the amount of shit this chick's covered me in! I'm clearly stressed and unhappy," she gasped, "and dammit where's that other chick gone?"

Zoe squealed from her hay bale: "Lauren's lost her chick, Lauren's lost her chick!"

"Just giving it the freedom we all crave in life. You'll understand that when you get older."

Rachel sighed. "That's it, isn't it? You want the freedom to do as you please and you don't like the idea you've been caught tied down to Trudy."

"I'm not tied down to Trudy."

"You'll upset me if you try to brush her off on Saturday."

"I won't."

"Good."

"Fine." Lauren took a deep breath. What had just happened? What had she just agreed to? "Anyone seen my chick?" she asked shyly.

Zoe giggled. "It wanted to come and have fun over here."

Lauren rubbed her hands down the sides of her chinos. "Of course it did."

CHAPTER SIXTEEN

"That guinea pig ejaculated on me!"

Rachel sighed. "Stop being so dramatic, Lauren."

"It did! It humped my forearm until it climaxed!"

"Stop it."

"I won't. I'm traumatised. It was bobbing up and down, getting faster and more frantic before it collapsed with hot sticky stuff seeping from its undercarriage."

"It probably just went to the toilet."

"I *can* tell the difference!"

"Since when have you been an expert on the bodily functions of guinea pigs?"

"It was bobbing and grunting. You don't do that on the toilet."

"I don't know…"

"You bob and grunt?"

"I'm just saying there's no way that guinea pig had sex with your arm."

"Why's it so hard to believe? What's wrong with my arm?"

"Nothing, but you accused that baby chick of emptying its bowels all over you."

"Everyone saw that!"

"And you said that llama spat at you."

"Look at my hair!"

"You accused the duck of being feral."

"I've got nicks on my ankle to prove it!"

"My point is, it's always them."

"Well, I didn't encourage that guinea pig. I didn't wine and dine it. I didn't woo it with roses."

"Hatty said that animals have an innate ability to mirror the thoughts and behaviours of others."

"Who's Hatty?"

"The woman!"

"She was talking about horses."

"God help you then."

"What?" Lauren followed Rachel's gaze to the huge Shire horse being led into the newer, more pristine barn they'd all moved to; this one was sectioned off into pens and the group was split up between more helpers.

"Let's hope he doesn't get frisky."

"I wasn't thinking about sex when I was holding that guinea pig, and I didn't have a sign on my white chinos that told that chick to squat and drop here. Likewise, I didn't request the llama to gob in my hair, and that duck… well that duck *was* just feral."

"No one else's guinea pig ejaculated."

"What's your point?"

"Hatty's right. Your anger and behavioural issues are surfacing through the animals' responses."

"We're here for Parker, not me."

"And look at him." Rachel nodded to the section of the barn where Parker was leading his little pony around in sensible circles.

"That man's helping him."

"He's not and you can't begrudge your godson his success. His horse is responding because he's an open and honest, happy little boy."

"My horse will respond." Lauren shook her head. "Oh, Hatty, why are you bringing me that buffalo?"

"This is Wilbur."

"No one else has a Shire horse."

"We like to match the temperament of the animals to the person involved. Wilbur's a bit old and sluggish."

"I'm twenty-nine and I wear white chinos and sandals!"

"He needs gentle encouragement. He needs calm."

"How can I be calm when your guinea pig—"

"Thank you, Hatty." Rachel took hold of the lead. "Lauren, here you go, you know the rules."

"Trust me I'm not going anywhere near its backside. I've been shat on enough times already today!"

Hatty gently waved the air with outstretched hands. "Calm, Lauren, calm."

"I'm calm, it's fine."

"We'll be right over here."

Lauren watched as the two women walked away. The three children had been given one horse and one helper each, with the adults paired up so they could take it in turns. Looking at Wilbur, Lauren was sure he couldn't possibly be a properly registered hippotherapy horse. Surely they'd have to undergo all sorts of extensive training like guide dogs. You couldn't just find a random Chihuahua and expect it to help you cross the road or tell you when to take your medicine. Likewise, you couldn't expect a wild seal to jump off a diving board whilst barking and clapping at the crowds. In the same vein, this old Shire horse couldn't be expected to foster change in a human – specifically, in her. In fact, it wouldn't surprise her if Paddy the gypsy strolled in with Sally the Shetland because sticking a horse in front of a few needy kids and claiming it could change their behaviour was a quick fire way to make money.

Lauren looked again towards Parker's pen. He'd now got his pony trotting around on the lead as he jogged ahead with giggles of delight. She sighed. Maybe it was a worthwhile scheme, but they'd obviously run out of money where Wilbur was concerned. She looked at the big shaggy horse. "Hello, Wilbur."

The horse turned its head and ignored her.

"I wasn't ignoring you. I was just looking over there at your friend in that pen. See him? He's trotting. Shall we do some trotting?" She lifted the lead and started to jog as best she could in her sandals. "Let's trot."

Wilbur yanked his head back, his huge feet still planted firmly on the floor.

"Ow!" She let go of the lead. "You've just given me rope burn!"

Hatty arrived back into her area. "So far, we can see that you like to run before you can walk and when things don't go your way you relinquish all responsibility."

"Hatty, this isn't a hippotherapy horse."

"Animals have been used for thousands of years in therapy."

"But this isn't one of the good ones."

"He can hear you. He can sense your disapproval."

"Good."

"Be honest with him. Open yourself up to change."

"I don't want to change."

"So neither will he."

"He's just going to stand there?"

"Yes. Why would he want to interact with you?"

"I don't know, Hatty, maybe I'm good fun."

"So show him." The woman made her way back out of the area once again.

Lauren turned to the horse. "Why the long face?"

"Oh good god, Lauren," shouted Rachel. "You need to do better than that."

"Stop shouting, you're scaring him."

Hatty chipped in. "Start by calling him Wilbur. People often respond better if you address them by their real name."

Lauren whispered. "You're a frikkin horse, you have no clue what I'm saying." She started to pace. "Okay then, Wilbur, let's get real shall we? Real and funny. That's who I am, that's what I do." She walked back up to his ear and whispered. "Yo mamma's so fat the horse on her polo shirt's real."

Wilbur stayed motionless.

"That was funny! You didn't find that one funny?"

Wilbur wasn't even blinking.

"What do you want from me? You want to watch me dance? I know! You want to watch me whip? Watch me neigh neigh! Get it! Neigh neigh!"

Hatty appeared next to her shoulder. "You try to use humour to diffuse awkward situations, don't you?"

"This isn't an awkward situation." Lauren looked around at the other pens and all the other interacting horses. "We're just having a bit of banter before we head off to plough a field."

"Be honest. Say what you need to say."

"Okay, I liked the idea of warming up with the smaller animals first, but whatever funding the NHS is giving you for these—"

"To Wilbur! Talk to Wilbur."

"About what?"

"Whatever's going on with you."

"It's embarrassing talking to a horse."

"It's called honesty. We're moving away, we can't hear you. Come on, Rachel, let's stand by the fence."

Lauren turned to Wilbur and sighed. "You're not interested in what I've got to say. No one's interested in what I've got to say."

Wilbur made a notable exhale from his damp, velvety nostrils.

Lauren looked up at his big brown eyes. "You are?"

The horse exhaled again, nudging his head towards her body.

Lifting her hands to his cheeks, Lauren spoke quietly. "Okay then, big boy, you see that girl over there? That's right, the one in the wellies and hoodie? No, not old Hatty, I'm talking about that hotty with the pretty face." Lauren smiled. "That's my Rachel." She lowered her voice further. "And I love her."

Wilbur lifted his large front leg and started to tap his giant foot.

"You like this, Wilbur?" Lauren was rubbing his cheeks. "You like this, old boy? Okay, I'll go on. I have to be quiet though because I can't let her hear. I've never said any of this out loud and I'm not sure I ever actually will." She stayed quiet. "I've told Trudy bits, but I've not gone into detail."

Wilbur changed legs and tapped with his other equally large foot.

"You want detail? Okay then, big boy, you're definitely ready?"

The horse whinnied and nodded vigorously.

Lauren smiled. "Well keep this to yourself."

The tail swished.

"Life's a really funny thing." She glanced around to check no one could hear. "It's short but long, and dangerous but safe, and most people spend their days in a nice but mundane way." She shrugged. "I don't want nice but mundane. I want the dream. The rollercoaster. The fly by the seat of your pants, grab every moment and dare to live life to the max. You get one shot in this world, Wilbur, and I've been having my shot, by myself mostly, and while it's been fun and while I've been happy, there's someone I want by my side." She smiled. "That pretty girl over there. And don't get me wrong, Wilbur, she is by my side as a friend, and we've had adventures and we've found fun, but she's never been in it like I have. She doesn't see our potential. She doesn't realise how incredible everything could be."

The horse nestled its head into her chest.

"And I have dreams you know, of our life together; of the laughter and the holidays. Of the romance. I'd show her true love. Real love. The kind of love that makes everything magic. The kind of love you see once in your life." She sighed. "I'm not making any sense, am I?"

The horse gently butted her with his head.

"Okay, let me try to be clearer. Rachel and I together would outshine all the stars in the sky. We'd have a power and an energy to rival the swell of the tides and the pull of the oceans. We'd be our own force of nature. I feel our potential every time we're close." She stopped as another head nudge made her chest feel warm and befriended. "So why don't I tell her? That's what you're asking? Well, I always say I don't want to lose what we've got; that something is better than nothing. But if I'm honest, I think I'm scared. I'm scared of rejection." She bit the inside of her lip and spoke at barely a whisper. "I'm so scared of rejection. But, Wilbur, you have to know that nothing scares me in life. I roll with the punches; I get up when I'm down. I've suffered loss and misfortune and I'm okay. I survive. But this? This is much deeper. I couldn't bear it if I was wrong. I think that's the bottom line. Imagine feeling something so deeply only to be told: no, it's not there."

The horse nudged her forward.

"You want to walk?" She grabbed hold of the rope lead. "Okay, big boy, let's walk."

Wilbur neighed heartily.

Rachel ran over. "Lauren! You did it!"

"I did do it." Her smile was wide.

"What were you saying?"

"I talked about Black Beauty. She's a dark horse, you know."

Wilbur stopped walking.

"Come on, matey." Lauren pulled on the rope.

"What did you talk about really?"

"Nothing."

"You're lying."

"I'm not!"

Wilbur lifted his head.

"See, he's still responding."

"He's not."

"He is! You're responding, aren't you, big boy?"

Wilbur threw his head up and forward in a humongous horse sneeze, spraying Shire snot all over Lauren's top.

Lauren gasped. "Eugh!"

Rachel looked carefully at the splattered t-shirt. "Oh well, never mind, another animal's excretions to add to your collection."

"Aunty Lauren, you look all gooey!" Parker was laughing from his pony pen.

"Parker, mate, I'm coming to you for some tips." Handing over the rope to Rachel, she tried to wipe away the wet mess. "Wilbur's all yours."

"Go on, Mummy, make him trot." Parker was leaning over the railings.

"She has to learn to walk before she can run, Parker. First she has to talk calmly and quietly. Then she has to—"

"Go, Mummy, go!" Parker was giggling.

Lauren turned back around. "God damn you, Rachel, you're like a jockey at the Grand National!"

"Mummy's great isn't she!"

Leaning against the railings of Parker's pen, Lauren smiled. "She really is."

"She must be a very honest person. My instructor told me if I was honest with my horse then he would do what I wanted."

"And he did."

"I know." The boy smiled. "I told him I wanted Mummy to stay with me forever. Just Mummy. No new daddy. Just Mummy and me."

Lauren frowned. "You don't want Mummy to meet someone and be happy?"

"She's happy with me."

Looking at her friend trotting round the barn with her horse, Lauren nodded. "Parker, my man, you've got it right there."

CHAPTER SEVENTEEN

Walking towards the exclusive Skyward restaurant along the pretty street with its perfect landscaping and elegant lamps, Lauren was reminded of the romantic dance scene in *La La Land* where the two main characters spoke briefly before saying everything they really wanted to say via the dance. She looked at the lamp post ahead. Why couldn't she express herself in some way, in any way, to Rachel? If Rachel were here, would she be able to shuffle ball change along to the lamp post and swing round it before Rachel caught her? Would they spin, twirl and tap their way around the small squares of shrubbery built into the pavements? She shook her head; of course they wouldn't; she couldn't even tell Rachel about Parker's barnyard disclosure. The only time she'd referenced it was to her horse, having gone back for another go with Wilbur. She'd been honest about how Parker's statement had made her feel and what it might mean for the future, resulting in a rather fast trot around the pen; but it was yet another dose of reality to spike holes in her dream. Lauren knew she'd never put her own feelings ahead of her godson's, no matter how much she felt like the ocean or the tides.

Huffing, she slowed her walk and lifted her eyes to the low evening light. Sometimes it really was rather ridiculous how lost she let herself get in the fairytale; as if dating Rachel was even a choice, and the fact she'd confessed everything to a great big Shire horse made it all so much worse!

"Finally she slows!" shouted Trudy, tottering along in the same bodycon dress from Tuesday night's cocktail session, this time accessorised with a pair of skyscraper heels.

"Don't be so raucous, this is the even posher part of town."

"There's no one around."

"They're being discreet, plus I'm never late to events."

"This isn't an event. It's a double date and the restaurant's just there."

Standing still, Lauren waited for Trudy to catch her breath. Maybe if Wednesday night's minibus ride home hadn't been so full of laughter and wails from delighted children and adults she'd have spoken privately to Rachel. But everyone was so happy having connected with their animals that she didn't want to dampen the mood. Plus Rachel was obviously an open and honest person, happy with her lot in life, because Wilbur had moved almost instantly for her. She clearly wasn't pining or lost, or angry and confused; she was just Rachel whose horse immediately loved her. Not to mention that she could raise murdered week-old chicks from the dead. There wasn't any reason at all to ask if she was okay. Just like there wasn't any reason to ask if Parker was okay. Everyone was okay, and she would go on this date tonight and be okay.

Deep down, Lauren knew part of this evening was about testing the water. If Rachel *was* going to date someone new and Parker *was* going to struggle with that change, she wanted that person to be Jenny, not her. Grimacing, she realised how awful that sounded, but Parker would no doubt be doubly upset if he thought he was losing his mother and his godmother all in one go. If Rachel went public with Jenny she could talk to Parker and gauge his feelings before putting herself in the mix as a better option. Not that Rachel even saw her as an option… and there she was, back to square one.

"Boss, I know I'm the one gasping, but you look pained and anxious." Trudy dropped her hands to her knees and exhaled. "We're meant to be head-over-heels in kinky lust."

"Maybe that's why I'm pained and anxious and will you please stand up straight? You look like you're doing Tina Turner's wide-legged dance."

"You need to put your arm around my waist as we walk in."

"You're not a cripple."

"Hold my hand then."

"Trudy, we're pretending."

"Exactly, so pretend." Trudy stood upright, her skyscraper heels doing a good job of levelling out the height difference between them. "You want to show Rachel what she's missing. You want to spark her jealous, possessive streak. You're not going to do that by marching in there alone."

"It shows I'm strong."

"It shows you're a shit girlfriend; plus the whole jealousy thing won't work."

"Fine," said Lauren, reaching over to hold Trudy by the waist.

"Now pinch my bottom."

"I'm not pinching your bottom!"

"Get into character."

"Who am I? A sex pest?"

"Pinch it!"

Lauren pinched.

"Hi there," said Rachel.

"I saw that," added the woman with the piercing eyes. "It's lovely to see a couple so lost in themselves they don't notice the passers-by."

Trudy stepped forwards and lifted her hand. "Trudy. She can't get enough of me; a real tiger this one."

Lauren stood motionless. Rachel's date was Amazonian. Tall and sculpted with silky hair blowing in the warm breeze and bare shoulders gleaming in the evening light. This woman would spin round a lamp post, no doubt about it, and her dress would ripple as she danced to the music of love.

Rachel interrupted the silent stare. "Lauren, this is Jenny. Jenny, Lauren."

"Nice to meet you, Tiger."

Lauren froze. She couldn't compete with that. The voice was too smooth and the greeting too teasing. What could she possibly do to come back? She couldn't say: hello She-Ra or: hi there Jet from Gladiators, or: do you mind tilting your head slightly as the bronzer highlighting your sharp cheekbones is blinding me. She looked up. She had it. "Rawwr," she said, with a claw swipe that ended up more half-hearted than assertive.

"Excuse me?" The eyes stayed focused.

Lauren paused. "Rawwr," she said again, wondering what was wrong with her and why she couldn't just say a normal hello. The perplexed stare cued her explanation. "I'm a tiger." She stood still. What in god's name was she doing?

"Shall we?" said the confident woman.

Lauren looked at the outstretched arm herding the group the final distance up the street towards the steps of the restaurant. This wasn't *Jenny's* gathering so why should *Jenny* take charge? *Jenny* didn't know anyone here, well, apart from Rachel's tonsils, but still, she should be the one blending into the crowd, not acting like group leader. "Let's," said Lauren, lifting her own hand and waiting for Jenny to move, channelling tiger like never before.

"After you."

"No, really." Lauren stood her ground.

Trudy shouted from the top of the steps. "We've just finished our starters up here."

"After you, Jenny," said Lauren, loudly enough for everyone to hear. She shunted her hand and smiled, nodding as the sleek panther-like woman finally moved, Lauren dancing up the steps behind her. One nil and winning.

"Shall we?" said Jenny, reaching for the door.

This time Lauren let her play doorman. "Lovely, I booked us a table," she said, waltzing in first, the adrenaline of being top dog adding a real buzz of excitement to the evening. Who cared if Jenny had gorgeous eyes, silky smooth hair and a body to die for? Who cared that Jenny was on a date with the woman she actually wanted? For now, all that mattered was this one-upmanship, and she was well in the lead. Skyward was the most exclusive restaurant in the area and she'd managed to get them the booking. "Lauren Hilliard," she said, looking over her shoulder for Rachel's approval.

The pause was long. "And how do you spell that, please?"

"Hill-i-ard. As it sounds."

The waiter lightly swooshed his finger down the list of names. "With an H?"

"Yes, with an H." Lauren kept the smile plastered on her face as she turned to give Rachel a reassuring nod.

"Not an S?"

"No, not an S." She turned again, expecting to see supportive eyes, but instead she caught Jenny's smirk.

"I have a Lauren Silliard here."

"Right, well that must be me then."

"You're Lauren Silliard?"

"With an H."

"Apologies. Follow me, please, Miss Shilliard."

Lauren kept her focus forward as she led the group through the glamorous restaurant. Jenny would be loving this, but the fact still remained that she'd secured the booking, mis-spelt name or not. Skyward was notoriously hard to get into, especially at such short notice, and it was her connection to a bride who'd hired the whole venue last summer that had got them seated. Taking in the intimate opulence, Lauren felt her walk become taller. This place was something special: large sparkling lights swirling out from the ceiling and wispy white drapes accessorising the tables and chairs like clouds floating in gourmand heaven, the white gloves of the waiters like doves swooping around. She glanced towards Rachel and raised her eyebrows; she'd be impressed.

The voice was gushing. "Jenny? Jenny, is that you, darling?"

Turning around, Lauren spotted the owner, a Mrs Josephine Betts, dressed to the nines, with arms outstretched pulling Jenny in for a cuddle.

"You should have told me you were coming, darling!" continued Mrs Betts. "Have you got your regular table?"

"It's fine, Josie, I'm here with friends."

Josie? She'd never said she was called Josie. "Josephine, hello." Lauren stepped into their space.

The woman's face was blank.

"Lauren Hilliard."

Still blank.

"Wedding planner? We hired Skyward last summer."

"Right, yes, you phoned on Wednesday. I think they're squeezing you in over there. We can't have that though, not if you're friends with my darling Jenny."

Lauren looked at Trudy and Rachel who were watching and wondering no doubt what the connection was between the two women. "It's fine," said Lauren. "It looks nice over there." She glanced towards the slightly dark corner and corridor that led to the toilets.

"I shan't hear of it. Come, come."

Jenny smiled and lifted her hand to encourage the group. "It is rather splendid."

"Is it like a secret room?" said Trudy, already tottering after the owner.

"It's our heavenly VIP suite. Jenny helped me with a legal issue a while back and for that I will be forever grateful."

Lauren watched as the party of four moved away. She looked back at the dark corner; what choice did she have but to slink along after them? Catching up with Rachel, she hushed her voice. "I always prefer to be in the main restaurant where you can feel the hubbub and get a sense of the atmosphere, don't you?"

"Stop being jealous."

Lauren signalled towards the two women who were enthralling each other with loud laughter and smiles. "You think I'm jealous of a mafia mob lawyer?"

"Yes, I do."

"Hey, this is me, this is us." She tried a gentle nudge. "No one comes between the yin and the yang."

"You're doing a pretty good job of that all by yourself, Lauren. Now go play tiger with Trudy."

"Wait," she reached out for her friend's arm, "*you're* not jealous are you?"

"Of Janette Krankie on stilts? Of course not."

"So why are you quiet?"

"Why are you making so many animal noises?"

"You want to be the kitty to my cat?" She thought she'd try.

"This was a bad idea."

"So let's sneak off to Nando's."

"Why would we sneak off to Nando's? I'm here with Jenny and you're here with Trudy."

"We don't have to be."

"Yes we do, now get in there and behave."

Lauren looked towards the white door through which Josephine and the others had just disappeared. "Looks a bit dark and dank to me."

Trudy's head popped back out. "Boss, come and get a load of this! It's our own private room, so bright and sparkly."

"Stop with the boss thing," said Rachel, walking to the door. "It's too weird."

"We can't reveal our actual pet-names," said Trudy, giggling as she stepped aside to let them both in, "they're even weirder."

Lauren tried to ignore her impressive surroundings. A baby grand piano in the corner, white, like the wispily draped table and chairs. The same lights swirling down from the glittering ceiling, this time made even more impressive by the small size of the room; in fact they looked like star-lit tornados. She focused on Trudy. "Please don't," she chose to say.

"Please, do," said Jenny, getting wind of the conversation as Josephine darted back out of the room.

Trudy smiled. "Nicknames? She's my love puddle and I'm Mr Binkle."

Lauren tried not to laugh. They were both so atrocious that she found them quite funny, only nobody else was laughing. Looking back at the blank stares, she finally focused on Jenny. "Haven't you and Rachel got pet-names yet?" Okay, so Love Puddle and Mr Binkle might not be the coolest names around, but at least she and Trudy had names, albeit two seconds old.

"Not yet, no."

"Oh, that's a shame." And she's back in the game.

"But if we did they'd be something like diamond, or precious."

"Sounds like an East-End Gollum."

The eyes narrowed. "Better than referencing a flooding issue and a strap-on."

Lauren froze. Goddamn it, Trudy, what else could Love Puddle and Mr Binkle possibly mean? She thought fast. "Mr Binkle's Trudy's nipple piercing." Standing still in the silence that followed, Lauren glanced towards Trudy's body-con dress. Now she was pretty sure that Trudy didn't have a nipple piercing, in fact she'd never been sure if Trudy even had nipples, her big work bras, always visible under her ill-fitting shirts, did a good job of covering all surfaces.

"And Love Puddle?" Jenny wasn't dropping her stare any time soon.

Trudy spoke loudly. "Well, my nipple piercing and I are going to take a seat at Jenny's table if anyone would like to join us?"

Lauren snapped. "You can't call this Jenny's table."

"Sorry about that." Josephine was back in the room. "Right, welcome to Jenny's table. Here's some fizz. My pianist will be coming in to tickle the old ivories in a minute."

Jenny was smiling. "A private pianist, what a treat. Is this okay for everyone?"

And there she was again, playing group leader with her special room and special treatment. Lauren flexed her fingers. There was only one thing for it. "Don't worry about the pianist, Josephine, I can play."

"Ralph's a concert pianist," added Jenny.

"I've got this."

Rachel's voice was quiet. "I thought you only played that one piece?"

"You know I did the grades in school." Okay, so she'd done grade one, which she'd failed, with the examiner describing her playing as clunky and mistimed, but she could bring out the skills when needed and often did on random nights out in random bars with random pianos surrounded by random people treating her like she was Mozart reborn.

"I'll leave you ladies to it then. Your waiter will be in shortly." Josephine signalled to the table. "Make yourselves comfortable and please take a look at the menu."

Trudy giggled as they were left alone, sealed into the private den. "This is so exciting. Thank you so much, Jenny."

Lauren locked her fingers together and stretched. "Right, I think I should play."

"Wouldn't you rather sit down and chat?" Jenny was directing everyone to the table.

What was it with this woman and her need to play traffic controller? "I'd rather make music. What is it they say?" Lauren smiled. "Those who create music live in harmony?" She'd totally just made that up, but the one song in her repertoire always brought gasps of applause and involvement from all who listened. "Shall I?" she said, feeling the adrenaline starting to pump.

"Lauren, you're usually tipsy when you play." Rachel was looking concerned. "And your audiences are usually tipsy too."

"How nice that we can all appreciate a quick tune while we're sober then." She walked towards the white piano and pulled back the stool. "Come on round and join in if you like?"

Rachel moved behind her and whispered. "You're not playing that song, are you?"

"Of course not." Lauren tapped the middle C. Okay, so it was that song, but that song always went down so well. She tapped again. It would only take five taps before people started to sing. *Du du, du-du-du, du-du-du, du.* Silence. *Da da, da-da-da, da-da-da, da.* Still silence. *Dar dar, dar-dar-dar, dar-dar-dar, dar.* Oh god, she was going to have to burst into song. She shouted loudly. *"We're gonna rock, around, the clock tonight."* Lifting her left hand, she really let rip. This was where things often went a bit pear-shaped, but the crowd's loud singing always pulled her through. Only this time it was just her and the silence. She tried to get the fingering right, singing as forcefully as she could to disguise the mis-hit notes. *"Put your glad rags on and join me, hon."* She paused as her right hand stumbled. *"We'll have some fun..."* Dammit, that was flat. "Join in, guys."

Jenny's arms were crossed. "What song is it?"

Lauren started again. She was good at the first bit. It only took one finger repeatedly hitting the middle C, then the E, then the G. *Du du, du-du-du, du-du-du, du.* "Come on, guys!"

"Is it *Eye of the Tiger*?"

"No! *Five, six, seven o'clock, eight o'clock, rock.* Am I singing on my own?" She carried on, she obviously was. *"We're gonna rock—"*

"I think we're going to sit down, actually." Jenny was back in her traffic controller position, guiding Rachel to the table.

Rachel clapped a loyal, yet hesitant, clap. Trudy did a nod of: "Great stuff, boss" while Jenny pulled back one of the chairs.

"Thank you," said Lauren, standing from her stool and waltzing over to sit on the offering.

"That was actually for Rachel."

"Let me," said Lauren, pulling back the chair next to her own. "Rachel?"

"I ought to sit next to Jenny."

"Trudy then. Come over here."

"Always putting me first, aren't you, my Love Puddle."

"We never did find out where that came from." Jenny was staring as she took her seat.

Trudy smiled. "Puddles are often deeper than they first appear, and fear not, my tiger, I'm talking about your intellect and skill set. Who knew you were so proficient in the piano?"

Lauren smiled. "People who don't play are always amazed when they know someone who can. Do you have any pianist friends, Jenny?"

"I play a little myself, actually."

"Give it a bash then." It was going to be *Chopsticks*. Everyone who thought they could play played *Chopsticks*. In fact, Lauren remembered this one night where there'd been three of them on the piano, two of them playing *Chopsticks* as she harmonised with *Rock Around the Clock*.

Jenny sat on the stool.

Lauren nodded to get Rachel's attention. This was going to be embarrassing. Jenny probably wouldn't even do the high plinkity bit.

The cough was introductory as the hands were lifted, the chords sounding out gently from the keys.

Lauren gasped. She was playing *Hallelujah*. The haunting and beautifully melodic, *Hallelujah*.

Trudy started to sway as Rachel started to hum.

"Sing the chorus if you like," said Jenny, moving her shoulders in time with the music like real pianists do.

"*Hallelujah*." Trudy and Rachel had their eyes closed. "*Hallelujah*."

No one had their eyes closed when she had been playing.

"*Hallelujah*." Jenny's voice was angelic. "*Hallelujah*."

Lauren looked around at the swaying room. "Let's liven this up a little, shall we?" She jumped up, shoving Jenny to the edge of the piano stool. "This isn't a prayer meeting. *One two, three o'clock, four o'clock rock*."

Jenny tried to shunt her sideways. "*Hallelujah*."

"*Five six, seven o'clock, eight o'clock rock*." Lauren wasn't budging.

Jenny's volume increased. "*Hallelujah*."

"*Nine ten, eleven o'clock, twelve o'clock rock*."

"*Halle—*"

"*We're gonna—*"

"*lu—*"
"*rock—*"
"*ja—*"
"*around—*"

"I'm terribly sorry, but what's all this noise?" Josephine was back in the room.

Both women jumped up from the stool, Jenny speaking first. "Sorry, we're stopping." She returned to the table. "It would be lovely if Ralph would come and play, thank you, Josie."

Lauren waited for the owner to leave before twisting slightly to reach out with one finger. She pressed the G four times. "*...the clock tonight.*" And there we have it. Winner. Sauntering over to the table with a new lease on life, she took her seat next to Trudy. "Shall we order some starters?" There was no way Jenny could come back from this.

"I have a little something for Rachel first."

Lauren watched on as her opponent reached under the table for her bag. Not an engagement ring? No, of course not, this was their first date. So what would you possibly bring someone on a first date?

"You'd have seen a bunch of flowers, so I thought I'd surprise you with a single red rose."

Lauren saw the gorgeous gift, kept safe in its carefully wrapped cellophane and could do nothing to silence Rachel's soft gasp of appreciation.

"And I have something for you too, Trudy," she said, cutting off any monologue of thanks as she prayed to god her bag would surprise her. It was like that old game they used to play at uni. Wallet top trumps. Who could produce the best thing from their purse? A driving licence would beat a taxi rank card and a condom would beat an STI clinic flyer. Her loyalty card to the local laundrette often did well, as did her Dad's American Express Gold Card that she kept for emergencies. The top trump card holder, however, was often the person carrying an organ donation card because it said so much about them as a person. But then again, a

National Insurance card was high value because it took real balls to carry that around on drunken nights out where wallets were lost or misplaced.

"I got you a little something," she said, still foraging around in the bottom of her bag. Dammit, Trudy didn't want a squashed tampon as a first date gift, nor would she want an open packet of tissues, even though they were the gentle nose-moisturising variety. "It's your favourite. I noticed you were running short the other day." She pulled out the clear lip gloss.

Trudy took the offering. "That's so kind of you, my Love Puddle."

"Why's the nib red?" Jenny was staring. "There. It's clear lip gloss and the nib's red. You've obviously used that over some red lipstick."

Lauren feigned offence. "I have not."

Trudy smiled. "I love it. It's the first gift you've given me."

"No, it's not."

"Sorry, no, I forgot about all those orgasms."

Rachel coughed before turning to Jenny. "I really love the rose, thank you."

"It's my pleasure."

Lauren swallowed her gasp as Jenny moved in for a kiss. There was only one thing for it. "I'm glad you like your lip gloss," she said, leaning in to Trudy as she kept one eye on the other side of the table, waiting to see if Jenny connected. Dammit, Jenny had connected. She puckered up and closed her eyes.

Trudy whispered. "I'm over here, boss."

Lauren moved to the lips, opening one eye to peep at the other embrace. It was close-mouthed, but Jenny was holding Rachel's cheek which made it appear more intimate. She reached up to stroke Trudy's hair.

"Don't make me static, boss," came the side-mouthed whisper.

"Shhh." There was no way Jenny was going to out-snog her. That's it, she'd have to moan. "Mmmm." It was loud and over the top.

"And what's happening now?" Josephine was back in the room with a platter of hors d'oeuvres.

Lauren continued her moaning as she squinted across the table. They were still connected. Jenny had to be holding Rachel in place.

"Ladies?"

It was like that school game where the loser was the first to speak to the teacher. No matter what they said you just had to stay silent.

"Jenny?"

Lauren saw the movement. And boom, they were apart.

"Sorry, Josie, this isn't like me."

Lauren moaned once more for good measure before pulling away. And yes. She had it. Another winner.

"We have here a selection of dips and our own wood-fired sourdough." Josephine placed the tray on the table before turning quickly. "I'm sure you can find their description on the menu."

"Josie, wait…"

Lauren looked to the door. "Maybe you should go after her?"

"No, no," Jenny lifted her arm to the back of Rachel's chair, "I'm fine here. If I recall correctly we have a smoky aubergine dip, a spicy beetroot and mint, a caramelised onion and black bean and a white bean hummus. You take your sourdough and build it your way."

"Wonderful," said Trudy, grabbing a slice of toasted garlicky bread. "You must come here a lot."

"I do."

Lauren raised her eyebrows. "With dates?"

"Clients actually."

"Ai ai." She wasn't sure where it came from but the silence and stare it induced was worth it. Who did Jenny think she was, reciting the list of dips. This wasn't her restaurant and these weren't her dips. "Dig in, Trudy," she said with a smile.

"I am. I've got the smoky aubergine and I'm adding some hummus," she said, double dipping the now laden piece of toasted bread into the white paste.

"You really shouldn't double dip." Jenny looked concerned.

"We're all friends here. Ooo, this is good."

"It changes the flavour of the other dips."

"You've never double dipped, Jenny? Lauren's a big fan of the double dip, aren't you, my tiger?"

Lauren picked up a slice of sourdough and shoved it from the spicy beetroot and mint into the caramelised onion and black bean. "Oh yes. You have to live a little."

Trudy smiled. "I thought all lesbians were fans of the double dip? It fills you up quicker."

Lauren couldn't help the crispy crumbs spraying from her mouth as she laughed. "Trudy. Too far."

Rachel stood up. "All of you, too far."

"What are you doing?" said Lauren, quickly out of her seat. "You can't leave."

"Just watch me."

CHAPTER EIGHTEEN

"You were so feral!" Rachel was arms crossed and angry, standing in front of the roaring log fire.

"It wasn't just me."

"It was all of you!"

Lauren pulled her legs tighter into her body and picked up the fluffy cushion from the sofa seat beside her. She shrugged. "Maybe we were just marking our turf?"

"I'm not a clump of soil!"

"Is that how I made you feel?" Rising to her feet, Lauren kept hold of her fluffy shield to protect her from the coming onslaught. The last thing she wanted was Rachel upset. Angry was understandable, but upset, never.

"You didn't make me feel anything. Not intentionally anyway."

Lauren paused at the way in which it had been delivered. "You're saying you wanted me to make you feel something?"

"I don't know. Maybe I'm being dramatic, but what I do know is if that's lesbian dating then I don't want any part in it. The bitching and the backbiting. The snide one-upmanship." Rachel moved to the vacated sofa. "A typical gang of women who don't even like each other."

Hanging her head in shame, Lauren felt rather pathetic standing alone in front of the fire with just the cushion for company. She'd tried to do the right thing, dashing through the restaurant after Rachel. Admittedly the shoulder-to-shoulder sprint-off that erupted between her and Jenny had caused a few raised eyebrows, especially when she'd flicked out a heel and caught the panther's ankle causing her to crash and become prey to an aghast Josephine. But it had been that distraction that had given her the edge, enabling her to catch up with Rachel and follow her into the cab she'd just hailed. For a split second, she'd thought about pulling Rachel back onto the street, twirling her around the beautiful lamp posts and dancing it out without having to say a word, but instead they'd sat in silence for the whole journey home. Then she'd sat alone, on the garden bench, hidden from view until Rachel's in-laws had left. Her gentle tapping on the lounge window and repertoire of sad yet funny faces, the only thing to bring a slight smile to Rachel's lips and eventual uttering of, "this better be good," as the front door was partially opened.

Lauren looked across at her now. None of this was good. In fact, it was all incredibly awful. Yes, there'd been snidey one-upmanship and bitching, but it was good-natured mostly, wasn't it? And they did all like each other sort of, didn't they? "I like you," she chose to say.

The reply was quick. "And Trudy?"

"She's my colleague."

"Oh, Lauren, I saw you pinching her bottom and you have nicknames. Plus, you kissed her for absolutely ages."

"It was all an act."

"Don't lie to me."

Moving over to the sofa, Lauren shook her head. "That kiss wasn't real, you know that."

"And the kiss in the bar?"

Lauren paused. "What bar?"

"The cocktail bar. Tuesday night."

More silence.

Rachel reached out to grab the cushion, pulling it into her chest. "And that makes you a really shitty person for A: not telling me, B: not admitting it's real and C: using her to make Jenny jealous."

"I wasn't trying to make Jenny jealous and I only didn't tell you because—"

"Oh yes you were. You sabotaged her beautiful *Hallelujah* song."

"And you couldn't get enough of her beautiful *Hallelujah* song. Eyes closed and swaying. You always said my *Rock Around the Clock* was your favourite."

"When we were drunk as skunks! But that restaurant was posh and you double dipped! I never knew double dipping was such a thing for you lesbians."

"It's not."

"It clearly is and so are nipple piercings and animal role-play noises and long, uncomfortable closed-mouth kisses."

"Yours was mouth closed?"

"Of course it was! We were in a posh restaurant."

"Your other one wasn't though."

"What other one?"

What option did she have? If she told Rachel about her Peeping Tom incident she'd come across even worse than she feared was the case; if she didn't tell Rachel about her dirty-kneed Peeping Tom incident her behaviour would be totally inexcusable. But she was already standing in front of the storm that was Rachel's disgust completely defenceless so what harm could it do? "Are you telling me that was the first time you and Jenny have kissed?"

"This is about you, Lauren. I saw *you* in the bar."

"You saw Trudy, drunk, taking it too far. I pulled away and left immediately."

The silence now belonged to Rachel. "Immediately?"

"Immediately."

The silence continued, finally giving way to a much quieter voice. "Well then you know it wasn't the first time Jenny and I had kissed."

"So does that make you a shitty person for A: not telling me, B: not admitting it's real, C—"

"I haven't not admitted it's real."

"So you do like her?"

"After tonight? No, I don't think I do." The shoulders shrugged. "That rose was sweet though."

"You'd have preferred the lip gloss."

"I think that was *my* bloody lip gloss!" Rachel laughed for the first time that evening. "You really are a total tool sometimes, Lauren."

"I know. I'm sorry."

"Oh, I'm sorry too."

"Can we just start at the start?"

"I'd like that."

"No lies?" said Lauren as she dared to take a seat next to her friend.

"I haven't told you any lies, everything just happened so quickly. You dashed off after the horse whispering on Wednesday and I had that WI day on Thursday. Then you had a wedding on Friday and now it's Saturday and we went ahead with the date."

"Were you thinking of cancelling?"

"Of course, but you were so quiet. I assumed if you had any doubts you'd message me."

"But you never replied to my gifs."

"What?"

"My gif message. It was a solve-it-yourself story."

"Two of them came through blank and I couldn't quite piece together the bottom bit, plus that was the day Jenny was messaging me and then she friend requested me on Facebook so I immediately did what anyone would do and started stalking her page. I did mean to ask you to send your message again but then Jenny asked me out for dinner so I dashed to find an outfit and a babysitter. I didn't want to ask you because I knew you'd talk sense into me." Rachel sighed. "But I was feeling carefree and I was flattered that someone was taking so much interest, so I went. Then I saw you."

"And then?"

"Well, then... Gosh, Lauren, this is so cringy. I'm grabbing a drink. We both need a drink."

"You slept with her, didn't you?" Throwing herself back onto the sofa, Lauren gasped as her friend walked away. "I knew it."

"I didn't..." The distant voice made way for the clunking around in the fridge and chinking of glasses. "I didn't sleep with her," said Rachel, coming back into the room carrying full glasses.

"But...?" Lauren accepted the offering. "Sit down. Let's calm this thing down."

"I can't stay calm," said Rachel. "I've been so foolish. She came back here, late. She was on this sofa. *We* were on this sofa."

Lauren tried not to look down and grimace. "And...?"

"And she could have been anybody. She could have killed me."

Lauren took a big swig of bubbles. She had to say it. "I'd have saved you. I was standing outside."

Rachel gasped. "You were not."

"I was."

"The text? You came?"

Lauren nodded before raising her eyebrows. "Did you?"

"No! I thought you were watching?"

"Is that weird?"

"Very, but strangely reassuring in a way. We just had a few heated kisses on this sofa."

Lauren tried again not to look down and grimace. "And...?"

"And that was it. She left. You saw all this? You knew about all this?"

"Why do you think my horse wouldn't move? Why do you think I went ahead with Trudy's ridiculous plan to pretend we were dating?"

"Trudy's plan?"

"Oh, Rachel, I told you what I felt in that gif message and you know I'm not good with my emotions."

"What you felt?"

"I'm a fool and I just want to go back to being the Laurel to each other's Hardy."

"Can I see the messages? You know I'd usually reply, it's just that everything happened so quickly. You must have known something wasn't right."

"I did. I just didn't expect you to act like this without consulting me."

"I couldn't consult you."

"You could. You always can."

"I've tried."

Lauren ploughed on. "Either way, you're right. Lesbian dating's for suckers and you're wise to stay out of this world."

"I want to see it."

"This world?"

"The messages, but, yes, maybe."

"I don't think that's wise."

"Hey, you saw me getting my freak on through a window and I've remained incredibly unfazed."

"Maybe that's because you saw me being freaked up in the bar and you know how much worse it is for the person who's watching."

"I just felt like you'd lied to me. I assumed this Trudy thing was a sordid secret and you'd both been laughing at me for not knowing."

"Oh, Rachel, of course not."

"So can I see what you wanted to say?"

"It doesn't matter now."

"It matters now more than ever."

Lauren sighed before pulling out her phone. "Fine. The last two gifs are the wrong way round. And the one of the sun's in the wrong place." She clicked onto the thread. "And I missed out a 'my'."

Rachel spoke slowly. "Hi Ray hell. I like what you did there. You could have done a shell gif as well."

"I know, keep reading. In fact don't. Or just do it in your head." She grabbed back control of the cushion and hid her face in it.

"You're the sun to shine."

"To *my* shine."

"The home to my heart."

"Don't, I'm cringing."

"If you want a nice woman…" The pause was long. "You say the last two are the wrong way round?"

Lauren nodded into the fluffy fabric. The room went silent. Should she peep? Could she peep? Lowering the cushion slightly, she saw Rachel wiping away a tear. "It's awful, I'm sorry."

The words were quiet. "Then I'm a great start."

"But I'm not though, am I? I'm cocky and competitive and I give really crap presents and I can't play piano for shit." She stopped as a finger pressed onto her lips.

"You're the home to my heart too, Lauren."

Looking into the kind eyes, Lauren knew she had to explain. "I shouldn't have let everything get this far and I shouldn't have offered myself up like that on a gif thread just because you've started to take an interest in women."

"Is that all it was?"

"No, it's…" She could feel herself getting lost in the eyes. Like it was the first time she'd properly allowed herself to look. "It's…"

Rachel spoke again. "All it is?"

What could she say? The woman of her dreams was asking directly, and the eyes weren't letting her go. "You know how I feel."

"That's just it, Lauren, I don't."

She couldn't speak. The silence was deafening. "Maybe I could show you?" she finally managed.

"How?"

"I'll try to be honest."

"With your feelings?"

"My thoughts, my feelings, maybe my actions. Like right now I'm sitting here scared. Scared to tell you how beautiful you are."

"Oh, Lauren, my lovely."

"Exactly. It's embarrassing. You don't want an embarrassing lesbian best friend constantly pining after you."

"If that's the truth then yes, I do." Rachel smiled. "You're the one always shying away from my attention."

"When?"

"Always! Forever! You've never shown any interest in me and you're always interested in women; you're interested in loads of women."

"You're straight!"

"You've had plenty of straight women."

"You were married."

"I'm not now."

The atmosphere was charged, neither able to avert their eyes.

Rachel broke first. "I've always liked you, Lauren."

"And I've always liked you too. That's why we're best friends."

"And you don't want to ruin that?"

"I never thought I'd have a chance to ruin that."

"But you'd want to if you could?"

"Ruin it?"

Rachel laughed. "I'm telling you I like you, Lauren."

"And I like you too."

"Romantically?" The voice dropped to a whisper. "Sexually?"

Lauren thought of all the times she'd romanticised their relationship. All the times she'd sexualised their relationship. The dreams of rampant physical contact after they'd frolicked through the fields. "Occasionally... maybe."

"So..."

"I don't want to be your phase, Rachel. It would kill me."

"Why would it kill you?"

"Because..." Lauren looked to the fireplace.

"I thought you were going to be honest?"

"You're not ready for this. You're not ready for any of this."

"If it involves bitching, backbiting and game-playing then, no, I'm not."

"And double dipping?"

Both women laughed.

Lauren continued. "We're good at this," she said, letting their gaze connect once again.

"So let's see where this goes."

"And that's what you want?"

"Don't you?"

"I'd rather do this thing properly."

"What do you mean by that?"

"I'd like to start at the start."

"You're going to wine and dine me?"

Lauren's smile was wide. "If you'll let me."

"As long as you don't double dip."

The pause was mischievous.

"Oh gosh it's a thing, isn't it?"

"Rawwr," said Lauren as she laughed.

CHAPTER NINETEEN

Sitting at her desk at the back of the shop, Lauren sucked on her pen as she twirled on her chair. Last night had been perfect. She and Rachel had smiled and laughed and slotted back into their normal, only this time her glances weren't secret; this time they'd been met and noticed and glanced at right back. This time, she'd said what she'd felt and meant what she'd said, her parting comment of, "I'd like to do this again soon," leading to Rachel's nod of: "Name the day and I'm there."

It was going to be an old school romance, she could feel it in her bones. A kiss there and then or a full on disclosure of the years of pain and torment wouldn't have worked. They'd opened up slightly and that was all they needed to spark this flurry of anticipation, this further attraction and nervous adrenaline. Picking up her phone for the third time that morning, Lauren typed another message: **And I forgot to say your eyes looked like an ocean last night.** It was cheesy but it was true and she'd vowed to be honest from this point onwards. Rachel would know what she was thinking and feeling and, yes, probably not quite as graphically just yet, but gently and slowly as their confidence grew. She smiled again as she grabbed hold of the table and initiated a huge spin on her chair. "I love my life," she screamed at the top of her voice.

"Yeah? Well I banged Jenny last night," said Trudy, entering the shop. "Or she banged me to be precise."

Lauren jumped up. "Trudy, that's great!"

"Why are you so happy, boss? My flaps aren't happy. I'm sure I'm going to get cystitis. I knew banging was bad."

"You had the big P?"

"Well, it wasn't a penis but something went in there."

"I'm so pleased for you."

"My flaps aren't."

"I'm not interested in your flaps."

"Jenny was."

"Enough."

"Fine, why are you so happy? Have you been asked to appear on The Proms playing *Rock Around the Clock*?"

"It was better than *Hallelujah*."

"It wasn't better than *Hallelujah* and FYI Jenny has a grand piano at home. Think *Pretty Woman* and Richard Gere."

"She hoisted you onto her piano?"

"I clambered up really."

"And she played? Oh, that's so tacky."

"She didn't play the piano if you get my drift. Think more harmonica."

Lauren winced. "Trudy, now I've got an image of you spread-eagled on a piano with Jenny tooting your flaps."

"They sure did toot."

"I don't want to know this."

"Stop talking about it then and make us a coffee. You don't think Rachel will mind do you? It just kind of happened. You two ran off and I stayed behind to nurse Jenny's shins. Apparently you kicked her, boss."

"I didn't kick her."

"You did kick her and I'm glad because that's how our nurse and patient role-play started."

"Is she okay?"

"I saw to her."

"Sounds like you did."

"I'll tell you all about it over coffee. I can't make it though; I've got sore flaps."

"We haven't got time, there's a problem with the kilts. Jerry's ushers didn't pick them up. They thought Jerry was getting them."

"And the shop's shut?"

"It's opening up for me in twenty minutes."

"You're so good."

"I know."

Trudy edged closer. "Why are you glowing, boss?"

"I might stay in for the vows."

"You never stay in for the vows."

Lauren smiled. "My outlook has suddenly changed."

****

Sitting on the back pew in the old village church, Lauren wiped away a tear. She believed them. Jerry and Jane had been one of the nicer couples to deal with, both coming to decisions together with a shared idea of their day being simple and sweet; and it was, or it had been so far. A few family and friends, all ushers now in kilts, and a sharing of vows that actually seemed, for once, to mean something real. All too often, she'd slip out of the church before the vows were taken. Hearing two people who'd spent the last few months sitting at her conference table bickering and criticising each other, suddenly promising to love each other for richer for poorer, even though one had accused the other of being tight with the money, or in sickness and in health when one had accused the other of exaggerating their head cold to get out of the flower-choosing sessions, always felt a bit false to her. Not today though. Today she believed it. Today was till death us do part.

Smiling, she followed the crowd out of the church. They were all headed to the quaint kissing seat at the side of the porch, the only requested photo location. The bride and groom had asked for the day to be captured as naturally as possible, apart from this one shot outside. Nowadays, nearly every couple paid for a top-notch photographer who'd spend hours gathering the troops for photos with a running order confirmed in advance and laboriously executed, often with the help of herself or Trudy because, no matter how good the photographer, someone had to go and find the great-aunt already drunk in the toilets, and the child hiding under the buffet table. Not today though. Today it was just Jerry and Jane, smiling as they sat either side of the seat.

Lauren studied the white-painted wrought iron's prettily curving design, made more magical by the long, relaxed branches of the weeping willow tree shielding the front of the porch. She breathed in the atmosphere; everyone was gazing at the pair with swoony eyes and sighs of contentment. The photographer was asking the couple to kiss. And there it was. True love. She smiled. She was going to kiss Rachel. It was actually going to happen. When and how, she didn't know, and she didn't want to know. She simply wanted it to happen naturally, not be staged or pre-planned. It would happen when it happened and that would make it all the more perfect. Because like the staged photos, as nice as it was to see the whole family clumped together on a pretty bit of grass as the photographer shouted 'cheese' from some tall-enough top window, the best photos were the ones where the people weren't posing: the confetti floating over the couple; the bouquet thrown into the crowd; the tiny flower-girl poking her finger into the cake: the tears during the speeches. All those things were real and what she had with Rachel was going to be real.

Lauren laughed at the scene unfolding in front of her. The photographer had asked for one more shot: the groom in his kilt sat on the bride's knee, teasing the crowd with a flick of the fabric. Catching Trudy's attention she tutted; all photographers were the same, always pushing for that last image, and even though funny shots weren't on the couple's list of requirements, Jerry and Jane seemed to be playing along.

"That's it, kilt boy, I want you to straddle your bride."

Jerry was laughing. "Facing her?"

"No, facing me! It's not your wedding night yet, you devil. That's it, straddle her knees. Now, princess, you lift his kilt at the back, that's it, flatten it down over your dress. Like that, yes, perfect. Now, kilt boy, give us a bit of a tease."

Lauren watched as Jerry leaned forward with a cheeky lift of the front of his kilt.

"Who wants to see him go higher?" shouted the photographer to the laughing crowd.

"I'm a true Scotsman," shouted Jerry back. "I'm not going higher. What do you think this is, my wedding night?"

The photographer laughed. "And that's it. I've got it. You need a hand up?"

"I'm not that heavy."

"Yes you are," said Jane, pushing her husband up off her perfect white dress.

Lauren wasn't entirely sure what happened next. It could have been the crowd's gasps, or the bride's screams, or the nauseating feeling of her own stomach lurching at the sight of the brown stain, horrifically visible on the silky white fabric.

The silence that followed was alarmingly eerie. Jerry simply staring at the smear, the crowd wide-eyed and the photographer silenced at last.

Jane was the one who spoke up. "You dirty bastard! You've put a skidmark on my wedding dress." Jumping up, she hit him with her bouquet of calla lilies, her voice turning into a scream. "My wedding dress, you dirty fucking bastard! I've married a bloke with a dirty fucking asshole on his wedding day! If you can't even clean your asshole today when will you clean it?"

The voice was quiet. "I'll clean it."

"Not on my fucking wedding dress, you won't. Daddy? Daddy, where are you? I want to go home!"

Lauren dashed to the bride's side. She'd never heard Jane swear and this was meant to be true love. If these two didn't make it, no one would. "Come with me, I can sort this out."

"She's coming with me." The father of the bride took his daughter under his arm. "And what are you all staring at?" he said, turning to the crowd. "You're only here for the free booze. And I never did like you, Jerry, you dirty-arsed kilt-wearing tosser."

"Jane, I can explain."

Lauren signalled the groom over. "Jerry, just give them a minute." She turned to the crowd. "Could everyone go back into the church please? The string quartet hasn't quite finished." She knew she'd be able to rely on the musicians, always well prepared to fill in for any unplanned waits. "Trudy," she said, getting her second-in-command's attention. "Jerry or Jane?"

"I'll take Jerry."

They both knew the drill. Many a time they'd had to calm last minute nerves and smooth out unforeseen hiccups, and admittedly while a groom leaving a skidmark on his bride's dress wasn't one of the regular mishaps, it certainly could have been worse. Quite how, Lauren wasn't sure, but she could solve this, it was her job. Dashing to the wedding car, she pushed through the melee of bitching bridesmaids and female friends. It always shocked her how quickly people could turn, suddenly saying all the things they'd secretly thought but never said before, entirely happy minutes ago to see their best friend / sibling / daughter go through with the marriage, yet the second the partner put a foot wrong they were set upon for all their past indiscretions as well as ruining The Big Day. And poor Jerry, he hadn't meant it to happen. Trudy would have him now, in the church, apologising, yet trying to make light of the situation. "It's a story to tell," she'd get him to say.

Tapping on the car window, Lauren asked to be allowed in. Jane was sitting in the back with her father, tears streaming down her face, the chauffeur staring straight ahead clearly not sure what to do, but the fact that Jane nodded and opened the door told Lauren all she needed to know. "Okay, here's what will happen. Twigworth Lodge is five minutes away. Your evening outfit's in your room, right?"

The bride nodded through snuffles and tears.

"We'll ask one of your bridesmaids to go in one of the other cars and fetch it. You can change in the vestry. Let's make Jerry panic for fifteen minutes. Trudy's keeping him in the church. Everyone will be giving him a real roasting. This wait will be all the punishment he needs."

"And then?" Jane's eyes were looking up expectantly.

"And then you walk back into that church in your evening outfit, you take his hand, you shrug and grin at the crowd and you say: shit happens."

Jane laughed. "Oh, Lauren, you're great."

"And so is he. Get back in there and get on with the rest of your day."

"Daddy, what do you think?"

"Whatever makes you happy, my darling."

"But I was so mean."

Lauren tried to avoid looking at the stain. "Blame the shock. You could have said much worse."

Jane shook her head. "I bet he feels awful. I've never sworn at him before. I was foul-mouthed."

"It won't do him any harm." Lauren pointed out of the window to the wide-eyed bridesmaids. "Shall I ask Mandy to go?"

"Yes please, and Sarah."

"Anything else I can do?"

"Forgive me for being so rude? Apologise for me?"

"I will, but there's nothing to forgive." Lauren smiled. "I need you two to make it. If you don't, there's no hope for any of us."

"We'll make it," said Jane.

Lauren climbed out of the car. "I honestly pray that you do."

CHAPTER TWENTY

Knocking on the barn door, Lauren waited. She'd usually just let herself in but she wanted today to be different.

"What are you knocking for?" asked Rachel, opening the door and pulling her friend in for a cuddle. "I missed you yesterday; how was the wedding?"

Lauren held onto the contact and peered at Rachel. "You missed me?"

"We agreed we'd be honest so, yes, I missed you."

"Have you always missed me?"

"Yes," said Rachel, smiling. "But I wasn't going to tell you that."

Lauren stepped back and looked at her friend through half-closed eyes. "Do you know how many years I've been hanging on to your every word, praying for that one little glimmer of hope?"

"You have not!"

Lauren lifted her shoulders. "Just being honest."

"Look at you, you cool cat, you don't hang on anyone's word."

"I'll be hanging on your next one. Do you want an adventure?"

"It's Monday. We always have coffee on Monday."

Rachel was right. For the past two years, ever since Parker had started in full time school, they'd spent the best part of the start of the week having a coffee and catch-up, mostly focusing on Lauren's weekend weddings, but also debriefing any other titbits of gossip. It was the one day Lauren ensured she was completely free from work and she always chose to spend it with Rachel. Today would be no different, even if their location and activity changed. "It's a simple question," she said. "And by the way, long greeting hugs like that one should definitely become our thing."

"But we have so much to discuss. Let's do coffee, gossip and hugging."

"We can do it in the car."

"Ai ai."

Lauren laughed. "That's my gag." She smiled. "Come on, I'll ask you again. Do you want an adventure?"

"Why do you look so mischievous?"

"I'm just showing you how lesbians do it."

"In the car?"

"And your raised eyebrows aren't mischievous at all, are they?"

"Wouldn't you rather just stay here and…?"

"In time."

"Exactly! You can't have been waiting years for that one glimmer of hope."

"Maybe I have, and maybe I want to savour every single moment of this build up. Maybe I want to woo you in a really old-fashioned and memorable way."

"Sounds interesting. Where's the adventure?"

Lauren smiled. "The safari park."

"What, *now*?"

"Yes, come on, we're taking my car."

Rachel rolled her eyes. "You're so daft."

"And you love it and, yes, we will be back in time for the school run. Fear not, I have it all planned out to perfection."

"The safari park? Is this a lesbian thing?"

"It's a fun thing. It's an adventure thing. It's a spend-quality-time-together-whilst-having-a-laugh thing."

"We do that wherever we are."

"Okay, so it lightens." Lauren reached down to the shoe rack by the door and found Rachel's pumps. "I don't want every single conversation to be about us and the should we or shouldn't we. The can we or can't we. Or the do you really feel it, is this really real, are we being foolish, etcetera, etcetera, etcetera." She smiled as she handed over the shoes. "We've said we like each other so let's see where this goes."

"The safari park, obviously," said Rachel, taking the offering and following Lauren out of the door.

Lauren pointed to her car on the driveway. "Your chariot."

"Are you sure this is wise?"

"We've just had that monologue."

"No, I mean the TT with all those animals." Rachel locked the door after them both.

"It's hardly a smart car," said Lauren, leading them across the gravel. "Plus we can open the sunroof."

"What about scratches?"

"There aren't any monkeys at Bidwell."

"Just rhinos and elephants, and that's a TT."

"Audis are built to withstand all sorts. We took Parker when he was little, remember? That was an Audi."

"That was Toby's Q7."

"And it was too tall. At least this time we'll be close to the action."

"Tiger level."

"Rawwr."

"Don't start that again."

Lauren clicked open the car and paused.

"Don't even think about it. I can get myself in."

"Rawwr," she said, more feistily this time, dropping into the driver's seat as she waited for Rachel to get settled. "But you're right. I don't think I am a tiger. I think I'm more of a bird. Free flying. Likes to soar. I got you a skinny latte by the way." She nodded at the drinks holder before reversing away from the barns. "What animal would you say you are?"

"Thanks," Rachel lifted the coffee, "but you're not. We had a guest speaker at the WI a while ago who gave a talk on the four Fs of animal personalities."

"Which are?"

"Feeding, fighting, fleeing," Rachel smiled, "and sex."

"The four Fs?" Lauren laughed. "Oh, I like what you did there."

"It did bring a number of titters from the WI ladies."

"I bet it did."

"Anyway each animal falls into one of those groups and birds are actually focused on feeding."

"I got us both teacakes." Lauren nodded to the brown paper bag between their arm rests.

"And have you done that because you are, in actual fact, a tiger who's focused on the fourth F?"

"Sex? Is a skinny latte and toasted tea cake all it takes?" She nodded. "Noted."

"Ha! I always love it when you get flirty."

"I never get flirty. Not properly anyway."

"There's that tiger again."

"So what animal are you?"

"The WI woman gave us a quiz and I came up as a herd animal."

"Which one?"

"Exactly." Rachel was laughing. "I wasn't even distinctive enough to be gifted an actual breed, just herd animal. A flee-er. Someone who finds refuge in the company of friends and family."

"That's a nice trait."

She shrugged. "You're definitely a tiger. I remember there being a big focus on brutal displays of strength."

"I'm not aggressive."

"No, but you're an incredibly driven woman."

"You're the driven woman; you're getting driven to the safari park."

"Not a good one."

"No, sorry. I apologise." Lauren tapped on the sat-nav, ensuring they'd avoid any traffic. "I did a quiz once that told me I was Joey from *Friends*."

"The funny one?"

"The male funny one."

"You do have certain masculine traits."

"Like what?"

"You take charge, you're organised, you lift stuff."

"I'm a lesbian. It's in all of us to show we don't need a man."

"What if you're a feminine lesbian?"

"I am!"

"More like me I mean."

Lauren laughed. "You're not a lesbian."

"Yet?"

"See, this is why labels are so awful. Stereotyping's awful too."

"But you'd be the man and I'd be the woman, right?"

"No, we'd both be the chopsticks."

"I'm teasing you." The smile was mischievous. "I know what I'm doing."

"Well, I certainly don't."

"You're cute when you get flummoxed. It shows off your vulnerable side."

Lauren felt warm fingers squeeze her thigh. She glanced down. "What are you doing?"

"I'm going to quiz you."

"On my highway code? Yes, you shouldn't distract the driver with hand-on-thigh placement."

"You want me to remove it?"

"No." The smile came naturally. "In fact it was always on my bucket list. To reach over and hold your thigh whilst driving."

"You thought about that?"

"Every single time you were here."

Rachel squeezed again. "You're a sweetie. Right. Question one." She looked at the sat-nav. "Forty-five minutes to Bidwell Safari Park. What turns you on?"

Lauren spluttered.

"You see, you think you've got control because you're driving the car, but you haven't got any control at all. I can ask what I like, look at what I like, pin you down with as many questions as I like."

"Who are you?" Lauren pretended to glance around. "Where's my Rachel gone?"

"You've just never seen me in flirt mode."

"I have. It used to involve two laps around the dance floor at Reflex trying to sniff out the action."

"This is mature me. This is inquisitive me. This is – answer my questions or I'll slide my hand higher me."

"We haven't even kissed yet!"

"And whose fault is that?"

"You want me to pull into the animal enclosure and have my wicked way with you?"

"If that's what turns you on."

"I'm not a man, Rachel. You don't have to please me."

"So lesbians instinctively know what the other one likes do they?"

"Mostly."

"But in particular?"

Lauren kept her eyes on the road. "I like everything."

"Why are your cheeks red?"

"My heated seat's on."

"No, it's not." The pause was teasing. "Are you embarrassed? The strong, confident, sex-mad Lauren Hilliard embarrassed by little old me?"

"I'm not sex mad."

"You have loads of it though."

"But it's not usually discussed and debriefed like this on the way to Bidwell Safari Park."

"Good. I want us to be different. I may not have the experience you have, but I could offer something new."

Lauren met the eyes. "Rachel, you have no competition." She looked back to the road. "No one compares to you."

"They might in the bedroom."

She met the eyes again. "They won't. We're already connected on such a deep emotional level that any physical interaction will simply enhance what we already have."

"I love it when you speak with such passion. That's what turns me on. Your spirit. You're so full of life and it's catching; it's empowering. I always feel I'm capable of anything when you're by my side."

"Why didn't you say this before?"

"Same reason as you."

Lauren smiled. "Okay, I love my neck being touched."

"And for me it's my nipples."

"Noted."

They both laughed.

"We're going to be fine," said Lauren.

"I know," agreed Rachel, lifting her hand to Lauren's neck.

"And, yes, continuing our highway code quiz, running your fingers up and down a driver's neck, no matter how sexily seductive it is, may cause a crash."

"You want me to stop?"

Lauren gently and slowly shook her head, encouraging the fingers as she did so. "Right. My question to you. What makes you happy?"

"You. Before Toby, with Toby, after Toby, you've always been my source of happiness."

"Really?"

"I always smile when I'm around you."

"And your smile's what I live for."

Rachel laughed. "Oh, aren't we so cute and femme."

"Stop with the labels. You'll get enough of that when you come out. Not as in come out come out, because you're not a lesbian."

"Yet."

"You might be bisexual, but even then there's no need to label. Just come out as proud to be who you're with."

"I'd be incredibly proud to be with you."

"Likewise."

Rachel was smiling. "Is this real? Am I really on my way to bagging Lauren Hilliard, every lesbian's dream?"

"I've been bagged up at that checkout for years, waiting for you to notice I'm there."

"You weren't. You were whizzing round in other people's trolleys."

"Maybe only to bide the time."

"Well, now I've noticed there's something in the bagging area."

"I should have got that voice to shout louder."

"You should have."

Lauren's sigh was one of contentment. "It's like we've been dating for years."

"And we've still got a good few miles to go yet." Rachel pointed at the moving map on the dash. "Right then. Next question."

"No, it's my turn for a question." Lauren thought for a moment. "What's your current goal in life?"

"To raise Parker well."

"You've already achieved that."

Rachel's shoulders shrugged. "Still a long way to go."

"And what if I put a spanner in the works?"

"You've been his level since he was born." The fingers tickled Lauren's neck. "Do you get it? Level? Maybe I am a bit butch. I've always liked my toolbox."

"Your toolbox is pink."

"It's true though. You've been such a constant figure in his life. He absolutely adores you."

"Which makes me slightly wary of this." Laying her hand over Rachel's, she locked their fingers together and dropped their hands to her thigh. "If this goes wrong."

"Hey, lady, you've always said to me you'd rather regret something you've done than something you didn't do. We're both mature adults. We'd never let anything negatively impact on Parker."

"But if he thinks someone's trying to replace his dad, or take you away from him?"

"It helps that you're a woman."

"Does it?"

Rachel nodded. "In a weird way, yes. There's no direct comparison. You're not replacing a relationship, you're a different relationship entirely. Plus you're not someone new. He knows you and he loves you and if a new 'us' means he gets to spend more time with you then he'll be nothing but happy." The smile was wide. "What's that thing you say life's all about?"

"I say life's for the living."

"Exactly."

"I say you should live life like it's going out of fashion."

"That was it, and you say: breathe like it's your very last breath."

"You pay attention?"

"Of course I do. Your take on life's inspirational. Maybe you are that soaring bird after all."

Looking across at her passenger, Lauren laughed. "I'd rather have that very last F."

"Ha." Rachel unlinked their hands and picked up Lauren's coffee, tapping it against her own drink in a 'cheers' motion before handing it over. "Here's to living life."

Lauren took the offering and smiled. "To living life."

CHAPTER TWENTY ONE

"This isn't what I meant by living life!" hollered Rachel as a long-horned gazelle shoved its head further through the open car window, butting its face into her lap.

"Stop holding the pellets down there!" instructed Lauren.

"Where am I supposed to hold them?"

"Out of the window on a flat palm!"

"Have you seen those teeth? I'm not having that beast bite my fingers off! Quick, close the window!"

"I can't, its head's right there."

"Drive then, to nudge it away." Rachel gasped. "Please! It's dribbling!"

"I can't drive with its head still in the window!" Lauren tried to shoo the animal back out of the car. "GET!"

"Get where?! It's chowing down on my privates!"

"So move the food!" Lauren tried to grab the cardboard box of pellets they'd bought at the entrance. "Dammit!" she said as they scattered into the well that housed her handbrake and gearstick.

"It's still here!" squealed Rachel, edging away from the creature that was clearly very happy where it was.

Lauren nodded. "Must be good chow down there."

"Nudge the car forward!"

Moving the gearstick, Lauren heard the loose pellets crunch into a powder that would be no doubt impossible to clean up. She released the handbrake to more crunching and eased the car forward.

"It's coming with us!" screamed Rachel. "Go faster!"

"I can't speed round Bidwell Safari Park with a gazelle hanging from the window!"

"Brake sharply then!"

Lauren braked.

"It's still here!"

"You've got loads of pellets between your legs, that's why. Throw them out of the window!"

"I can't get to them. Use some from the box."

"We need to save those for the buffalo."

"I'm *not* having a buffalo chow down on my privates!"

"Fine, I'll scoop them up." Lauren tried not to laugh as she shoved her hand under Rachel's bottom, encouraging it up and off the seat.

"Now it looks like I'm loving it!" squealed Rachel, nodding at her raised pelvis.

"Lift higher."

"I'm high enough!"

"Now shake. Free up the loose ones."

Rachel shook.

Lauren brushed the leather, collecting the stray pellets into her palm, unable to avoid the strange stares of the family in the slowly passing car and the mother who'd covered the eyes of her child. She nodded, as if to say: all's fine; lifting your pelvis and shaking it in a gazelle's face is a regular occurrence in the African Plains section of the park.

"Can I come down yet?"

"No, they're still staring."

"Who's staring? Oh gosh, Lauren! Let me get down. That bloke thinks it's a right show!"

Looking at the man whose eyes hadn't been covered, Lauren signalled with her spare hand. "Move on," she mouthed, as her hand gesture scattered more pellets. "Dammit, these things are going everywhere."

"Throw them out of the window. Make it go away."

"Come on, Bambi," said Lauren, leaning across Rachel's seat as she enticed the creature with a handful of food. "That's it. Up you come."

"Now throw them!"

"Don't shout so loud!" gasped Lauren, dropping half the pellets into the gap of the open window.

"It's gone! Drive drive drive drive drive! I'm doing my window up!"

Lauren watched as the window rose, showering the car with lost pellets. "Try to collect them up so nothing else goes nosing around down there, and next time keep your hand flat and out of the window."

"There won't be a next time."

"Yes there will, the camels are round here."

Rachel took the box of animal food. "It says you can't feed the camels."

"Everyone feeds the camels."

"But it says you can't."

"We'll just encourage them over."

"I don't want to encourage them over."

"They'll love you; just like that gazelle loved you. You're like Doctor Dolittle."

"Maybe I should tell them to piss off."

"Rachel!"

"What? Doctor Dolittle could speak to the animals, couldn't he?"

"Yes, but he didn't say piss off!"

"Sorry, I'm all of a panic."

"You're not. You're loving this."

"In a giggly, can't-breath-through-the-fear kind of way."

"The camels are calmer, look." Driving up a small incline, Lauren followed the road around a corner. There weren't many cars on the two mile route that took vehicles through the different enclosures, probably because it was school term time and a Monday, so they'd been able to veer from side to side, pulling in whenever they wanted, on whichever side of the road the animals happened to appear.

"What are they doing?" asked Rachel.

"For the sake of womankind, you need to encourage them over."

"Are they…?"

Squinting, Lauren tried to make out the scene. "That's one camel, female I presume, on her knees, minding her own business as that other camel humps her from behind." She paused. "And it looks like there are two more, no, make that three more, huddled right there having a good old gawp."

"Look at her face! She's not impressed at all. Don't pull in! What are you pulling in for?"

"Shake your box at them."

"Don't be vulgar."

"The box of pellets."

"I knew what you meant. It's fine. He's finished. He's moving away."

Lauren pointed as another camel mounted the kneeler. "They're taking it in turns!"

"Eugh! How awful!"

"And she's still just collapsed there on her knees with a right face on her."

"Wouldn't you have a face on you in the circumstances?"

"I don't know, I've never had sex with a man."

"That's a camel."

"Same thing. I feel I should beep."

"Won't that call the ranger?"

Lauren nodded. "Good, we need to make him aware of the gang bang."

"I've heard gang bangs are meant to be fun. I'm not sure that camel's even noticed." Rachel continued to stare. "Eugh, and a third! They're quite literally queued up and taking their turn."

"You've heard about gang bangs?"

"Stop looking so sniffy."

Lauren pointed. "That camel looks sniffier."

"She's probably thinking: just put it away."

Lauren laughed. "They're trying!" Pressing the window button to 'open', she leaned across Rachel's seat. "I need to shake the box."

"Why's it always on my side? And what on earth's going on with his mouth? Oh no, Lauren, this one's choking! Look! Quick, shake that box!"

Lauren gasped. "It looks like he's got a pair of bollocks hanging out of his mouth!"

"Who knows what they were up to before we arrived!"

"It's not funny, Rachel, he's choking!"

"On a mouthful of bollocks! Beep the horn! Summon the ranger!"

Lauren did one long beep, keeping her eye on the frothing camel.

"Again!"

"The ranger's coming, look." She pointed to the camouflaged jeep that was speeding their way. Lauren opened the window on her side.

"Ladies, what's up?" asked the man, dressed for a safari.

Lauren spoke quickly. "Those camels have been taking it in turns on top of that one kneeling camel and now this one's gone too far and gobbled on something he shouldn't, which he's now regurgitating, and this female camel's simply nose-in-the-air taking no notice whatsoever, and I know that's what straight women do and I should probably just leave him to choke to death, but this is a family park and, see, there are mothers covering their children's eyes." She nodded at the same slow moving car that had previously passed them and whose driver was still ogling them. "It wasn't us," she mouthed in defence.

The ranger looked at the scene. "It's fine. It's the camel's doula."

Lauren stared. "You mean that sac of mouth-bollocks is normal?"

The man nodded. "In preparation for mating, the male camel heaves up that pink sac called a doula. It hangs out of the side of the mouth and makes the camel drool excessively. The female camel is supposed to find this quite arousing."

Lauren pointed. "You think that face is aroused?"

Rachel leaned across the car into the conversation. "They've all been having a go."

"Isn't the animal kingdom weird and wonderful?" The ranger grinned.

Lauren grimaced. "You sound envious."

"Do you know that a porcupine will urinate on a female before mating?"

"Again, a little too much pleasure in the way you say that."

"Facts are facts, and my favourite is the argonaut octopus who is able to detach an arm full of sperm and let it swim over to the female to fertilise her."

"Is this a family talk that you give to all cars?"

"Just the ones accusing the camels of dogging." He tipped his hat and winked. "You're the ones watching all this."

Rachel pointed at Lauren as she passed the blame. "She pulled us in."

"I thought we should help her. *You* thought we should help her!" Lauren sounded aggrieved.

"She looks perfectly happy to me," said the ranger, waving them on. "Keep moving through the park please and only use your horn if it's absolutely essential."

Lauren looked at the kneeling female with the bollock-mouthed camel frothing behind her. The female's haughty and superior expression hadn't changed once; she obviously didn't give two hoots about what was going on. "Last time I help you, lady," she muttered at the camel.

"Let's drive away in disgust," said Rachel.

"How do I do that? Wheel spin?"

"Slowly, with your nose lifted high like that camel's."

Lauren laughed. "Are all straight women the same? Just lying there and taking whatever your dangly-bollocked bloke gives you?"

"I think I may have done her camel face once or twice." Rachel paused. "But you need to stop making out like lesbian sex is so much better."

Lauren did a deliberate shudder as she pulled away from the scene. "It's *sooooo* much better."

"Why?"

"I wouldn't know where to begin."

"That makes two of us then."

"You'll be fine. You'll actually get some orgasms."

"I got orgasms."

"Every time?"

"No, of course not."

"My dear sweet Rachel, how surprised you shall be."

"You're not trying to turn me on at Bidwell Safari Park, are you?"

"Is that a bad thing?"

"Yes, I can see a rhino taking a really big dump."

"Rachel!"

"What? And even though that ranger probably has a story about it being used as some sort of mating ritual, the animal kingdom just isn't where my lust is at."

"I'd be an animal." She'd thought it, so she'd said it. "In the way I'd protect you," added Lauren, quickly realising it was far too soon for her friend to hear all the ways she could sexualise the most normal of situations.

"Oh, I thought you meant in the sheets."

Lauren laughed. "Would you like that?" She paused briefly. "You dirty animal." Again, maybe too soon.

"Shall we head home and see?"

"No! We have the elephants and the big cats, not to mention the walk-around areas where we can hold insects and watch bats." She nodded. "And that ranger failed to mention the interesting fact about dragonflies. Did you know the female dragonfly will often fake sudden death to avoid male advances? Google it. It's true."

"Are you stalling?"

"No, just working the clutch. Safari parks are known to ruin your car clutch, all the stopping and starting."

"You don't have to do that laughing distraction thing anymore."

Lauren looked at the eyes. "I just think we should take things slowly."

"Why?"

She knew what she wanted to say: Because once I rip those clothes off I won't be able to stop. Once I let you in properly there's no going back. Once we go there my heart won't return.

"Just say it, Lauren."

"I want you to be sure."

"You're the one stalling."

"All those pellets in my damn gearbox."

Rachel smiled. "Oh, lovely, who thought it would be me having to go easy on you? I can't promise this is who I am or who I'll be, but I want to find out."

Lauren shook her head. "I'm not sure I'm okay with that risk."

"But we're just seeing where this goes. Is it Parker? He doesn't have to know anything yet."

"You want him to know?"

"Of course I do."

"But what is there to know?"

"Well, nothing if you don't hurry up through the big cats and take me straight home."

"Why do you want to go home?"

"Because as much as I love seeing the frothy-mouthed camels with their bollock sacs swinging around their jaws I'd rather see you."

"You're seeing me now."

"I want you unprotected. I want you alone." Rachel's fingers were back on Lauren's neck. "I want you looking at me." She squeezed. "Talking to me; quietly and softly without turning away."

"Do I turn away?"

Rachel nodded. "You turn away."

"Maybe I'm shy."

"Ha! That's the funniest thing I've heard since that octopus sperm arm story."

"Vulnerable?"

"Ha! Even funnier!" Rachel paused. "Why would you be vulnerable, Lauren? I understand the Parker thing, but we both know we'll always be friends. We've got too much history to be anything else."

Lauren kept her eyes on their route.

"So unless you're already completely head-over-heels in love with me and couldn't bear for me to break your heart, there's nothing to fear." The laughter was kind. "I should be the anxious one with you and your seven month cycle of girlfriends. I've got till Christmas on a good run."

"That's not funny."

"Which bit?"

"Any of it."

Rachel removed her hand from Lauren's neck. "So off to the bat cave we go."

"Don't be like that."

"Why not? Come on, Lauren, tell me why not."

Looking out of the window, Lauren held on to her words. *Because I already love you*, she said, for only her heart to hear.

CHAPTER TWENTY TWO

"Boss, you're a total and utter failure." Trudy was sitting on the wedding shop's purple sofa shaking her head.

"I know," said Lauren, as she curled herself into the armrest of the upright armchair. "I dropped her home and made my excuses."

"What's wrong with you?"

Lauren shrugged. "I guess I'm struggling with revealing everything and scaring her off, and playing it too cool and staying just friends."

"Even friends go in for coffee."

"But she seems so eager."

"And that's a bad thing?"

"She's been in my life for so long. Can you imagine how incredibly random it is to think we're just going to start snogging?"

"I thought you'd pictured all this, boss?"

"I did and it was romantic and magical."

"So make it romantic and magical. You can't have honestly thought your first kiss was going to be in the bat cave at Bidwell Safari Park?"

Lauren smiled. "We held hands in there. It was cute."

"You're not fourteen."

"But I want to take things slowly. She's new to all this."

"Don't you put this on her. This is all you, lady. You're scared of opening up."

"But it's so typical of the lesbian to bombard the straight girl with the declaration of undying all-consuming love before they've even shared their first kiss."

"Better than making her think you don't feel it."

"I don't know if *she* feels it."

"She's *said* she feels it! You need to tell her, boss!"

"And make everything incredibly serious from the outset?" Lauren sighed. "And I'm anxious about making things physical because I know once I do then I'm lost forever."

"Look at you! You were lost years ago!" Trudy nodded. "Just think of me if it helps."

"What?"

"When you're getting physical."

"Don't."

"You need to wine and dine her. Do it the old-fashioned way."

"I was doing that."

"You took her to the safari park! You took her to a normal laughing Lauren place. You need to show her your serious side."

"That's too heavy. No one wants to see that."

"She clearly does."

"She made a joke about me being in love with her."

"Just stop stop stop stop STOP with the over-analysing. She likes you, she wants to see where this goes, so just go."

"And if she turns back?"

"Well then she turns back."

"And I'm left heartbroken."

"You'll mend."

"That's just it, I don't think I will. I've never felt this before. I'm tough and resilient, but when I'm with her my heart feels like it's floating."

Trudy groaned. "Floating? Really?"

"Yes, with tiny little wings that are fragile and delicate."

"Boss, that's enough."

"Exactly. If you don't want to hear it then she certainly won't."

"It's about her, so she will. Honesty's the biggest ever turn on."

"Is it?"

Trudy nodded. "Jenny told me my lady bits looked like a beautiful flower press."

"A flower press?" Lauren sat up straighter. "That wooden thing with the bolts?"

"I imagine she meant more the flowers concertinaed together. Either way it turned me on."

"Thinking of your own bits all squashed up together?"

"Hey, you're in no position to offer any sort of judgement or guidance. Just get yourself round there and open your heart."

"I can't. Camilla and Ian are en-route."

"Tonight then. Cook her a meal."

"I'm not a good cook."

"Try. Just bloody well try."

Lauren watched as her second-in-command stalked over to the round conference table. "*Sorry.*"

"For what? And don't say it in that tone of voice."

"For whatever's made you annoyed."

Trudy spun back around. "There's a big difference between someone who's insecure and someone who's a total wet lettuce." She pointed her finger. "You're at risk of seriously fucking this one up, boss."

"A tad harsh?"

"It's not. Put yourself in her position. She's told you she likes you and you're running a mile. She knows your previous dating history and what an uncommunicative commitment-phobe you are. I say it takes balls to do what she's done."

"I'd never end it with her."

"She doesn't know that! She just sees you shying away and making excuses."

Lauren nodded. "I need to tell her, don't I?"

"You need to tell her!"

"I'm going to tell her." She stood up.

"So go and tell her!"

Lauren walked to her desk at the back of the shop. "I'll tell her tonight."

"Tell her now! I can handle Camilla and Ian."

"They'll be expecting me."

"And who's more important?" Trudy clapped her hands towards the door. "Just go! Go and give her your heart."

"You think?"

"Damn yes!"

The smile slowly crept from Lauren's mouth to her eyes. "Fine, but first you need to give me that lip gloss."

****

Standing in front of the big wooden door, armed with just a third-hand lip gloss and a nervous constitution, Lauren questioned her resolve. This wasn't magical or romantic, it was Tuesday morning and cloudy. Rachel would no doubt be curled up in front of the log fire learning Spanish or arm-deep in flour, baking cakes. Or out; Rachel was probably out. On hearing the latch of the lounge door, Lauren panicked, Rachel was definitely in. Glancing down at the lip gloss, she knew she was poorly prepared. She couldn't woo Rachel with this. There was only one thing for it. She'd have to hide. Darting behind the boxwood topiary tree, Lauren held her breath as the front door was opened.

"Hello?" said the voice.

Lauren froze. What in god's name was she doing? Keeping her knees bent and her back against the wall, she dared to glance up. Dammit, there was her car.

"Lauren?"

Lauren struggled up as best she could, sauntering back around the boxwood with as much swagger as she could muster. "Sorry, I dropped something."

"What are you doing down there, you dafty?"

"I thought I'd bring you your lip gloss."

Rachel took the offering. "Thank you. Haven't you got any appointments today?"

"I have."

"So why are you here?"

"To give you your lip gloss."

"The one you stole from me then gifted to Trudy?"

"That's the one."

"Well, thank you. And is there anything else I can help you with?"

Lauren smiled. "You're enjoying this aren't you? And what happened to our long-hug greetings?"

"I'm intrigued as to why you'd be skulking around my bushes."

"I've been wanting to skulk around your bushes for years."

Rachel laughed. "Do these lines usually work?"

"I said I'd be honest. I always have a running commentary in the back of my mind."

"Maybe it should stay there."

"Should it?"

"If it involves skulking around my bushes, then yes."

"And if it involved soulful laments about the way you stand on your doorstep with the breeze in your hair and the sun on your skin?"

"It's cloudy. But that would be better."

"What about the way I look at your lips when you talk?"

"Carry on."

"The way I picture them moving to me."

"I'm listening."

Lauren took a deep breath. "The way I adore you with every inch of my soul."

"You, my lovely, are the simplest yet most complicated person I know." Rachel was smiling. "Why couldn't you say all this yesterday?"

Lauren shrugged. "I'm shy."

"You said that already."

"You still don't believe me?"

"I know you, Lauren; I've seen how you are. When you want something, you get it. Absolutely nothing fazes you. You're the most cut-throat woman there is."

"I sound like a bitch."

"But you're my bitch."

"Am I?"

"If you want to be."

Lauren laughed. "So hang on a minute. Rachel Moore, the prim and proper housewife from the posh barn conversions just asked me to be her bitch."

"And that's how you see me, isn't it? Prim and proper."

"You're telling me you're really a sex fiend?"

"With you I think I might be."

"Can we go on a walk?" Lauren looked skywards. "See, the sun's trying to break out." She nodded. "And that's what I came round for: to surprise you with a spontaneous May morning walk."

"You're wearing your work heels."

"There's a pair of my trainers just there." She pointed through the doorway at the shoe rack.

"And that Ralph Lauren suit?"

"It's due to be cleaned."

"Where will we go?"

Lauren thought fast. She'd had absolutely no intention of embarking on a Tuesday morning walk in her high heels and work gear but it suddenly seemed the most natural thing in the world. "My look-out point."

"This sounds interesting. And where do we find this look-out point of yours?"

"It's just on the hills."

Rachel passed over the shoes and reached for her jacket. "Your car or mine?"

"Yours," said Lauren smiling. "It's my turn to touch your leg while you're driving. Plus I'm still knee-deep in pellets."

****

Sitting on the wooden slats at the look-out point, Lauren smiled. She'd never brought anyone here before. It was the place she came for quiet reflection and appreciation, because that's all there really was to do half-way up the hill looking out across the open heathland. There were plenty more beautiful spots across the hills that weren't as barren or dry, where you could find purple moor grass and evergreen fescue instead of this dusty bracken and scrub, but there was something about its simplicity that drew Lauren back time and time again.

She'd stumbled across the place a couple of years before when wandering the area looking for the perfect spot to watch a solar eclipse, sitting herself down on what looked like a boardwalk even though it led nowhere and had no visible purpose, just stuck in the centre of the hill. Maybe this was it, she thought, reaching down to take Rachel's hand, just somewhere to stop and take stock. That's what had happened on that March morning when the moon had covered the sun, the brief darkness making way for a light that opened up the expanse in front of her, as if saying: this world's yours, it's open and free and the possibilities are endless. Lauren smiled. Well, here she was now, the impossible dream sitting right by her side.

"It's beautiful," said Rachel. "So quiet and peaceful."

"Coming here always relaxes me."

"Do you come here a lot?"

Both women smiled at the line.

"You're getting good at this," said Lauren. "Twice a month maybe. Just to sit and think."

"And what do you think about?"

She shrugged. "You mostly."

"Even before?"

"Always." Crossing her legs under her, Lauren turned to face her friend properly. She wanted Rachel to read her eyes and feel her meaning. She reached for her hands to connect them completely. "I think about you every day, Rachel. I always have done. You've had a hold on me since the moment we met."

"In what way?"

Lauren smiled. "For eleven years I've known it was you."

"Oh, Lauren."

"Wait. I want to say it."

"You don't have to say anything."

"I need to." She took a deep breath. "You have that special something that draws others in. You're one of those magical people, Rachel, and I've been content," she paused, "in fact I've been incredibly lucky to be by your side. I haven't had some great plan to make you mine one day, but I've certainly imagined the fairytale; this fairytale."

"Why haven't you told me?"

"Because the thought of losing you is unbearable." She squeezed the fingers. "You're the best thing in my life."

"Why would you lose me?"

"You get scared. You run. You don't feel it too."

"I love you, Lauren. You know I love you."

"As a friend."

"As a friend, as my rock, as that one person who's always been there."

Lauren spoke softly. "But I'm *in* love with you."

"There's no difference."

"There is. I feel you in my heart every day, Rachel. You consume me. You're my first waking thought and my last dream at night."

"But the girlfriends?"

"Weren't you."

"But you've shied away from me so many times, Lauren."

"Because this is real. It means everything to me. When I kiss you I want you to kiss me right back. Not because it's something you want to try, but because it's something you *have* to do. Something you *need* to do."

"I've needed to kiss you for a long time."

"I don't believe you."

Rachel shrugged. "I might be a bit late to the party but I'm here now and I don't want you questioning why, or analysing any suggested confusion, or allocating any labels to my desire. I just want to admit to feeling that desire so we can see where this goes."

"It could take you anywhere on Tinder."

"But my desire's for you."

"How do you know?"

"Because I look at you and imagine."

"Since when?"

"Since forever. You're a gorgeously strong and inspiring woman, of course it's crossed my mind."

"But not enough to ever properly act on it?"

"I was married and you were dating, plus you never showed me a single jot of interest when I did get drunk and become flirty."

"Trust me, my private monologue did."

"And what's it thinking right now?"

"It's thinking: *Kiss me.* It's thinking: *Just lean forwards and kiss me.*"

"So say it."

Moving her gaze to the expanse of possibilities, Lauren took a moment to absorb the sheer peacefulness of the scene. "I want you to kiss me," she said, her eyes back on Rachel.

"And I want to kiss you too. Just promise you won't doubt me again."

"I won't."

Rachel was smiling. "Good, because you won't have to."

Lauren watched as the space between them disappeared, the song of a lark somewhere high above the only sound to break the silence. Rachel's lips were on hers, her hands on her cheeks as the sun shone down on their love. Lauren closed her eyes as the warm breeze danced around them, their mouths parting wider for more.

CHAPTER TWENTY THREE

"We should have done this sooner," groaned Rachel, her back up against her barn's wooden door. "You have to come in."

"I can't come in," said Lauren between the searching kisses, "as much as I want to."

"I want you to."

"I want to."

"So come."

"I will, but not now."

Rachel reversed their positions, pinning Lauren against the door instead. "Tonight. I'll cook."

"I'm only hungry for you."

"Internal monologue?"

Lauren nodded as she tilted her head back, letting Rachel's mouth move to her neck. "I'll rein it in."

"Don't you dare. This is so incredibly perfect."

Lauren kissed again. "Outside your barn in broad daylight, getting it on with another woman?"

"Getting it on with you."

"We are, aren't we." She moaned, completely overwhelmed with desire. "I have to go or we'll end up in your box tree."

"As long as I'm on top of you, I don't care where we are."

"Is that your internal monologue?"

"Just my rampant desire. Honestly, Lauren, I want you so much."

Lauren kissed back with as much force as she was receiving. "Unfortunately, so do Camilla and Ian," she said, managing to edge herself sideways. "In a different way, of course."

"Go." Rachel stepped away. "Before I change my mind."

Lauren moved back in for another embrace, pulling Rachel's body into her own. "Don't you ever change your mind."

The groan was deep. "After those kisses, how could I?"

Lauren smiled. "Good. I'll see you at seven?"

"Six-thirty."

"Won't Parker be up?"

"Sleepover at Rosemary and Ken's."

"Don't."

"He loves it."

"He hates it. Take him to Boing Zone after school, wear him out, I'll come round at seven."

"That, my lovely, is why you're so special."

"I'm not coming between you."

"You won't." Rachel smiled. "Apart from tonight, when you'll definitely be coming between me."

Lauren felt her stomach lurch. "Did you really just say that?"

"I said it and I'm going to say an awful lot more. Keep your phone on. I don't care how bad Trudy claims this crisis is, I'm about to offer up some light afternoon relief."

Lauren moved in for one final kiss. "I'm so turned on."

"Well, it seems you're the twist to my tap too."

Lauren laughed and raised her eyebrows. "Is that so?"

"Appears that way," said Rachel.

Lauren groaned as her hand was taken and placed between Rachel's legs. "What are you doing?"

"Whetting your appetite for later."

Lauren felt her own knees buckle.

"You did that to me."

"I haven't done anything yet."

"Well, my lovely, I'm already there."

****

Dashing from her car towards the shop, Lauren still couldn't breathe. Rachel had been so forward and confident… and wet. And yes, she'd only felt it through her trousers, but it was there: her desire, and she had been proud. Lauren groaned. That was the biggest turn on: a woman not afraid to be real, feeling everything fully, not scared to let go. Rachel would be a screamer, she just knew it; she'd never thought it before, always imagining she'd come quietly, embarrassed at the pleasure she'd received, but not anymore. This new Rachel was feisty and fiery and so much hotter than she could ever have hoped. Lauren approached her business premises and focused. She had to concentrate on the task in hand. Trudy had said it was bad, but just how bad was yet to be seen.

Opening the door to the shop, she gasped. Camilla's mother-in-law, Ma'mar, was face-first against the side wall in her wheelchair, Camilla was arms and legs folded on the high-backed armchair facing the back wall, and Trudy was in the middle, arms held out to both bristling hostiles. "Where's Ian?" she chose to say.

"In the toilet," growled all three women in unison.

The most elderly of the group craned her neck. "Could you please take my brake off?"

"Don't you dare," snapped Camilla, also craning her neck to the new arrival.

"Trudy? Why's Mrs Brennan been wheeled to the wall and put on lockdown?"

"I had to separate them."

"Only useful thing she's done all morning," snapped Camilla.

Moving over to the wheelchair, Lauren released the brake and turned the woman back around. "I'm so sorry, Mrs Brennan, this isn't how we do things around here. How can I help?"

"I would like to sing at the wedding."

The Cruella de Vil lookalike jumped up from her seat. "You shall not be singing at the wedding!"

"Tina thinks I'm good."

"I'm Trudy, my lady, and you're great."

"She's not!" snapped Camilla. "Lauren, listen to this!"

"I can't perform on command in this heightened state of anxiety."

"You have to. If you're Whitney or Celine, you perform."

Lauren looked at the old woman, struggling to spot any sort of likeness. "Shall we all just sit down and have a cup of tea?"

"No," said Camilla's mother-in-law. "If she wants to hear it again she can hear it again."

Lauren watched as a small silver harmonica was pulled out of a leather handbag that had been resting on the old woman's knees. The breathy buzz sounded loudly.

"And what note's that?" snapped Camilla.

"My note." The warbly voice started to sing. "*In the bleak midwinter—*"

"You are NOT singing *In the bleak midwinter* at my June wedding!"

"Gosh, are you two still going?" asked Ian, appearing from the door that led to the shop's small bathroom.

"Says you, Mr Weak Bladder!"

"Camilla!" Lauren couldn't help herself.

"Yes, Miss Hilliard?"

Lauren paused. "Shall we all just take a minute?"

Camilla sniffed. "Ian's taken twenty."

"Getting away from you, no doubt," muttered the old woman.

"Ma'mar!" gasped Ian.

"Ladies, ladies, ladies," calmed Trudy, raising her hands once again between the two women.

"Are you going to wheel me against that wall again?"

"No, she's not," assured Lauren, "and I can't comprehend what could have led to such a manoeuvre; I can only apologise once more."

"Mrs Brennan threw her harmonica at Camilla."

"It fell. Now, where was I?" The instrument buzzed again loudly. "*Frosty wind made moan.*"

"You can't sing that, Ma'mar."

"But it reminds me of Camilla."

Ian tried to stand straighter. "Camilla, my darling, what if Ma'mar sang a different song?"

The harmonica sounded a much lower note before the voice sounded out in a gravelly fashion. "*This is the road to hell.*"

"Right! Back against the wall." Camilla marched towards the wheelchair.

"Listen here, you." The old woman's bejewelled finger was wagging. "I've been moved off the top table and told I have to eat from a tray on my lap at the side of proceedings. I've been banned from the bridal procession and family photos in case my wheelchair leaves track marks on your ghastly gown, and I've—"

"Ian." Camilla cut her off.

"Yes, my darling?"

The hand made a dismissive wave towards the door.

"What?"

"Push her away."

"Onto the open road?"

"If you have to."

"Surely she can sing something short?"

"At my wedding? Never!"

"It's my wedding too."

"And that can be rearranged," came the reply before Camilla's whole demeanour suddenly changed. "Sidney," she said to the open shop door, "my hero. What a pleasant surprise."

"Camilla Riggins."

Ian stepped forward. "Soon to be Brennan."

Sid ignored him completely, taking hold of Camilla's hand and pulling her in for a twirl. "The Rig to my Sid."

Camilla giggled. "The fold to my flower."

Trudy interrupted. "You did all this last time, Sid. How can we help you?"

"Just bringing round my portfolio. Camilla's asked for two hundred pieces of hanging origami, made from tracing paper obviously. Nothing shall obstruct the sight of this beauty. So here's some of my work and I'll obviously be needing her fast-finger folding skills to help me finish off."

"Is that what you were doing here the other morning?" asked Trudy.

Camilla dismissed her with a wave. "I wasn't here the other morning."

"You were. Wednesday morning wasn't it?"

"I've started Pilates on a Wednesday morning."

Ian spoke up. "You didn't go back to fiddle with the pre-nup, did you?"

"You've not got anything worth fiddling with."

Trudy whispered. "I bet Sid has though."

Sid pulled Camilla in for another twirl. "And I'd love to accept your kind invitation to the wedding. Top table you say?"

"This man will not being coming to our wedding," said Ian, "and he will not be sitting on the top table while poor Ma'mar here is silently gagged and bound with a TV dinner on her lap."

Camilla sniffed. "Didn't I tell you he could get vicious? You wouldn't think it, being all arty and whatnot, but I'm right to ban booze at the wedding."

"Wise, my dear Rig, very wise."

Ian moved to the wheelchair. "Ma'mar, we're leaving."

Zhooshing up her hair, Camilla laughed. "For good?"

"Believe it or not, my darling, I love you." Pushing his mother towards the shop door, Ian continued to talk. "And I shall marry you in just over two weeks."

"Shall you now?"

"Yes, I shall, and you're to end this ridiculous charade right away."

"I like it when you get firm."

"I know you do; now help me open this door."

Camilla moved to the front of the shop and did as instructed. "Rig?"

"Leave your portfolio with the ladies; I'm sure they'd like to see your fine finger work."

Trudy whispered again. "Not in a million years."

"And that muttering really needs to stop, Tracy." Camilla pointed at the old woman in the wheelchair. "You're worse than his mother."

"It's Trudy, my lady and…" The door clicked shut. "…and they're gone."

"Do they have any other appointments scheduled in?" asked Sid, as he watched the trio disappear down the road.

Lauren re-opened the door for his exit. "Everything's been ready for months but Camilla keeps popping in with new queries and dramas, and you're no help bringing your origami to the table at such late notice."

Sid ignored the gesture, instead moving his head from side to side as if calculating something of huge importance. "Third of June, two weeks on Saturday. I'll have to work quickly. Camilla's fast fingers will help, no doubt."

"Don't get involved," said Lauren, tapping on the open door. "We'll see you soon."

"She wants you to look at my portfolio."

"Sid." Lauren sighed as she let the door close in on itself. "Camilla's a client, and I'll always be supportive, but…"

"But what?"

Trudy cut in. "But Camilla's clearly a people collector. She doesn't want you or your origami. What she does want is for you to want her."

"I do want her. We…"

"You what?"

The solicitor paused. "Nice chap is he? This Ian?"

Moving over to the coffee machine, Lauren shrugged. "I've seen all sorts come through here and I never judge. The ones you think are going to make it often never do, and the ones you believe have no chance seem to go the distance." She lifted her hands heavenwards. "I have no clue what makes a relationship work.

Couples can be strange. Those two clearly like to bicker, or she does, while he's fine playing second fiddle. You'd never play second fiddle, Sid."

"I would for my Rig."

"Go back to your shop. Forget about the origami. I'll say the pieces are too distracting for the audience."

"The audience?"

"That's what Camilla likes to call her guests." Lauren popped a coffee pod into the machine before lifting herself onto the counter. "The day's about her, Sid. Her whole existence is about her. Don't get caught up in something that's got nothing to do with you."

"I don't think Camilla Riggins would be too pleased to hear you talking in such a manner."

"She's been Camilla Hollop and Camilla DeLacy since you last knew her and she's soon to be Camilla Brennan."

Trudy jumped up next to Lauren. "Yeah, and I don't think her fiancé would be too pleased to hear about your secret trysts."

"Get down, Trudy."

"Sorry, boss."

Lauren waited for her to slide off the counter. "Sid, you need to forget all about her."

"But she's my Rig."

"She's Ian's Rig, well Brennan, actually no, is she still a DeLacy or has she...?" Lauren coughed. "Either way, you need to man up."

"I do?"

"You do."

Sid nodded. "Thank you. That's exactly what I'll do. You've been a great help, Lauren. I'll see myself out."

"Did he think either of us were moving?" asked Trudy as she watched the solicitor make his exit.

"Hey, I was holding that door for a good two minutes."

"You do realise you've just sparked him into action?"

"I've done nothing of the sort."

"Yes, you have and I do love the way you've suddenly started doling out the relationship advice. You sounded very wise. The afternoon was a success I assume?"

Leaning back on the counter, Lauren groaned. "Mmm hmm."

"You're official?"

"Let's just say Rachel and I are that strange couple who might actually make it."

CHAPTER TWENTY FOUR

Crossing the gravel driveway, Lauren knew her assessment was right: She and Rachel were a strange couple. Best friends of more than a decade, one gay, one straight, one opting for family, one for career; both suddenly coming together in an explosion of perfect compatibility. She moaned with sexual arousal, the idea of exploding as they came together had been on her mind all afternoon, especially since Rachel's texts had begun. The first one simply read: *I want you.*

Reaching into her back pocket for her phone, she scrolled to the message again. It was like an instant aphrodisiac; three words she never thought she'd hear: *I want you.* So powerful. Words that evoked such emotion and returning desire. The next one had been more explicit: *On the kitchen counter.* Lauren laughed. Oh, how many times had she imagined that? And the third message simply read: *Naked.*

Lauren bit on her lip. Of course they'd seen each other naked before, but she'd never stared, or studied, not openly anyway, and the idea that Rachel's body would be hers to admire and enjoy was in equal measure the most thrilling yet terrifying part of all this: that they were actually going to get physical. She bit her lip even harder. Eleven years was nowhere near enough preparation. Putting her hand on the latch, she took a deep breath and clicked the door open as quietly as she could. This was it. This was the start of their story.

"Welcome," whispered the woman standing at the entrance to the lounge holding a sparkling blue Venetian masquerade ball mask up to her face.

Lauren stared down the hallway. "Rachel?"

Rachel pulled the mask away. "Of course it's me, shhh, just listen." The mask was back, the feathers now swaying with the movement. "This is our story. Please come this way."

Lauren kicked off her shoes and placed them on the rack. She'd made an extra effort with her outfit this evening with a marked departure from her usual chilling clothes, but she was a long way from the masked beauty trussed up in a gown leading her into the lounge. "I just went for smart jeans and top," she whispered, not wanting to speak at full volume until the heavy door was firmly closed. Parker was usually a good sleeper, but she didn't want anything to scupper their chances of a romantic night in.

"It's okay, I have your mask here."

Lauren laughed, the lounge door safely shut. "I recognise this."

"You wore it at our freshers' ball. I'm not sure how I ended up with them both but, you know me, I never throw anything away that has value."

Lauren lifted the stick, peeping through the extravagant mask's eye holes. "Why does this have value?" she asked.

Rachel stepped in closer. "Because it was the first time I tried to flirt with you."

"What?" Lauren peeped over the feathers. "You did not!"

Bending over the coffee table, Rachel lifted the first of the large placards from the pile. She took two steps back and smiled. "I did."

"Are we about to have a *Love Actually* moment?" Lauren pointed to the pile of cardboard that remained face down on the table.

"I'm doing one better," said Rachel, flipping the sign in her hand.

"It's a photo!" Lauren took a step forward. "Look how young we are! And you're right, they are the same masks!"

"Of course they are."

Lauren held out her hands for the picture. "May I?"

Rachel handed over the huge photo. "You were dancing, holding your mask up to your eyes and I waltzed over to you. I think I was trying to get into the Venetian spirit even though they were playing Destiny's Child at the time. Anyway, I waltzed over and curtseyed and asked for a dance."

"I remember."

"We used one hand for our masks and we held hands with the other. You twirled me."

"Did I?"

"And I tried to do a backwards fall, imagining I would look like a damsel in distress, horizontal in your arms and you'd look into my eyes and just kiss me, but you didn't. I stumbled and you dropped me and we ended up getting thrown out for being drunk."

Lauren laughed. "That's right! I remember. We went back to the halls of residence via the Scrumpy Jack shelf at the corner shop. But we definitely didn't almost kiss."

"Because you dropped me."

"I did not!"

"You did! Can we do it again?"

"The drop? Our bones are older. I don't think it's wise."

"The twirl and the fall."

Lauren laid the placard on the sofa and moved next to Rachel. "What was I doing dancing alone?"

"Being you. Being cool. And I simply sashayed over."

Lauren laughed. "If you did it like that it's no wonder I dropped you."

"Put your mask up, let's make it authentic."

"You have the music?"

Reaching for the iPod remote, Rachel clicked. "Destiny's Child at their finest."

Lauren laughed. "Perfect for a masquerade ball."

"Dance then."

"I'm dancing."

"And I'm making my move." Rachel nodded. "We were drunk. I don't think we spoke. We just held hands and started to jig."

"Awkwardly like this?"

"Exactly like this."

Lauren smiled as the music and the sight of Rachel's warm eyes sparkling through the feathers transported her back in time to one of their very first nights out together. "I remember. And I remember you looking absolutely sensational, like you do now."

"Let me twist and fall."

"And this time I've caught you," said Lauren, smiling. "And this time I'm staring. This time I'm looking straight into your eyes."

"And I want you to kiss me, just like I wanted you to kiss me back then."

"You were on the floor and it was obviously just a drunken whim."

"But now I'm in your arms and this time it's real."

Lauren leaned in, pressing her lips gently to Rachel's. She closed her eyes and lost herself in the re-enactment. The music was old school and the mask's feathers were tickling her nose, but the moment was perfect and the kiss was sublime. At the same moment they opened their eyes and looked at each other.

"Do you need me to get up," asked Rachel, a big smile spreading across her face. "I think I'm a tad heavier now than I was back then."

"I wouldn't know. I dropped you."

"And I'm glad you did because that kiss was more perfect than it would have been eleven years ago."

"You're right. I'd have had double vodka and Red Bull breath."

"And I'd have freaked out about kissing a woman."

"But you wanted to?"

Rachel moved back to the coffee table, placing her mask on it as she picked up the next placard. "Yes. Just like I did here." She spun the card round to display the photo.

Lauren squealed. "That's the night of spin the loo roll! Look at us! What the hell were we wearing?"

"Satin shirts were in."

"Satin shirts have never been in, especially not orange ones."

"The loo roll tube spun to us. Do you remember?"

"Of course I do. I had concussion for two days."

"I wanted it to happen."

"You did?"

"Yes. Can you remember what was playing?"

"It was at that strange girl's house. Who was she obsessed with? That singer. Deepish voice?"

Rachel smiled as she clicked the iPod forwards a song.

"Sade!" squealed Lauren.

"It was playing all night. Here, take a seat."

"On the tiles?"

"On the bobbly rug, and pass me that bottle, we're more sophisticated now."

Lauren went over to the fireplace and the wine rack where Rachel kept her bottles of red. "Wait, the fire's not lit. I've only just noticed. What's going on? Where's the real Rachel gone?"

"You don't like it too warm. Plus, I want you to strip off because you want to, not because you have to."

"I like it. Where do you want me?"

"You were sitting alone on the far side of the circle."

"Why was I alone again?"

"You were always alone. And I can't remember who spun it." She took the bottle and twisted. "But it landed on you," she twisted again, "then on me."

"And I think I crossed the circle on all fours at such a speed I sent you flying."

"No, it was me! I jumped onto my knees and cracked you with my head. We both ended up face first in that stinking carpet."

"Weren't you pleased the game ended there?"

"No. I wanted to kiss you."

"Oh, Rachel, I never knew."

"And I'm glad you never knew because now we get to spin and kiss without all those weirdos looking at us."

"Are you sure we weren't the weirdos?"

"Gosh no."

Lauren laughed. "So Sade's playing, the bottle's been spun; I'll try to get over there in a slow and sexy fashion."

"You do whatever you need to do."

Lauren stayed facing forward, advancing feet first.

"Let me know when you're starting."

"Ha! I'm doing it!"

"That open-legged spider thing?"

"How would you get across?" Lauren stopped.

"I'd smoothly shift onto all fours and prowl my way into your space."

Lauren let her legs drop down. Rachel was sexily slinking her way over the bobbles with an exaggerated swaying of her bottom, like a lioness out on the prowl. "You're so hot," she said.

"And I'm going to crawl right on top of you."

Lauren clutched her legs together and leaned back on her elbows, allowing the lioness to seize her prey. She looked up at Rachel on all fours over her. "You have me where you want me."

"Where I've wanted you for a very long time."

Lifting her hands to Rachel's hair, Lauren tucked the loose curls behind her friend's ears before pulling the full weight of her body on top of her own. She moaned. Rachel's lips were on hers, her tongue in her mouth; there was no space between their bodies. Lauren rolled over so she was on top. She wanted more, she needed more, she had to taste deeper. This was the climactic moment of her dreams, the dreams she'd had for so long; the moment where they took each other, really took each other. The groan from Rachel only worked to encourage her so she pinned Rachel's arms out on either side, parting her legs with her own, their bodies pressed hard into each other. "I've wanted this for so long," she gasped.

"So have I," said Rachel, taking hold of Lauren's wrists and grappling her into the same arms-out position, turning her over so she was in charge.

"Keep kissing me. I'm happy with kissing."

Rachel pushed her thighs between Lauren's.

"And that. I'm happy with that too."

"And this?" asked Rachel, releasing one wrist as she lifted the bottom of Lauren's shirt.

Lauren felt the contact on her stomach, her insides spiralling into a rampant frenzy of arousal. Rachel's smooth hand was moving slowly up her side, skin on skin. She gasped and took Rachel's lips back onto her own, moaning into her mouth as Rachel's fingers wandered further, closer to her breast.

"Was it your nipples you like being touched? Or was that just me?"

Simply hearing the words nipples and touched come from Rachel's mouth was enough to send Lauren over the edge. This was happening, this was really happening. She tilted her chin up, forcing Rachel's mouth to move to her neck, a sigh of arousal sounding out as the fingers brushed over her bra, Rachel's thumb already working her breast through the fabric.

"Oh, you do like this, don't you," said Rachel with a smile. "And what if I pull your bra down?"

Again, the words bra and down coming from Rachel's mouth were as much of a turn-on as the actual act itself. Lauren screamed as the hand moved fully onto her skin, her nipple clasped between two of the fingers. "Rachel!"

"Yes?"

Her words were drawn out. *Fuck. Me.*

"Now?"

"As in *fuck me* you're so…" she gasped again as the fingers started to work, "*good*!"

"And we've still got our clothes on. What if I unbuttoned this?" Rachel's other hand moved to the shirt. "And this? And then, oops, this button here?"

Lifting her head, Lauren watched Rachel pull the shirt open.

"Oh and look, your bra's come down."

Lauren gasped as her breast came into full view, her nipple hard under the fingers. On feeling Rachel's mouth back on her neck she dropped her head back and closed her eyes.

"And what..." Rachel's words were punctuated with tiny kisses. "If I..." The kisses moved lower. "Were to..."

Lauren moaned as the lips made contact with the swell of her breast.

"Kiss..."

"Oh Rachel."

"You..."

Lauren gasped. "Oh hell."

"Here?"

The sensation of Rachel's mouth tight against her nipple was too much to hold in. Lauren sighed in joyful ecstasy, grabbing her hands to the back of Rachel's head, fingers pushing up into her hair. "Oh Rachel!" she cried as the tongue worked forward and back, the teeth grazing gently, slowly increasing their pressure.

Rachel's eyes were wide. "Wow."

"What?"

"You're incredible."

Lauren exhaled. "I'm not doing anything."

"I have your nipple in my mouth."

Lauren's body convulsed. Words she never thought she'd hear. This was enough. This was more than enough. This was heaven. She pulled Rachel up gently, prising the mouth away from its target. "You're the incredible one," she said, before rolling her friend onto her back.

"I haven't finished."

"This will never finish." Lauren smiled. "This hasn't even begun."

CHAPTER TWENTY FIVE

Seated, with her legs lifted under the table onto Rachel's lap, Lauren sighed with contentment. They were in the dining room, looking like Brad Pitt and Angelina Jolie in that scene from *Mr and Mrs Smith*: half naked, clothes torn, battle-scarred from the high-energy frantic confrontation moments before, destroying the house while devouring each other. She smiled. "That was old-school heavy petting."

"I came!" Rachel laughed. "Twice!"

"So did I!"

"Really? I made the lesbian queen Lauren Hilliard come? Actually come?"

"Twice, and my jeans haven't got lower than my buttocks."

"I'm sure there's something we can do about that, but first," Rachel was smiling, "this is why we're here," she smiled again, "for a nice dinner out."

"I've already dined out and it was delicious."

"Really?" Rachel spoke with an edge of doubt.

"Mouth-wateringly!" Lauren watched as Rachel screwed up her nose. "You don't believe me? You want me to show you again how tasty you are?"

"Don't! Look, my cheeks have gone red."

"Only because we've been fucking."

"Lauren!"

"What? I get it; it's the two things that worry the straight girl the most: can I make another woman come and will she really like to chow down? Well I'm telling you now, that gazelle was right to stay face-first for so long."

Rachel laughed. "And I'm okay?"

"You're moreish, didn't you hear my screams?"

"Not as loud as mine."

"Poor Parker."

"He's fine. I wore him out after school and if he hears anything he'll just assume it's the TV."

"What are you usually watching at night then, missy?"

"Ha," Rachel was laughing. She paused. "This is fine, isn't it? In fact, it's more than just fine, it's natural. It's better, even better than we were, and we've always been pretty awesome." She laughed again. "Anyway, stop distracting me."

"You're the one being all dreamy."

"Yes, well, we've done the masked ball and the house party, and the New Year's Eve DJ party with bottles of Blue WKD. So now we're..." she reached down for the next placard that she'd brought in from the lounge, "at the Thai curry night."

Lauren studied the picture. It was the three of them: her, Rachel and Toby. "Right," she said.

"He's part of both of us and I can't ignore the time he asked for a threesome."

"He was joking!"

"We spoke about it."

"You did not!" Lauren moved off her chair and folded her arms, daring to look down at the photo once more.

"Of course we did. Lots of straight couples have that threesome fantasy and surprise surprise, most men don't want another man involved in the action."

"He didn't like me like that."

"He liked the idea though, of seeing us together."

Lauren's arms stayed folded. "I'm not sure I'm happy with this one."

"It's fine, I just know you like Thai food and I've had a red curry in the slow cooker all afternoon. I said I was cooking didn't I and we've not eaten a thing yet."

"I have."

"Ha. Let me go and grab us two bowls."

Lauren watched as Rachel disappeared out of the room. It was strange seeing Toby's face looming so large on the cardboard photo, but Rachel was right, they shouldn't ignore him. She turned it face down. "But I'd rather you didn't watch."

"I heard that," said Rachel, back in the room. "Is that why you said no at the time?"

"I didn't think he was being serious."

"It had to be an off-the-cuff remark to start with."

"Which I batted away."

"I know you did."

"You can't honestly have wanted a thing with me and him at the same time? I'm a lesbian; I'd have been grimacing and," she shuddered, "ewww no. Just no."

"I think maybe I thought having you in that way would be better than not having you at all."

"Why have you never said any of this, Rachel? It's just ridiculous."

"You've always been so distant."

"I've flirted! I've innuendo-ed!"

"You do that with everyone."

"I've silently stared and imagined."

"So why have *you* never said anything?"

"Because I didn't want to ruin what we had. Because I didn't want you to dismiss me, to make me feel like I was wrong for harbouring these thoughts."

"What thoughts?"

"Well…"

"Go on." Rachel passed over a steaming bowl and handed Lauren a fork and spoon. "Sit down."

"Well." Lauren took the offering as she followed the instruction. "I didn't want you to say I wasn't falling in love. To say I wasn't in love. To say I couldn't be in love." She started to stir the fragrant contents of the bowl. "But I was. I have been since forever." She looked up. "I am."

"Oh, Lauren."

"And let me guess, it was just the three of us at the curry? I was alone again?"

"You were. But only because you chose to not bring your girlfriend. I can't even remember who was on the scene at the time. Can you?"

"No." Lauren shrugged. "But that's only because no one's ever really meant anything to me before."

"But I have? You've liked me from the start?"

"I've loved you from the start."

Rachel sighed. "And then I went and married Toby."

"And I'm glad you did, because this is our time, Rachel. It wouldn't have worked at any of those other points." She signalled to the placards strewn around the room. "You weren't ready."

"Me?"

"Yes, you. There's a difference between having a fantasy about someone with the occasional idea that a kiss at a certain time might be fun, and actually knowing with all your soul that you need to be with that one person. You're my one person, Rachel."

"And I feel it too."

"Do you really though?"

"This whole rampant sexual wanting of women might be a bit new but, trust me, I'm totally on board with that now." She smiled. "The other things you had to offer I've always wanted, I've always loved. Your companionship, your strength, your humour, it's been there; you've always given it to me. I got the odd orgasm from the hubby because that's what people do. I followed the straight path. I didn't have some great internal debate or to-ing and fro-ing, I loved him and I got married, that's how life works: people get married and have kids." She paused. "But I knew I was getting so much from you that I should have been getting from him. You're my best friend, Lauren, and it was easy to blame my occasional crossing the line attempts on the drink, but if I look closely I think I've always wanted you like that."

"But you shouldn't have to think. You should just know and this is all so retrospective."

"That's where you're wrong. Everyone's story is different. Sexuality can be strict for some and fluid for others. Some people make really well thought through choices, while others just follow their lust. Some people don't realise what they want until it's too late, and some people change all of a sudden and for no apparent reason." She smiled. "I fancy you, Lauren, more now than ever. You're my rock, my soulmate, all of those clichés, and I want you – sexually and emotionally. I want you exactly as we've been before and so much more on top of that too. And I'm sorry if you think I should have seen you as a real and credible option from day one, maybe I did, but you didn't seem to give me anything back. I don't know, I just know we're here now and I feel it just as much as you do."

"But I love you. I'm in love with you."

"Don't you get it? I'm in love with you too."

Lauren bit the inside of her lip, overwhelmed with emotion, not sure of the words.

Rachel spoke again. "I love you, Lauren."

Pushing the bowl to one side, Lauren moved from her seat and walked around the small table, dropping onto her knees in front of her friend. "You can't let me believe this. If you have one single jot of doubt you simply can't let me believe this."

"I'm not going to hurt you. You can let yourself go." Rachel reached out for Lauren's cheeks. "You're not alone anymore."

Lauren held onto her tears, managing to emit a small laugh instead. "I sound like a right loser."

"Well, you're my loser now."

"I am a loser, aren't I?"

"Yes."

"Ha. That's why I love you."

"And if we're done with the curry I have one final picture to show you."

Standing up, Lauren composed herself. There was a fine line between welcome emotion and someone with a worrying instability and she'd always felt it important not to burden others with woes or doubts. If Rachel was saying she loved her, then she'd just have to believe that she loved her. Lauren smiled, she couldn't help it. "You love me?"

"Yes, I love you."

"You're in love with me?"

"Yes, I'm in love with you."

Reaching out a hand to her friend, Lauren pulled Rachel from her seat. "Say it again."

"I'm in love with you."

"Say it again," she shouted, twirling her friend into her arms.

"I love you!" came the laughing reply.

Lauren stopped the movement. "Will you get it on a t-shirt?"

"Only if you get one too." The voice was serious. "In fact, why don't we get ones that say: I'm in love with her and an arrow pointing left and right? We could walk around with our arrows pointing at each other."

"What a perfect first item of clothing for us as a couple."

Rachel nodded. "On it. Right, stop twirling me and come and look at this." Reaching for the next photo, she smiled as she turned it over. "The Blackpool tour."

"Crikey! Those same satin shirts! And this was two years later. We so needed a new wardrobe back then!"

"We were poor students."

"Who chose to spend their money going on tour to Blackpool. What was it even a tour for? We didn't play in any official teams."

"Crazy Katrina organised it."

Lauren peered at the five girls in the photo all crammed into a crappy Blackpool B&B. "What happened to Crazy Katrina?"

"On that night she ended up on a ferry to the Isle of Man, but in general I have no clue. We must hunt her down; she always was such a good laugh."

"She wasn't! She had that weird thing with the matches!"

"Yes, I remember!"

Lauren nodded. "Always carried a box of matches around, randomly lighting them and flicking them wherever she was."

"Probably in jail for arson now."

"Or a fire breather."

"Anyway, my point is," Rachel tapped the photo, "this was the night we ended up sharing a double bed."

"Did we?"

"Yes, and I took hours to pluck up the courage to hold your hand under the covers."

Lauren laughed. "I definitely don't remember this one."

"You must!"

"Nope."

"Did I take too long? Were you already asleep?"

"Clearly, because an under-the-covers hand holding experience would be etched into my memory."

"I wondered why you were so unresponsive. I thought you were pretending."

"I was probably passed out. It *was* the Blackpool tour. No one remembers anything from that weekend."

"Apart from Crazy Katrina's phone call from the Isle of Man." Rachel frowned. "You really don't remember?"

"No!"

"Right, well I'll have to remind you." Rachel took Lauren's hand and led them from the room.

Following her friend towards the guest bedroom she already viewed as her own, Lauren understood why it was the obvious choice. Rachel's room was at the top end of the barn next to Parker's, so it made sense for them to stay as far away as possible. Plus Rachel's room had that whole you-slept-with-your-husband-in-here thing going on, so she was relieved by the direction they'd taken; relieved in the most nervous yet excited of ways. They were en-route to a bedroom. An actual bedroom. Her and Rachel.

"Do you have a pair of shorts and a t-shirt for me?" she heard herself say. "That's what we all wore to bed back then."

"I still do now, and you have pajamas in the drawer."

"I only put them on in the mornings when I come out to the kitchen."

"You sleep naked?"

"Don't you?"

"No! I wear shorts and a t-shirt."

"Old school. Are we going to re-enact it?"

Rachel closed the bedroom door behind them and reached for the two piles of nightwear. "I prepared them earlier. Shorts and t-shirt times two. I'll change in the en suite. You change in here and get into bed. Turn off the lights and snuggle under the covers. I'll come in after a night out on the Blackpool strip. Try to stay awake if you can."

"I'd have stolen some of Crazy Katrina's matches to keep my eyes open if I'd known you were planning on making a move in bed!"

"You sound excited."

"I *am* excited!" Lauren smiled. "You know I walked into the barn tonight believing our story was about to begin, but you've shown me we've been living our story for years; this is just the next chapter."

"You, my lovely, are the words on my page."

"Arr, I like that one." Lauren smiled. "And if I could write, I'd write a novel for you."

"Just get your nightwear on and pop into bed, that's good enough for now."

Lauren laughed as she watched the door to the en suite click shut. Throwing off what remained of her clothes, she pulled on the shorts and t-shirt. This did feel romantic and giggly; somewhat childish, yes, but that's who they were. There was no awkwardness or shyness, just a natural progression of how they'd always been.

Lauren laughed. And they'd always been hilarious. They always would be hilarious, just now with the added bonus of rampant hot sex. Pulling back the covers she jumped into bed and reached up to switch off the lights. How many times had she lain in this same position thinking about Rachel, obsessing and debating what every little interaction had meant. They should have just spoken to each other, openly and honestly. Lauren shook her head but, no, it would never have been perfect like this. On hearing the creak of the en suite door, she closed her eyes and felt the covers flick back, the bed sinking on one side. Lying there in silence, she imagined what it would have been like if she *had* been awake that evening. She'd have been lying there like she was now, aware of Rachel, knowing she was inches away. She didn't move. Rachel wasn't moving either. This would have been torture if she *had* been awake.

Lauren stretched out an arm. She'd have stretched out an arm in the hope of an accidental touching of skin. Dammit. Rachel wasn't there; she hadn't stretched far enough. What would her next play have been? Lauren paused. The other girls would have been in the room so whatever she did would have had to be silent; she couldn't just whisper: are you awake? Lauren exhaled heavily, smiling as she heard a similar heavy exhale from the other side of the bed. That would have been their signal. Both knew the other was awake. She tried again, crawling her hand further into the middle of the cool sheet. She stopped. She wouldn't have gone further than the middle, she'd have waited for Rachel to make the next move – which Rachel would never have done as it was back then and that was how it was. Lauren paused, feeling the finger brush against her own. But this time Rachel *had* made a move too.

Slowly, Lauren let their little fingers lock around each other. That's all it took, two little fingers reaching out to connect; the simplicity of the touch having such a deep meaning; nervous excitement flowing through her like never before. This was their first lingering contact. A contact that spoke much more than words. Lauren smiled in the silence. This was everything. This was knowing.

"Remember the other girls were in the room," came the whisper.

"I clocked that," said Lauren, jolted from the haze of the moment.

"We wouldn't have been able to talk."

"I know."

"Shush then."

Lauren couldn't help the smile that spread across her face. What would she have done next? She was right handed; she'd have got her right hand involved in the mix. Rolling gently onto her side and keeping their little fingers locked, she let her right hand graze Rachel's leg as she settled into her new position. She could have claimed it was an accident. Smiling wider, she felt the thigh nudge back against her fingers, Rachel's way of encouraging her touch, so she let her hand find the leg once again. She'd have brushed gently, moving up the side of the shorts and onto the stomach. The stomach was a safe area, an area where she could let her fingers gently stroke the skin, no aim of going anywhere, just moving in their own time.

Lauren felt Rachel's little finger curl tighter onto her own as she continued to move her hand across the soft stomach. Rachel was enjoying this. She was wanting more. Slowly, Lauren's fingers climbed up past the belly button, stroking the area just below the breasts. She'd never have had the courage to go higher. This was still safe. This was still friendly. Lauren tried not to laugh at the sudden downwards shunt in the bed. Rachel had brought her breasts to her hand. Pulling the covers away from Rachel's face, Lauren snuggled in closer, letting her fingers ride up the curve of the skin. She swallowed. Rachel wasn't wearing a bra and this thought alone made her ache. She'd seen Rachel's breasts on many occasions before. They were perfect, round and full, with the most kiss-able nipples. But now they were hers for the taking. Walking her fingers higher, Lauren circled the target. Rachel had talked about her nipples before and if their earlier encounters were anything to go by, then they were certainly the way to turn her right on.

Dancing around the area, Lauren ignored the shifting of Rachel's body that was urging her to take her completely. Lauren knew where the fingers were wanted, but she also knew that the nipples could wait. The accidental odd brush against the hardness would be enough to send waves of anticipation through Rachel's body and Lauren wanted to make the most of her time. Rachel would already be ready and waiting, but this was where the most fun could be had. This was where anticipation was often more satisfying than the actual event itself. Rachel was clearly desperate for her nipples to be touched and squeezed, worked in the fingers and pulled in a pleasurable way. And because Rachel was desperate for this, Lauren knew she'd be picturing it, feeling it already, urging her on, so when there *was* that odd brush and that first gentle squeeze, it was magnified one hundred times over. Likewise, when the fingers did finally get rough, the intensity would be too hard to describe.

Lauren studied Rachel's face in the darkness. She could just about make out her closed eyes and that she was biting her lip. Moving her mouth to Rachel's cheek, she planted a gentle kiss on the skin, taken aback by the instant turning of her head and mouth-on-mouth action. Would they really have done this? Lauren continued to kiss, taking the nipple between her fingers and squeezing. Maybe they would have to mute Rachel's sounds, silenced by their open mouths and pressured connection. Lauren eased her fingers away as she moved her mouth to the ear. "Shush," she whispered as she slid her left arm under Rachel's neck, reaching her hand back down to the breast. The moan sounded again so Lauren clamped her mouth back onto the lips, only easing up as she softened the rhythm with her fingers, teasing the nipple so gently, until squeezing once more, her mouth back in position covering the gasps.

"I need it," said Rachel, grabbing hold of Lauren's free hand.

"Shush, you'll wake up Crazy Katrina."

"She's on a ferry on the way to the Isle of Man."

"Shush!"

"No, I really need it, Lauren."

"And you're going to get it," she whispered. "I'm going to slide my right hand down to your stomach. I'm going to play with the top of your shorts. I'm going to slide my fingers under the waistband and I'm going to stroke your skin for an hour."

"An hour?! I can't take an hour!"

"You can if I bring my mouth down to your other breast." Lauren groaned as she took the pert nipple between her lips.

"Oh fucking hell, Lauren, bite me!"

"Stop that, you'll wake up the girls."

"I don't care if I toot the horn on the Isle of Man ferry. I want you inside me. I want you fucking me. I want you doing that thing that you did out in the lounge."

Lauren lifted her hand from the waistband. "I think I'd actually go in this way," she said, walking her fingers up the inside of Rachel's thigh and into the loose leg of the shorts.

"I love my thigh being tickled! Oh fuck, where are you going?! Why have you stopped? Keep going!"

"Shush! You'd have had to let me do it my way then, so let me do it my way now."

Rachel inhaled sharply. "What the fuck is that?!"

"Why are you so sweary?"

"Because you're... you're... What the fuck are you *doing*? Oh hell this is hot!"

"I'm just squeezing your outer lips together."

"It feels like you're kneading a bread roll and inside the bread roll there's my clit and it's getting pounded and worked and you're not even touching me. Oh, Lauren, this is good, this is so fucking good!"

Lauren silenced the cries with her lips, devouring the words as she worked with her fingers. This was the dream. This was the closeness. This was her friend's pussy in the palm of her hand.

CHAPTER TWENTY SIX

"Parker!" screeched Lauren as the little boy dive bombed onto the bed. She usually screeched because his bounce was so forceful and elbows-first, but this time she screeched because Rachel was still under the covers. "What are you doing?!"

"What I always do, Aunty Lauren. Wake up, wake up, wake up!"

Lauren tried to pull the covers higher. "Why don't you go and get yourself ready for school?"

"My clothes aren't out. Let's do the castle!"

"Go and put your clothes on first."

The laugh was bouncy. "Don't be silly! We never do the castle with clothes on."

Parker was right, they only ever did the castle in pajamas. It was their early morning ritual. Wake Aunty Lauren up with a screeching elbow in the face, get her to hoik her legs into the air, lifting up the covers like the turrets of a castle so he could climb them and slide down again, often bony knees first. This morning, however, he was super early and she hadn't even been mildly awake; nor had the beautiful body lying next to her that was now shrivelled into the tightest ball against her thigh.

"I need to get my pajamas on first. Go and grab me a glass of water from the kitchen, would you please?"

"Did you and Mummy have a party? It's a bit of a mess in there."

"Something like that."

"Shall I get her a glass of water too?"

"I think she's in the shower."

"No she's not."

"Isn't she?"

"No, she's lying right there."

Lauren widened her eyes. "Is she?"

"Why are you being so silly this morning, Aunty Lauren? Wake up, Mummy; I know you're under there too!"

"I don't think she is. Come on, go and get some water so we can do the castle."

"Here she is!" yelled Parker, dashing to the other side of the bed and yanking the covers back.

"Oh hello," said Rachel, with static bed hair and red face. "I wanted to come and play castles too. Let me find my shorts and t-shirt."

"Why are you both naked!? Have you been doing some adult kissing? Zoe from PP always talks about adult kissing. You do adult kissing naked."

"No, I don't think I've heard of that sort of kissing," said Rachel, sliding out of the bed and onto the carpet.

"Sounds gross," added Lauren, reaching down to the floor in a desperate attempt to find any sort of nightwear.

"What are you doing then?"

"Checking for spots," said Rachel, now on all fours hiding behind the bed. "Like I do to you."

"Does Aunty Lauren have spots?"

"Three that stand out," muttered Rachel.

"Did you have to squeeze them?"

"I did indeed," she said, her head peeping back up.

Parker grimaced into the bed. "It hurts when Mummy does spots, doesn't it."

Lauren coughed. "Well, if they've got to be squeezed they've got to be squeezed."

"Did you scream?"

The nod was serious. "I did indeed."

"Are they all gone now?"

"They might need another seeing to."

"Can I watch?"

"No, now go and get us some water so we can all play castles." Lauren waited for her godson's exit before sliding out of bed and racing around to find clothes. "What are you doing on all fours?" she asked Rachel.

"No clue!"

"Well get up and get changed!"

"He saw us naked! In bed together!"

"He often comes in here before I've got changed."

"But I'm not there hiding under the covers too!"

"My acne's never been a problem before."

"Oh Lauren, should we tell him?"

"Just get off your hands and knees and get some clothes on."

"That's not what you were saying last night."

Lauren laughed. "Here," she said, throwing a t-shirt in Rachel's general direction. "Put this on."

"This one's yours."

"It doesn't matter, just get back under the covers and lift up your legs."

"We haven't got time for that now!"

"The castle!"

"Oh right. What time is it though?"

"No clue. Last time I looked it was five a.m. and we were still snogging."

Rachel smiled. "We were, weren't we." She turned to the door and shouted. "Parker, what time is it, please?"

The young boy returned to the room wobbling two tall glasses of water. "The big hand and the little hand are both on the nine."

"So that means it's…"

"Quarter to nine?"

"Quarter to nine, that's right." Rachel gasped. "No, it can't be!"

"Quarter past nine?"

"No!"

"Nine to nine?"

"No, it's… Let me go and look." Rachel pulled her t-shirt down past her bottom, scuttling quickly from the room.

Lauren heard the shriek.

"It's quarter to nine!"

"Yessss," whistled Parker.

Lauren took the water glasses and placed them on the bedside table. "I think you're late for school, buddy."

"My clothes weren't laid out and you always say we've got time for the castle."

"Not today!" wailed Rachel, back in the room, t-shirt no longer pulled down. "Quickly. I need to get you ready!"

"I'll get him ready. You go and get yourself ready."

"Goodness, there's the doorbell! It'll be the Amazon man! It's always the Amazon man! Get the door please, Parker. I'll get your clothes."

"I'll get his clothes, you get yourself ready." Lauren took the dressing gown from the back of the door and followed Rachel out of the bedroom. "Wow, what's happened in here?" she said, looking around at the mess of placards, bottles and clothing strewn from the hall to the kitchen to the lounge.

"We happened in here," said Rachel, dashing up the stairs. "I'll throw his clothes down. Parker, get the door please!"

"It's Uncle Trevor."

"What?! Don't open it!"

"I've opened it."

The man's voice was confused. "Hello, I wasn't expecting anyone to be in. Shouldn't you be at school, Parker the pumpkin?"

"Yes, but Mummy and Lauren had a party and Mummy was checking Lauren's—"

"Trevor!" Rachel was back at the bottom of the stairs with a pile of school uniform. "Sorry, we're all in a bit of a rush."

"All?"

Lauren made herself visible in the lounge doorway. "Hello."

"You don't usually stay on a week night, do you?"

"Aunty Lauren stays all the time and I'm too old to be called Parker the pumpkin."

Trevor nosed his way through the hall. "Quite the party." He looked around. "What's with the big photos?"

"You couldn't take him to school, could you?" Rachel was talking fast from the bottom step as she awkwardly clung on to her t-shirt, pulling it as low as it would go. "I'd really appreciate it, Trevor. It's all been a bit manic this morning."

"I haven't got my car."

"We always walk." She passed the pile of clothes to Parker in as ladylike a fashion as she could muster without exposing too much flesh. "Quick, get yourself changed. It's hot dinners today because you've got PP tonight, so you don't need your bag. Just grab his coat would you please, Trevor. You know the way, you've done it before. Lauren, help him with his clothes, would you?"

Trevor continued to examine the scene. "Just the two of you, was it?"

"Trevor, please, come back into the hall, I need your help."

"She needs me," he said with a smirk and a nod directed at Lauren.

"They don't close the gates until five to nine; if you walk fast enough you should just about make it. If not, you'll have to go round to reception and sign him in."

"I know the drill." He looked again towards Lauren. "I've done it before. By the way, your dressing gown's inside out."

"And your beard's only half there."

"Very quick for someone who clearly drank a lot last night." He turned to the stairs. "You should have asked Mum and Dad to have him, Rachel."

"Spur of the moment."

"Those photos don't look spur of the moment. What were you celebrating?"

"Our friendship," said Lauren. "This was all me."

"Please, could you just take him quickly?" Rachel turned to her son. "We'll both pick you up from school and take you to PP."

"Will we?" Trevor beamed.

"I was talking about Lauren, Trevor, not you, but thank you."

"I've not been to one of those sessions for a while."

"Sorry, it's classroom-based today, numbers are restricted. And I didn't mean to sound rude, I'm just in a bit of a muddle."

"Next time then."

"It's his last session."

"Like none of it ever happened."

"Trevor."

"What? I have to say it. Here you are, partying away."

"School, please." Rachel turned to her son. "Parker, I love you. I'll see you later."

"Bye buddy," said Lauren, giving him a pat on the back.

"And there I was trying to do the right thing," continued Trevor, "walking round here when I knew you should be out so as not to disturb." He pulled an envelope from his pocket. "Mother wanted me to hand deliver this. It's an invitation to the Macmillan coffee morning at the surgery next week. She's still trying to push us together, Rachel, but I do have a certain level of self-respect, which I'm now very proud of if this is how you conduct yourself on a school night."

"It was a one-off Trevor, and you should have just posted it through the letter box if you were trying to avoid me."

"I heard squeals."

"Mummy was doing Lauren's—"

"Parker, please, just get yourself off to school."

"You'd send him alone?"

"I'm sending him with you! You know what, Trevor, don't worry about it. I'll go and get changed."

"No, we're going. You can always count on Uncle Trevor."

"Byeeeee," said Parker.

"Ladies," said Trevor, moving out of the door, only to pause for one final statement. "Use this time to clean up. This place is a mess."

Lauren waited for the front door to shut before dashing out of the lounge. "The Amazon man indeed!" she gasped.

"At least you had your dressing gown on! My flaps were hanging out!"

"They don't hang out."

Rachel flopped onto the stairs, letting everything hang out. "What a disaster."

"It's fine."

"Look at the place."

"He knows we party."

"But our clothes!"

"We'd just woken up."

"And Parker tells him we were naked spot checking each other?"

"It's what girls do."

"Do they?"

"He wouldn't have a clue."

"He's right though. I'm usually out of the house at this time."

"That's a good sign then. He knows he's no longer in the race."

The smile crept onto Rachel's lips. "You won it last night."

"Did I?"

"You know you did."

"Should we have a re-run this morning?"

"Don't you have to go to work?"

"Yes."

"Go on then."

Lauren walked to the bottom of the staircase. "Sit two steps higher up."

"Why?"

"Because I'm going to kneel down here." She kissed Rachel's mouth. "And while this is a lovely position to taste your tongue, I want to taste your lips."

Rachel groaned. "You want to fuck me on the staircase?"

"I thought last night's dirty mouth was a drunken thing?"

"It's a you thing. You bring out the beast in me."

"Well spread your legs like a straddled giraffe and lift them over my shoulders."

Rachel laughed. "I've heard of people having funny sex before, but I never thought I'd have funny sex. It's always been so serious for me. So straight-faced with hardly any talking. This is just so…"

"This is an extension of us. We're not going to be Queen of the lols in all other aspects of our relationship and stay silent for sex. Why can't I call you a straddled giraffe?"

"Fine, and I'll call you one of those dingo dogs with its tongue hanging out."

"Oh fabulous, I wonder what our offspring will look like?"

"Get on all fours and I'll tell you."

"As soon as you get your giraffe legs straddled. Hurry up, I'm hungry."

Rachel snapped her thighs closed. "I forgot to give Parker his breakfast." She jumped up and edged past Lauren. "I'll have to chase after them with a Nutrigrain bar."

"And his teeth!" Lauren stood up. "We haven't cleaned his teeth."

"Or given him a wash!"

"Or brushed his hair!"

"Oh, Lauren, we're such bad mothers!"

"We?"

"Our first morning on the job together."

Lauren was smiling.

"What? This isn't funny, hurry up, we can still catch them."

"You're bottom-less. I'll go. I'll take the car."

"The school's only five minutes away."

"Exactly, if I drive I'll be there in one."

"And you'll go in wearing your dressing gown?"

"If I have to," she smiled. "I'm one of those mothers."

"Oh Lauren."

"What? Top shelf of the cupboard, aren't they?" She dashed into the kitchen before returning to the hall and scooping up her keys. "Back in a jiffy, and why didn't I just take him in the car in the first place?"

"I was in a panic. Trevor was snooping around. It's all I could think of to get him out of the lounge."

Lauren shoved on her shoes. "Don't move a muscle."

"You want me back in the straddled giraffe?"

"Hell yes I do."

"I might get cramp."

"Let's hope so."

"Really?"

"No, that one didn't work. I'm getting all silly with this mission-deliver-nutrigrain-bar."

"Go!"

"I'm going!" Dashing out of the front door, Lauren raced across the drive to her car, reversing and turning in a spray of gravel past the barns and out onto the road. They wouldn't have got far as Parker was a slow walker, always stopping to admire some piece of nature, or pick up a hidden treasure that would then get re-discovered in a pocket a few weeks later having gone through the wash once or twice. "Gotcha," said Lauren, seeing them at the end of the road about to turn into the school. She beeped and waved as she buzzed down her window, pulling the car onto the kerb. "Quickly, eat this before you go in," she said, handing over the cereal bar.

"You've not had any breakfast?" asked Trevor.

"It was a one-off," answered Lauren. "It's fine, he never eats much. They get toast at break time and he likes to save himself for that."

"Is this true, Parker?"

"Yes, well I do like to have *some* breakfast," said the boy as he ripped open the wrapper.

"Dear me, Lauren, what *is* going on? Is Rachel having some sort of late-onset breakdown?"

"It was one night. Just girls having fun. My fault. I surprised her. Parker's fine, aren't you, buddy."

"My hair feels a bit itchy."

Trevor tutted at the mess of curls. "Hasn't it been brushed? I think I should head back and have a word."

"It's fine. She wanted you to see him in." Lauren tooted her horn. "Bye guys!"

"But I should—"

Buzzing up her window, Lauren spun the steering wheeling into a U-turn and headed back to the barns, thankful they'd been late and therefore avoided the usual jam of cars. She looked in her mirror as the two entered the playground, the teacher on the gate ready to lock up once the last 'almost-on-time' parent had delivered their child. She sighed. Trevor had got a point; this morning hadn't been ideal, but it was a one-off and they'd spoil Parker rotten after PP tonight. Refocusing on the road, she increased her speed, feeling a quiver of excitement race through her body. Maybe she wouldn't put Rachel straight into the straddled giraffe just in case Trevor did come back, but they could have coffee and intertwine their limbs and laugh and chat and be happy.

"Honey, I'm home!" she shouted as she banged her way back into the barn.

"Did he get in okay?" Rachel was tidying around, still dressed in the t-shirt.

"Nutrigrain in hand."

"What a trouper. Right, I've collected all the photos but I can't find my list."

"What list?"

"I made a list of all the times I wanted to kiss you."

"As well as the photos?"

"I only had the afternoon to sort out my *Love Actually* moment, as you called it, so I scribbled down as many of the times I could think of before heading to my computer to find any corresponding pictures, which I then emailed to the photo shop in town. I picked it all up within the hour."

"Did you take the list down there?"

"No, I was sure I left it here."

"Have you found my bra?"

"Nope."

"Carnage. Carnage I tell you."

"Worth it though," said Rachel with a smile.

"Just drop all that on the sofa."

"What if Trevor comes back?"

"He'll see us enjoying a coffee still in our pajamas like most school-run mums do after a big night out."

"Do they?"

"You read about it in the papers. Mums dropping their kids off whilst still in their slippers."

"We're not going to be those sorts of mums."

"Why do you keep calling me mum?"

"Lauren, my lovely, you've been playing that role to Parker for I don't know how long. It makes sense that you'd get the official job title once we're together."

"Once we're together?"

"Once we've gone public. Once we've eased everyone into this."

"Once we know Parker's okay?"

"He's the least of my worries. He loves you so much, Lauren." She laughed. "And he was so matter of fact in the way he asked if we'd been adult kissing."

"I like the sound of this adult kissing."

"Naked apparently."

"Ooo, shall we have coffee first, just in case Trevor comes back?"

"You think he's okay?"

"Trevor? I think he's fine and, like I said, it's progress. He seems okay about being out of the picture."

"But will he be okay knowing you're the new painting?"

"I like that." Lauren smiled before shrugging. "It's got nothing to do with him."

Rachel dropped the placards and pieces of clothing back onto the sofa. "Yeah, let's just do this our way."

"You know I'm a tidy freak, don't you?"

"And you know I like clutter."

Lauren smiled. "Well if that's our biggest obstacle I think we'll survive."

****

Unfolding the sheet of paper from his pocket, Trevor bent down to the boy. "One last thing, Parker, before you go in." He tapped the list. "Is this Mummy's writing, or Lauren's?"

CHAPTER TWENTY SEVEN

Walking into her shop doorway with Rachel close behind, Lauren smiled at the scene. Trudy was in the upright armchair leading the meeting with bride Deloris and groom Jim. All three were leaning over the coffee table, smiling and nodding at the large photos of chairs spread out across the surface. It was a relatively new thing, this insistence for all seating in all venues to be dressed with chair frocks and bows, with some companies even offering chairs that had trains just like the bride's, or flowers that matched the bouquets.

"I told you she'd be fine on her own," whispered Rachel.

Lauren tilted her ear to the mouth, urging the lips to brush her skin. "Say it again."

Rachel's mouth moved closer. "I told you she'd be fine."

"This is why I don't have a bell on the door. We can hover here unnoticed with your lips on my neck."

"Is that where you like them?"

"I like them everywhere. Your closeness sends shivers of—"

"Boss, thank you for coming."

Lauren stepped forward, about to chastise the inappropriate address when she realised Trudy wasn't being cheeky or sarcastic, just authoritarian.

"Deloris has requested thrones for the top table and I wanted to confirm where we hired the elegant ones from. All Dressed Up, wasn't it?" The focus was back on the client. "We used one company where the red was rather garish and the material rather cheap and I'm not having anything garish or cheap at your wedding."

"She could have asked me that by text," whispered Lauren.

"She's obviously trying to impress you."

Lauren raised her voice. "That's the one." She turned to the clients. "You're in safe hands with Trudy. Anything else I can help you with?"

Trudy rose from her seat. "No, we're just about done. Our next appointment's in two weeks." She reached out a hand to the happy clients. "You've got my number so don't hesitate to call with any queries or ideas."

Lauren watched as Trudy escorted the couple to the door, another professional handshake seeing them out of the shop. "Is that a new suit?" she asked once the door had closed.

Trudy did a twirl. "Zara."

"Wow!"

"And a new top too."

"Which I notice isn't a shirt. Double wow." Lauren smiled. "You extended that meeting until I arrived, didn't you? So I could see you all professional and in charge."

"Ignore her," said Rachel, leaning in to give Trudy a warm kiss on the cheek. "You look great, and you're doing a great job."

Trudy's eyes darted to Lauren.

"She's right. You are, and thank you for hosting that meeting. It's nice knowing I have someone I can rely on."

"Were you tied up with something?"

Rachel laughed. "That's happening tonight."

"Rachel!"

"It's fine, boss, Jenny had me chained to the bedpost last night."

"Stop. I don't want to know."

"I do," said Rachel, taking Trudy's hand and leading her back to the sofas. "I heard your news and I'm happy for you both. The perfect ending to a disastrous date."

Trudy frowned. "I never thought you liked me."

"I always thought you liked Lauren."

"Everyone likes Lauren."

"That's why I'm tying her down," said Rachel, laughing. "Plus we need to become best friends so you can give me advice if she's in a mood at work, or if she talks to you about our sex life."

"I won't be talking to anyone about our sex life," said Lauren. "Now, who's for a coffee?"

"Sorry, boss, I'm meeting Jenny at Starbucks."

"Now?"

"If that's alright?"

"Fantastic, shall we all go?"

Trudy and Rachel shared a glance. "Is that wise?"

"Like you said, we all need to make friends and form bonds."

Trudy coughed. "It's too early for foursomes, boss."

Lauren grimaced. "How have you gone from someone who doesn't like their tides parted to someone so sexually advanced?"

"It's Jenny. She's amazing in bed. But I did say it was *too* early for foursomes."

"She doesn't look *that* amazing in bed." The grimace continued.

Rachel shook her head. "Please, don't start this again. No more competition, we've both made our choices."

"No harm in heading over to Starbucks then," said Lauren, moving back to the door.

****

Crouching next to the gutter grate, Trevor started to click. There wasn't a lost glove down there, but the three women passing by on the other side of the street didn't know that. Nor did they know he was about to focus his camera on them.

****

Upon entering the green-themed coffee shop, Lauren took hold of Rachel's hand.

"What are you doing?"

"Holding your hand."

"Why didn't you hold it walking down the road?" Rachel's eyebrows rose. "Because there was no sign of Jenny?"

"Of course not. I wasn't sure you were ready for that yet."

"This isn't the twelve-hundreds, Lauren. I'm just a professional woman going for coffee with my girlfriend."

"Ooo, I like that. So you *will* consider something more full-time at the shop?"

"That's where we *should* be, at the shop, discussing my options, except now we're in Starbucks parading our lesbianism for Jenny's benefit."

"It's not for Jenny's benefit, she's not even here yet, but you're okay with it?" Lauren squeezed the fingers. "Calling me your girlfriend?"

"Boss, she just told you this isn't the twelve-hundreds."

"Trudy, if you were wearing one of your normal shirts she might be mistaken into thinking it was."

"But she isn't," said Rachel, moving into the queue, "and I'm fine."

"Honestly?"

"You already know my view. You lesbians don't have the monopoly on same-sex love. Other people *can* get involved without having to internally combust with self-doubt and confusion. Nowadays people just go with the flow." She stretched up their arms and looked around. "See, no one cares. Woo hoo! We're holding hands."

Lauren laughed. The two baristas were busy making coffee and the scattering of customers were engrossed in their chats. She glanced out the window, suddenly clocking the Amazonian figure of Jenny approaching the shop. "So what if I kissed you?" she asked.

"I am here too, boss."

"I'd question your timing because Jenny's just arrived."

"She's not here is she? I hadn't noticed. I just wanted to kiss you."

"You've been tracking her through the window."

"I have not!" The laugh was false. "Now come here." Lauren ignored the tall woman arriving beside them, instead pulling Rachel in close as she planted a huge open-mouthed kiss on her lips.

"Ladies," said Jenny.

Lauren didn't pull away. She had a reputation for long kisses to uphold.

The instruction was loud. "Trudy."

Lauren opened one eye. Jenny had pulled Trudy in for a full-on embrace.

"Next!" shouted the barista.

Someone coughed behind Lauren, but there was no way she was going to pull away first.

"Are you in the queue for coffees?" asked the voice.

She couldn't respond.

Someone moved past her.

She peeped at the scene. Dammit, it wasn't Jenny. But Rachel's wide eyes were millimetres away staring back at her in annoyance.

"I don't think she's enjoying that, love," said the same voice from its new position at the counter.

Lauren reached round for the back of Rachel's head, trying to get more into the moment.

The voice spoke again. "Her eyes are still open."

"Okay," snapped Lauren, pulling away and addressing the critique, dismayed to see that Jenny hadn't yet released her woman. "You shouldn't be watching," she said to the man.

"Hard not to, but this couple seem more into it than you."

Lauren looked to Jenny who finally released Trudy.

"Nice to see you again," came the purr.

Lauren growled. "Likewise."

"You two don't like each other, do you," said the man piping up once more.

"I'm not sure I like them either," snapped Rachel.

"Nor me," added Trudy.

"Yes, you both do, now what'll it be?" Lauren reached for her purse.

Jenny stepped forwards. "No, no, on me."

"For goodness sake I'm getting them," said Trudy. "You lot go and sit down."

"Can I come and sit down too?" asked the man.

"No," said all three women in their first display of lesbian solidarity.

Trudy continued. "Jenny, your usual espresso?"

"Lovely thank you."

"I'll have a double espresso please," said Lauren with a smile.

Rachel sighed. "Just a normal skinny latte for me thank you."

Trudy turned to the barista. "One espresso, one double espresso, one skinny latte and one hot chocolate please."

"Can I take your name?"

"Trudy."

Lauren thanked Trudy for paying before holding her arm out for longer than Jenny so as to guide the group to the table near the window. Her shop was just about visible at the end of the street on the other side of the road so it was the perfect place to sit and have coffee. They'd often nip out for lunches or drinks, especially on weekdays when drop-ins were low. Weekends were the time where people would pop in without appointment, having noticed the shop and suddenly become curious about the possibility of a planner for their big day; but it was nice to see if she was missing any potential custom, hence their current position by the window.

"Anything going on?" asked Jenny.

"Nope, all quiet," said Lauren, continuing to stare down the road instead of across the table.

"Business not great?"

She turned to the eyes. "No, it's wonderful, busier than ever."

"For goodness sake, you two," snapped Rachel. "You're both successful, you're both gorgeous, you've both got your girl, so stop acting like blokes."

"They'll shout when it's ready," said Trudy, arriving to take a seat. "Everything okay?"

Lauren and Jenny nodded like chastised schoolgirls.

"We're all great, Trudy," said Rachel. "Now tell us about bride Deloris. I hear you're taking charge on this one."

Trudy smiled. "Am I?"

Lauren smiled too. "It's yours if you want it. You've really proved yourself over the past couple of weeks and I honestly love the new suit."

"Jenny took me shopping."

Lauren connected again with Jenny's eyes, still egotistical, still gorgeous, but this time she spotted a slight softness in the way they were shining. "It looks great," she said.

Jenny's response was genuine. "Only because Trudy's wearing it."

"Oh, that's sweet of you," gasped Trudy. "Look at us, it's a right little love in."

"Turdy!" came the shout.

Trudy spun around.

"Turdy!"

"Here we go again. Why am I so hard to remember?"

Jenny stood up. "I'm not having this!"

Lauren watched as Jenny snatched the tray of mugs from the barista.

"It's Trudy. Her name's Trudy." The gorgeous eyes were narrow.

"It says Turdy here."

"Well your till girl's clearly got issues. That wonderful woman sitting there's called Trudy. It's not a hard name, it's her name. Trudy."

The barista nodded. "I'll have a word. Sorry, Trudy."

Trudy's cheeks flushed as the tray was placed on the table. "You're my hero."

Lauren smiled as Jenny returned to her seat. "Thank you."

"What are you saying thank you for, boss?"

Lauren shrugged. "It's nice to know you're being looked after, that's all." She took the double espresso and lifted it to her lips. "And if I'm honest, I hate shots of coffee like this."

Jenny reached out her hand. "Truce?"

"Truce," said Lauren, smiling. "Oh, Trudy, you always bring out the best in us, don't you? And you're right, this *is* a nice little love in."

Rachel giggled. "Shall we give that man in the corner something to talk about?"

"And you've certainly come out of your shell, haven't you?" added Jenny.

"It's Lauren. She's just amazing in bed."

Trudy cut in. "Well, Jenny does this thing where—"

"Hang on. You two better not start competing now." Lauren was about to laugh, but instead her attention was drawn to the window. "Isn't that Camilla and Sid?" She pointed. "Yes, it is. It's Camilla and Sid. Over there, about to pass Nando's."

"They're probably just touching up their origami," said Trudy, staring over the road.

"Again?"

Jenny was nodding. "I don't know who they are but there's definitely some touching up going on."

Rachel shook her head, also eyeing the couple. "No, that was just a friendly arm rub. Is this the bride you were talking about?"

Jenny looked at Trudy. "And the solicitor from next door that you mentioned?"

Trudy nodded. "Lauren thinks they're having an affair."

Rachel laughed. "Sid's not having an affair with that woman. She's far too glamorous for him."

Jenny studied the couple crossing the road. "I'm with Lauren on this one. Look how they're walking. They're in each other's space."

Rachel continued to stare. "You said Sid knew her from school didn't you, Lauren? And no one has affairs this close to a wedding."

Lauren and Jenny shared a glance.

"What?"

Lauren spoke first. "I've seen it all. People are shits."

"And I'm just coming from a lesbian perspective," added Jenny. "You get the action when and where you can find it."

"I'm not sure I like this," said Rachel.

"Nor me," added Trudy.

Lauren laughed as she wiggled her eyebrows. "Well you two are the only pairing not to get it on yet, so if you need to bond over this, feel free."

"Trudy?" said Rachel.

"I actually rather quite like Jenny."

"No, I mean what are your thoughts? You think they're messing around?"

"I hope not."

Lauren took another sip of espresso. "And even if they were, it's none of our business."

Rachel was frowning. "You'd have to say something though."

Jenny shook her head. "You should never say anything."

"Trudy?"

"No, I still don't think you and I would work out."

"The moral duty! Where do you stand on the moral duty?"

"On partner swapping?"

"On telling the injured party! Surely the groom has a right to know?"

Lauren reached out and rubbed Rachel's arm. "Never tell the truth if you know it'll hurt them."

"Really?"

Jenny nodded.

"Is this a lesbian thing?" continued Rachel.

Lauren continued. "It's a kindness thing. Don't say something just to ease your own conscience."

"Trudy?"

Trudy shook her head. "Honestly, Rachel, you're being rather pushy."

Rachel sighed as she lifted her latte. "Let's just hope I never need to hear the truth from any of you."

Trudy tapped the table. "Fine. I find you attractive, but your weird fashion sense is not quite for me."

CHAPTER TWENTY EIGHT

Sitting in the classroom at the community centre, Lauren smiled. Today's PP group leader for the final session was Sheila, the most outdoorsy of the small team of counsellors who ran the on-site sessions, and it looked like she was about to give in.

"Please, please, please, please, please can we do it outside?" begged Parker and his little friend Zoe in unison.

The woman looked out of the classroom window. "It is nice and sunny."

"We'll let you give us that bird talk again," added Parker.

Zoe groaned.

"Now there's an idea." Sheila was on her feet. "Maybe we could have a short walk through the park while Josh moves this kit to the nature reserve. Give me a second. I'll just see if I can find him. Adults, please make sure they don't touch anything."

Lauren looked to the huge pile of multi-coloured pool noodles that were stacked in the middle of the room. Nothing about these sessions surprised her anymore. They'd done all sorts of activities and completed all sorts of tasks, each with a surprising lesson to be learned. Today they'd probably learn that life was like a pool noodle: invaluable when used correctly.

"What do you think the moral of the story is this session?" she whispered to Rachel. The small group of adults and children in the room weren't listening, but she liked the closeness her hushed tones encouraged.

Rachel leaned into her ear. "Always tell the truth?"

"You're not still talking about that are you?" Lauren said, pulling away. "Camilla's my client. I offer couples a service, but I don't get involved in their private lives."

"Maybe you should."

"No one knows what goes on behind closed doors."

"But the poor husband-to-be deserves to know what he's getting himself into."

"He knows."

"That she's cheating?"

"We don't know that she is."

"You and Jenny seem to think so."

"We're the hardened, battle-scarred lesbians."

"You pair were the ones inflicting the damage no doubt."

"Only because we weren't with the loves of our lives."

"You think she's serious about Trudy?"

"You know what?" Lauren nodded. "I do. The way she defended her against that barista." She whispered again. "Standing up for your woman's a sure sign that you're smitten."

Rachel stood up.

"What are you doing?"

"Standing up."

Lauren laughed. "Look at you, Dr Hilarz."

"I am, aren't I," said Rachel with a giggle.

Lauren tugged her back down. "And I know you're right about the Camilla-Sid-Ian love triangle in theory, but people have their own secrets and it's up to them whether they're able to live with them or not."

"Could you live with a secret?"

"Oh god, yeah."

Rachel laughed. "I'm in for a rocky ride with you, aren't I?"

"Not now I've found my soulmate. Scratch that. I always knew we were soulmates. I should have said: not now my soulmate's all mine."

"And I am."

Lauren stood up and went to the centre of the room, reaching for one of the long pool noodles. She returned to her chair and looped it over Rachel's back, dragging her in close. "You're my life support."

Sheila's voice was loud. "Lauren! How did the children manage to leave them alone, yet here you are, pool noodle in hand?"

"Oh no, was this a test? See which naughty child can't leave temptation alone?"

Rachel whispered. "I don't want you to leave temptation alone. I want you to grab it and ravish it with both hands."

Lauren whispered back. "Noted. Let me just put this pool noodle away first."

"Anyway. Great news," said Sheila, continuing. "Josh can set this up in the nature reserve while we're taking a quick bird watching walk."

"Ai ai," muttered Lauren.

Rachel growled. "You can look but you can't touch."

"Follow me, troops," instructed Sheila, who was one of those people who just battled on through any murmurs and disruption.

Lauren continued to whisper as she rose from her seat. "Not even the tits?"

"Fine, and I'll take the woodcock."

"Would you?"

"Not anymore." Rachel laughed. "One-upmanship gone wrong. Let me try again."

Guiding them out of the room, Lauren watched her friend with eager eyes. Rachel was the only person who'd ever been able to make her snort with laughter, and while she found lots of people and situations funny, Rachel had the ability to make her laugh with not just the odd snigger, but a laugh that saw you spray drink from your nose as you erupted with uncontrollable howls. She nodded as they walked down the carpeted corridor towards the community centre's main entrance. "And don't mention the cockatoo either."

"I wouldn't, that's old school."

"What have you got then? I'm excited."

"Fat balls."

Lauren laughed. "Don't. Sheila loves talking about her husband's fat balls and how they attract all sorts of birds to their garden."

"Shall we loiter at the back like naughty children on a school trip?"

Looking towards Parker and Zoe eagerly following Sheila's quick march at the front, Lauren nodded. "We're already there."

"Hold my hand then."

"Really?" Leading them out into the sun, Lauren looked around. The community centre had been built next to a lottery-funded nature reserve with wooded scrubland on one side where local school children could come and take part in the Forest School initiative that was sweeping the nation, aiming to get children outside and active, even though there was a play park and café on the other side that they chose to frequent over the dirt and the trees. But Sheila's walk, that she'd already led them on twice over the past couple of years, saw them move around the nature reserve, through the play park and into the scrubland, searching for birds she insisted were there, even though no one else ever saw them.

"There!" hushed Sheila, halting the group at the entrance to the park, inadvertently forcing Lauren and Rachel to catch up. "Who can hear the woodpecker?"

Everyone stayed silent.

Sheila lifted her binoculars. "It's in the bushes."

Lauren whispered. "I knew Sheila had birds in her bushes."

"Stop stereotyping," said Rachel, squinting in the general direction of the supposed wood-pecking action. "She *is* making it up though."

Parker yelled. "I see it!"

"Oh and now it's gone." Sheila dropped her binoculars back around her neck and resumed their brisk pace. "Onwards!"

"Swallow!" shouted Rachel.

Sheila squinted before nodding. "Oh yes, well done."

"She sounds miffed," whispered Lauren. "Your swallowing skills must be better than Sheila's."

Rachel silently shuddered. "Not anymore."

"Why do it in the first place?"

"That's what you did. You swallowed."

Lifting her face to the sun, Lauren drew in the fresh air. "And at no point did you ever think, hang on, isn't sex meant to be nice?"

"Shush!"

"It's fine. They're miles away. Sheila's probably showing them her chaffinch."

"Ha! Oh, Lauren, you always make me smile."

Linking their arms together, Lauren pulled Rachel in close. "And you always brighten my day."

"But you're the one who makes everything such fun."

"Just cheap gags."

"No, it's you. There's something special about you."

Lauren smiled. "And you've only just noticed?"

"I've always noticed it, but I'm now fully understanding and accepting of how much it turns me on."

"I've laughed you into bed? It wasn't my hot body or amazing smile?"

"It was you." Rachel reached for the hand and squeezed. "It was all of you. I'm so incredibly happy and so totally and utterly in love."

Lauren felt a wash of contentment surge through her body. This was all she'd ever wanted: Rachel, standing beside her, holding her hand while she said she was happy. It was the dream, the goal, and even though she'd pictured it numerous times over the years, forever romanticising their relationship and scripting out this moment, the feelings evoked were so much more than she could have imagined, her fantasy nowhere near as all-consuming as reality actually felt. To hear her say it. No prompting. No imagined script. Just Rachel, with the sun on her face and the truth on her lips.

Lauren glanced ahead before turning to Rachel, tenderly kissing her, only pausing at the sharp drilling sound in the distance. "Woodpecker!" she shouted.

"Not anymore, thanks," mumbled Rachel, stepping away as soon as she noticed the group's attention had turned.

"Sorry, I heard one," said Lauren with a shrug.

Sheila lifted her binoculars and made a large sweeping movement with her head. She shouted. "No. I don't think you did."

"Right, no." Lauren nodded. "My mistake. I think it was more of a purring pussy."

"Onwards again," Sheila instructed, marching her followers forward.

"You did not hear one!" laughed Rachel.

"A woodpecker? I did." Lauren interlocked their arms and walked faster in an attempt to keep up with the group. It was one thing to get lost in the moment and another to do it with a bunch of bird spotters just metres away. "Don't you find your senses are more attuned when we're together? Like now. If it was anyone's arm locked into my own it would just feel like anyone's arm locked into my own."

"Poetic."

"Thank you. But my point is my whole body senses you, it responds to you. It feels alight with energy and sparks of friction."

"Stop it, you're turning me on."

"I'm on."

"We can't leave Parker."

"I know! I'd never suggest that."

"It crossed my mind."

"It did not!"

Rachel shrugged. "Maybe for a split second."

"You bad bad woman."

"Tell me how bad."

Lauren moved her arm out of the link and wrapped it around Rachel's waist, looking behind them to the path that was slowly becoming more wooded as they entered the scrubland. Checking that no one was about, she smiled; the park was disappearing into the distance and the benches were empty. "You're bad," she said, pushing her palm down the back of Rachel's jeans as she squeezed the buttock. "Very bad."

"And what do you want to do to me?"

Lauren kept them walking forward, close enough to be part of the group, but far enough away not to be heard. She moved her hand more to the centre, parting the cheeks with one finger.

"I didn't even let Toby do that!"

Lauren pulled her hand back out.

"What?" laughed Rachel. "I was joking."

"He *did* do that?"

"Well no, but I might, and why have you stopped?"

Lauren shook her head. "I know he's part of us, but in the moment? Really?"

Rachel laughed. "We weren't actually going to have a booty-tickling moment as we trailed after Sheila on the way to a pool noodle session were we?"

"I don't know. I can see myself getting carried away with you. Haven't you had that before? All sense of good judgement simply flies out the window when you're in the moment?"

"Umm, we kissed on a group walk and I let you stick your hand down my trousers, so yes, I get it."

"You *would* get it if I had my way."

"How would you give it to me?"

"Right now I'd take you over to that tree."

"No, that one looks too knobbly."

"Okay that one, it's smooth, it looks like a silver birch."

"Aren't they poisonous?"

"No. Either way, there'd be a tree with you pushed against it. Me on my knees, your one thigh wrapped over my shoulder, my mouth between your legs."

Rachel groaned. "Were you imagining this last time Sheila took us on a walk?"

"We went den building afterwards didn't we? I imagined me fucking you in the wigwam we built."

"You did not! Is that why you lined the floor with those big leaves?"

"I wasn't actually setting it up for that, but I've pictured you everywhere, and I've pictured myself taking you in every way possible."

"Are you a pervert?"

Lauren laughed. "I don't think so."

"I think I might be, because I want us to act out every possible way."

"Well the sooner we get this pool noodle session over the better."

"Mmm, pool noodles."

Lauren laughed. "Really?"

"Yeah."

"Pervert."

****

Sitting on the wooden logs that surrounded what was usually the camp fire, Lauren puzzled at the pile of pool noodles, arts and crafts, and odds and sods that had been brought out from the community centre. It was all spread across a large tarpaulin with Sheila standing to one side rubbing her hands together in glee. "She likes them too," whispered Lauren.

Rachel tutted. "Shush, this is the important bit."

"So," began Sheila, "does anyone know what these are?"

Parker spoke up. "Things that help you to swim!"

"You still need floats?" said Zoe with a giggle.

"He doesn't actually." Lauren was nodding at the group. "He's got his one hundred metres badge."

"Yes, they're floats," continued Sheila, clearly wanting to keep things on track.

Rachel whispered. "I love how you always stick up for him."

"She's just a little upstart." Lauren stared at the six-year-old. "I still haven't forgiven her for calling me poo bum or stealing my chick."

"But he'll have to learn to fend for himself one day."

"Not while I'm around."

"Bless you, but he will."

"And Lauren." The voice was sharp. "What about you?"

Lauren looked up at the group. What was Sheila asking her? "I don't need them!"

"That's exactly the attitude we're trying to avoid." Sheila raised one of the brightly coloured foam cylinders. "The question was: when you've learnt to swim what do you do with your noodle?"

Lauren thought for a moment before nodding once more. "Nope, still don't need it."

"So you throw it out?"

On sensing the tuts from the other group members, Lauren paused. "Of course not. I hand it over to someone else."

"You could, I guess."

"That's not the right answer? This isn't about passing on our knowledge and skills?"

Sheila took a seat on a log, her binoculars dangling between her legs. She was shaking her head. "These sessions are almost over and I hope that none of you are ever in a situation where you need to pass on these skills."

Lauren noted more tuts.

"This is about adapting." Sheila lifted her hands. "You no longer need us. We're the pool noodle. You can swim. You're survivors." She smiled. "But you don't just forget about us or throw us away. You don't stop using the skills we've given you, you utilise them in your lives moving forward."

Rachel whispered. "I told you this was the good bit."

"This is the bollocks bit," muttered Lauren.

"Only because you got told off."

The sharp voice returned. "And your thoughts, Lauren?"

Dammit, what was Miss Chaffinch asking her this time? She looked around at the group. No one was helping.

Zoe put her hand up. "You could cut it up and put it on the springs on a trampoline to stop you from getting hurt. That's what my mummy does."

Lauren watched from narrowed eyes as Zoe's mummy basked in the congratulatory nods. "I've got it," she interrupted, reaching out to grab a blue noodle from the centre of the circle. Wrapping it over her head and holding the two sides down by her neck, she shouted: "Hair! You could make hair!"

Everyone stared at her.

Zoe spoke first. "No one has blue hair and that's hardly useful."

"They do actually, and it might be if you're bald."

"My aunty has cancer and all her hair's fallen out. Putting a pool noodle on her head won't make her feel better."

Lauren sensed the disapproving atmosphere and slowly lowered the foam tube. "I'm sorry to hear that." She spoke again quickly, without really thinking. "But maybe you could make her a sword to battle that cancer away." She tried to jab the pool noodle from side to side but it swished in a very unsatisfactory and rather limp manner.

"I want useful ways to reuse a pool noodle," said Sheila, back in charge. "We'll have three rounds, ten minutes creation time in each round. Feel free to pair up," she looked at Lauren, "or work alone, and we'll re-group on the whistle."

"Come on then, Parker," said Lauren, standing up and shoving the pool noodle between her legs. "Jiggly, jiggly, jiggly."

"I think I'm going to work with Zoe and her mummy."

Lauren's pool noodle wilted. "Oh, okay. Rachel?"

Rachel grabbed the blue foam, dragging Lauren back onto her log. "Who makes a pool noodle willy?"

"Everyone! That's the first thing you do when you pick one up! At least I didn't do the silly walk with it grasped between my thighs. Are we pairing up?"

"I think I've got this."

"You're working alone?"

"You know I like creative stuff."

Lauren watched as Rachel grabbed a pair of scissors and some multi-coloured marker pens from the centre of the circle. "Can I help?"

"You're creative too."

"I'm more practical."

"So make something practical out of your pool noodle."

Lauren looked around to the rest of the group who were all beavering away. She shrugged. "Alright then, Mr Pool Noodle, what are you?" Shoving it back between her legs, she smiled. "I've got it. Round one to Lauren Hilliard."

Rachel looked up. "Whatever it is you should decorate it."

"Fear not," said Lauren, pushing the arts and crafts materials around in search of string, "I'm on it." She laughed. "Quite literally."

"So," said Sheila, sounding the whistle after the ten minutes had passed. "Who would like to begin?"

Lauren smiled as the first group produced their super-sized tic-tac-toe board. It was fun, but really, it was only four pool noodles on the floor crossing over each other. Likewise, the marble run, made by cutting the cylinder down the middle, was good, but the marble could only roll straight down in one direction. Rachel's mix and match creature blocks were sensational, with the pool noodle cut into three small pieces and pushed onto a stick, the cat, robot and human she'd drawn on each side able to be twisted to form funny bodies. The current cat head, human tummy and robot legs bringing applause from the group.

Lauren stood up. Mix and match creatures was fun, but there were limited combinations so actual interest and play time would be short lived. Her creation, however, was magnificent. "Let me introduce, my hobby horse," she said, trotting around the outside of the group on her pool noodle. "She's called Fluffy."

"She stole our idea!" wailed Zoe.

Zoe's mother comforted her daughter. "No she didn't, darling, look. She's only tied a piece of string round a pool noodle. Ours has hair and eyes."

Lauren glanced over to the brilliant thoroughbred horse now on display. Zoe's group had folded the top of the pool noodle over and kept it in place with an elastic band to form the head, two googly eyes had been stuck in position as had nostrils and a wonderful mane made from coloured string was cascading down the back of the horse's head. She looked again. It even had ears. Slowing her trot, Lauren got off her blue foam and used the frayed length of string to drag it back to her log.

"You're right, Mummy," said Zoe, "that's just a piece of string tied round a pool noodle."

"All are great," said Sheila, clapping her hands at the group. "Shall we go again?"

"I'd rather not," groaned Lauren.

Rachel whispered. "Where was the effort?"

"The reins!" gasped Lauren, pulling on the string.

"The reins of a horse come from both sides. That looks like you're taking your pet snake on a walk."

"Can I go with you for this one?"

"No. I'm already half way there."

"Can I copy?"

"I doubt it."

Lauren lifted her pet snake. "It's okay, big boy. I'll make people like you."

"Put the violins down and get involved."

"Boom! Got it!"

"You're not making a violin are you?"

"No, of course not." Lauren yanked the piece of string away and held the long tube in front of her body. "Diddla, diddla, diddla, dowwwwwww!"

"What's that?"

"Guitar riffs."

"At least try to make it look like a guitar."

Lauren strummed again. "It does."

"Add some strings or something."

"Ooo, thank you." Working quickly, Lauren avoided the temptation to look over at Parker, Zoe and Zoe's mother. She'd definitely win him back with this one.

"So," said Sheila once more when time had run out, "who's ready for round two?"

Lauren smiled as the cup holders for warm drinks were displayed, and nodded as the door stoppers designed to avoid fingers getting trapped in doors were presented: a slice in the top of the pool noodle enabling it to fit along the door edge – good, but not great. Rachel's creation was better, but it followed her previous theme. This time there were letters on the three small cylinders, allowing the user to twist the section and create words. Lauren gave a thumbs-up. Interesting, but again quite limited once all the words had been made.

"And Lauren, what have you created?"

Lauren stood up, channelling Bill and Ted as best she could. "Diddla, diddla, diddla, dowwwwwwww!"

Zoe spoke first. "That's just another pool noodle with a piece of string tied to it."

"The string's going lengthways this time," said Lauren, continuing to strum.

"Well, we have a toss game," said Zoe.

"I bet you do," muttered Lauren under her breath, watching as Parker and Zoe flung circular pool noodle quoits over tall pool noodle tubes.

"Wonderful!" gasped Sheila.

"Thank you, thank you," said Lauren taking a bow.

"She was talking about our toss game," snapped Zoe.

"Oh sweetie, she knows she was," said Rachel addressing the grumpy child. "Lauren here just likes to go for the laughs."

"There's nothing funny about being rubbish," said Zoe.

Parker got up from his log. "I'll go with you this time, Aunty Lauren."

"Oh Parker, honestly there's no need."

Sheila clapped. "Time for your final round. Let's go!"

Rachel smiled. "Now stop playing the fool, Aunty Lauren, and do something good."

Lauren opened her arms to her giggling godson, letting him push her off her log as they hugged. "Right, buddy, what shall we make?"

"Let's make them pay." Parker looked towards Zoe and her mother and snarled.

"I like it. Any ideas?"

"Something huge!"

Lauren glanced around the wooded area. "Got it. You can climb, right?"

"Please don't climb any trees," said Rachel looking up from her twistable maths sums mix and match creation.

"Mummy, we have to beat them. They were laughing at Aunty Lauren."

"Aunty Lauren wanted people to laugh at her."

Lauren gasped. "I did not! I thought my snake and guitar were brilliant."

"I thought it was a horse?" said Parker.

Rachel rolled her eyes. "Exactly."

"Come on," whispered Lauren, "over here." She grabbed a handful of pool noodles.

"Don't we need anything else?"

"String."

Rachel laughed. "I'm so glad I didn't know you in school. You'd have been a disruptive influence."

"Life's short, live it." She pointed upwards. "Right. See that tree there?"

"Parker's not climbing that tree there."

"I can climb it!"

"Rachel, he's fine, get back to your mix and match maths game. Predictable, by the way."

"What are we making?" asked Parker.

"A wind chime," said Lauren leading them towards the thick tree trunk.

"But they won't make any noise when they bang together."

"We could tie some stones to the bottom. Plus it'll look really colourful hanging from up there. You get yourself to that first branch there and I'll pass bits up to you." Lauren tied string to the first pool noodle.

"She won't tell us it's just a pool noodle and string again will she?"

"Not when we have five of them, all different colours hanging from the branches. Do you need a leg up?"

"Please be careful," shouted Rachel from her log. "In fact, I'm bringing my stuff over there."

"Mummy, you don't have to watch me all the time."

"It's not you I'm worried about, it's Aunty Lauren."

"She's not coming up."

"Nope, you're right, you've got this, big man," said Lauren, smiling as her godson pulled himself onto the first branch. "Great job, now let me pass you this first noodle. See if you can tie it around that branch there." Lifting onto her tip toes, Lauren pushed up the first section of wind chime.

"I think I need to go higher."

"That's high enough, Parker," said Rachel, now working at the bottom of the tree.

"Aunty Lauren, I think I need to go higher."

"It looks good there, buddy."

"But Zoe might beat us."

Lauren smiled. "Maybe one branch higher then."

"Be careful, Parker."

"He's fine, aren't you, mate?" Lauren looked up at the exact moment Parker's shoe slipped.

"Watch out!" yelled Lauren as the boy fell from the branch, arms flailing, hands unable to get a grip on anything, body falling from the tree as his head knocked into the trunk.

"Parker!" screeched Rachel.

Lauren lunged forward and reached out with both hands, thrown to the ground as she caught his falling body.

"Mummy!" Parker was screaming, lying in a heap on top of Lauren, tears immediately pouring down his cheeks.

"He's fine, he's fine, he's crying." Lauren lifted her head to the body on top of her own.

"Mummy!" continued the wail.

Rachel grabbed her son, cradling him in her arms. "For god's sake, Lauren! I'm not losing him too!"

Lauren pushed herself up on her elbows, rubbing the bottom of her back where it was already throbbing. "Excuse me?"

"You and your stupid ideas!"

"He slipped!"

"You were encouraging him to go higher!"

"I was not!"

"You were! Always playing the fool!"

"I'm fine, Mummy," said the small voice from its nestling place in the tight arms.

"You're not fine! You're all I've got, Parker."

Lauren looked at the scene and dusted herself off. "I'm sorry, buddy," she said, attempting to rub his head, but Rachel drew back.

"It's not your fault, Aunty Lauren."

Rachel's voice was shaky as she turned her back on her friend and glowered. "It's always her fault."

CHAPTER TWENTY NINE

Sitting on the sofa in Rachel's lounge, Lauren waited. She'd hung around as Sheila administered the ice pack and followed at a slight distance on the walk back to the car. She'd helped make the dinner, albeit in silence, and offered to put Parker to bed, a request approved by Parker but denied by his mother; hence her solitary position on Rachel's sofa. She was hurt, deeply, but she wasn't childish, and stropping off wasn't the right option; she cared about Parker and wanted to see him okay.

On hearing the latch and creak of the door she turned her head. "How is he?" she asked, tracking Rachel as she walked to the fireplace. She watched her kneel and reach for the box of firelighters.

"He's okay," came the eventual reply.

"It was an accident."

"I know."

"So why lash out? And we don't need a fire."

The curls spun around. "I'd just seen my son fall out of a tree! He came crashing down, hitting his head as he fell. What was I meant to think?"

"That it was an accident."

"I was in shock! I snapped."

"At me."

"People lash out."

"But you lashed out at me. You're lashing out at me now!"

"Because we need a fire."

"No, we don't." Lauren moved from her seat and crouched next to Rachel. "I'm here for you."

"And we're here *because* of you."

"You really think that?"

"No one else asked him to climb that tree."

"But I caught him."

"And next time what if you don't?"

"I'll be more careful." Lauren took the firelighters out of her friend's hands. "I'm sorry. That's all I can say."

"I was scared."

"I can understand that."

"He's all I've got."

"He's not all you've got. You've got both of us. You've got me."

Rachel gasped before clasping her hand to her mouth as if in a delayed realisation. "I didn't even act like that when Toby fell." Her head was shaking. "What's wrong with me?"

"Remember when that car hit me?" said Lauren, helping her bewildered friend away from the fireplace and guiding her to the sofa. "I was driving along that road into town, the one with the high houses and driveways on the slope. Remember?" She waited for Rachel's half nod. "Okay, well suddenly this car just reversed down one of the drives and straight into the road, T-boning me and sending my car into the oncoming traffic. Only it wasn't being reversed. There was no one in it. Its handbrake had failed and it just rolled straight down the hill and into the road, hitting my car in the process." Lauren took a deep breath. "Every time a vehicle pulls up to a junction I'm driving through, I flinch. It's always there, the worry I'll get hit again, and it's irrational and the chances of it happening a second time are miniscule, simply because the chance of it happening the first time were so slim. For me to be driving past at the exact moment a car's handbrake failed was a real case of wrong time wrong place." She reached out and rubbed Rachel's leg. "And I know you're going to think it's a silly analogy, but I can understand your reaction. Yes, your reaction hurt me, but you couldn't help it. Something bad happened in your past, so now whenever you think something like that might happen again, you panic."

"But I've been fine."

"That's the first close call we've had."

"There'll be others?"

"Loads," said Lauren with a smile. "But I'll be there to catch him."

"And me? When I'm throwing myself into a tizzy?"

"I'll catch you too."

"Oh, Lauren, I'm sorry."

"It's fine, honestly. There's a big difference between people saying things in the heat of the moment and people saying something pre-planned or prepared."

"I've never wanted to question or accuse you before."

"Exactly."

Rachel smiled. "You're the Doctor to my Phil."

"I'd rather be the fill to your hole."

"Does that one work?" The laughter was there.

"Beat it and I'll tell you."

Rachel smiled. "I've been so silly."

"Forget about it. Come on, you're beating my statement."

"Fine. I'd rather be the six to your nine."

"Ooo," Lauren laughed. "Just let my tea go down first."

"Oh, Lauren, I love you."

"And I love you too."

Rachel smiled. "Don't change. He needs one of us to be daft and adventurous."

"You're adventurous."

"Am I?"

"You said you'd try the straddled giraffe."

"Just let my tea go down first."

"Ha! Can we kiss and make up?"

"You've got nothing to make up for, but I have."

"You haven't."

"Well, let's celebrate our ability to get over tiffs quickly and logically then."

"And how should we do that?" asked Lauren, before spotting Rachel's wicked smile. "Where are you going? Why are you sliding off the sofa? You're not crawling back to that fireplace are you? Crazy Katrina and her match fetish had a much deeper effect on you than I first realised."

"Stop talking."

"Why?"

"Because I'm on my knees. I'm taking your trousers off."

Lauren lifted her bottom as her zip was undone and her trousers pulled down. "Please don't put a firelighter up there."

Rachel burst out laughing. "Stop it! I'm being serious, and I'm being sexy, and I'm slowly peeling your knickers away from your waist."

Lauren lifted her bottom again. "They're meant to be low-slung hipster briefs, so I've no clue what they're doing up by my waist."

"Whatever they are, they're off." Rachel threw the knickers over her shoulder. "And I'm going in."

"Do you want to leave a trail of breadcrumbs in case you get lost?"

Rachel smiled. "I know my way around."

Throwing her head into the cushions, Lauren gasped. Rachel had gone straight in, tongue first, mouth clasped tight to her lips. She groaned and tilted her pelvis upwards in time with the onslaught. Rachel's mouth was so wide and her tongue so deep, her lips pushing in all the right places. Lauren groaned again and tilted her head to the side, her eyelids fluttering in pleasure. "Parker!" she screamed catching a glimpse of the boy.

"My head hurts."

Rachel threw herself upwards. "Oh sweetie!"

"What are you doing?" asked the boy.

"Nothing. What woke you? Your head?"

"There's someone's at the door."

"Is there?"

"I'll go and get it."

"No, Parker, wait—"

Lauren reached out and grabbed Rachel's arm. "Let him go. Help me with my trousers."

"I didn't hear the latch!"

"Where are my knickers?"

"I don't know!"

"Did you shut it behind you?"

"How long was he there?"

"Seconds. Milliseconds." Grabbing her trousers, Lauren lifted herself into the legs, stumbling forwards as she caught her foot on a section that was still inside out. "Oh fuck it," she gasped, falling to her knees.

"Who is it?" shouted Rachel.

"It's Uncle Trevor, Nana Rosemary and Grandad Ken."

Rachel gasped. "Shit!"

"Help me up!"

The voice boomed from the doorway. "Father, I rest my case."

Both women turned to look at Trevor, arms folded, a large art portfolio slung over his shoulder, flanked either side by his parents.

Scrambling for the button on her jeans, Lauren hauled herself up using the arm of the sofa. "What are you doing here?"

"We might ask you the same question," continued Trevor.

"Cup of tea, anyone?" Rosemary's hands were clasped in front of her body.

"No one wants a cup of tea, Mother. What we want is the truth."

"What truth?" asked Parker, squeezing past the three adults all squashed into the doorway.

Rachel moved forwards and put her arm around her son's shoulder. "Let's get you back to bed."

"Can't I stay up and watch?"

Trevor sniffed. "Is that what he usually does? Is that what he was doing?"

"Bed, Parker," said Rachel, pushing him past the group in the doorway.

Lauren glanced around, unable to focus on anyone or anything, until her eyes spotted her knickers, gusset upwards hanging from the edge of the coffee table.

"I've already seen them!" said Trevor, dashing over to grab the lacy underwear. He lifted the knickers between two fingers.

"Put the lingerie down, son," said Ken.

"It's more evidence."

"Of what?" asked Lauren, reaching out to swipe back her belongings. She missed.

"Ha!" said Trevor, waving them about in front of her face.

She grabbed again.

"Both of you, stop it." Ken's voice was firm. "If we're doing this, we're doing this properly."

"What? A game of catch the knickers?" Lauren realised it wasn't an appropriate comment, but what the hell did they want?

"He's down," said Rachel, re-entering the room. "Can I get anyone a drink?"

"A cup of tea would be lovely," said Rosemary.

"No one's having a cup of tea," snapped Trevor. "Everyone needs to sit down and listen."

Ken moved towards the sofa. "Let's give Trevor his moment."

"This isn't my moment, Father, and believe it or not I'd rather not be having a moment at all. But he was my brother and I owe him the truth."

Lauren shook her head. "Oh, Trevor, what is this? You don't have to listen to this, Rachel."

"Yes, she does. You've been in her ear for too long."

"We're friends, that's what friends—"

"And THERE'S the first lie!"

"Trevor!" snapped Rachel, stepping between the pair before taking a breath. "Let's just calm this thing down."

Lauren gasped. "You don't need to calm anything down. He's the one who's come marching in here accusing you of... what even is this, Trevor?"

"I'm not accusing Rachel of anything. I'm accusing you of—"

"Stop with the accusations." Rachel held her ground. "Trevor, you're right. You found us out. Lauren and I are in love. That's what this is about, isn't it?"

Lauren felt a sorely needed warmth as the hand took her own and she smiled as her fingers were squeezed. "You don't have to," she whispered.

"Shush, and Parker's fine by the way. I told him it was a thigh spot."

"Damn acne," muttered Lauren.

"You're admitting it?" spluttered Trevor, glancing around, momentarily lost for words.

"It's not about admitting anything. Rosemary, Ken." Rachel turned to her in-laws. "I loved your son very much, but two years have passed and I've come to realise that I see Lauren as more than my friend. She's my rock and I love her."

"Right. Well if that makes you happy, dear," said Rosemary.

Trevor swung his portfolio from his shoulder, slamming it onto the coffee table. "You've not seen this yet, Mother!"

"And she doesn't need to," said Ken with a sigh.

"You said we should come round!"

Ken continued. "They've admitted the truth."

"No they haven't!"

Rosemary frowned. "Where was I when you showed your father all this?"

"Making a cup of tea!" shouted Trevor.

"For goodness sake," gasped Lauren. "It's a school night. Parker's in bed. Rachel's told you the truth, so let's leave it at that."

Trevor sneered. "Not when you're the one lying."

"Excuse me?" Lauren watched on as a crumpled sheet of A4 was pulled from the portfolio and slammed onto the table.

"You've always wanted her." Trevor pointed at the scruffy handwriting with a jabbing finger. "Eleven instances of you wanting to kiss her. Eleven!"

"What's this, dear?" asked Rosemary, finally coming in from the doorway to peer at the list.

Trevor continued. "This isn't a recent thing, Mother, it's been planned over many years. Desire. Lust. Revenge."

"Stop it," said Lauren, looking to Rachel for support. "That's not even my writing."

"Yes, it is. Parker told me." Handing the list to his mother, Trevor nodded. "Read it for yourself. It says: Times I wanted to kiss you. It's underlined. There are eleven instances. They date back to before Toby was even around. He didn't stand a chance, poor chap. She even tried to lure him into a threesome."

"Why would I want a threesome with a vile man?!"

"You thought he was vile? Is that how it happened?"

"How what happened?!"

"Is that *why* it happened?"

Rosemary's voice was quiet. "My son wasn't vile."

"Oh, Rosemary, I know that." Lauren glanced to Rachel who'd taken a seat on the sofa. "Rachel, you know I know that. And I didn't mean vile like that anyway, I was talking about men in general. You know – figure of speech and all that."

"Getting ourselves in a bit of a fluster, aren't we? Were you flustered back then when my brother said no to your threesome?"

Ken coughed. "That's enough, son."

"It's not enough," bellowed Trevor, scrabbling into the folder and pulling out a photo. "She has her now, in the grasp of the alternatives. Four of them, openly kissing in Starbucks. It was obscene."

"You were spying on us?" Lauren was aghast.

"And it's a good job I was because poor Rachel here has no idea what she's getting herself into." He reached for the next photo.

"Rachel, you need to stop this." Lauren tried to ignore the show at the table. "You need to tell them about the list."

"We're well past the list now," said Trevor, banging on the next photo. "Here she is, being molested on a Positive-Purpose walk. An event designed to remember my dead brother."

Lauren looked at the photo that had been taken from behind. Her hand was down the back of Rachel's pants, the group of bird spotters clearly visible ahead. She squinted at the image. Admittedly, it didn't look great.

"How is that even slightly appropriate?" Trevor reached for another photo. "And worse, here they are kissing, with the group of children just meters away."

Lauren tutted. "There's nothing wrong with two women kissing."

Rosemary was shaking her head. "Oh, Rachel, at a PP session?"

Lauren waited for Rachel's response, filling the silence when it didn't arrive. "It doesn't look great, but—"

"But nothing." Trevor's voice remained raised. "You finally get what you've always wanted and then what?" He slammed the last photo onto the table. "History repeats itself."

Rosemary's gasp was dramatic. "Parker!"

"I caught him!" said Lauren, staring in shock at the photo of her godson mid-fall. It looked awful, captured just after his head hit the trunk, a look of pain and fear across his face, his body horizontal as his arms flailed at the air.

"Yes, Nana Rosemary?" said the voice in the doorway.

Rachel finally spoke. "Get back to bed."

"What's Aunty Lauren done wrong?" Parker started to cry. "Why's Uncle Trevor shouting at her? Is it the adult kissing?"

"He knows?" Trevor's voice was aghast. "You've exposed him to *this*? What kind of mother are you?"

"Stop shouting at Mummy."

"It's not your mummy, Parker, it's your Aunty Lauren. I'm shouting because of your Aunty Lauren. Tell him, Lauren," said Trevor. "Tell him what you did to his dad."

The little boy frowned. "What did you do to Daddy, Aunty Lauren?"

Lauren was open-mouthed. "Rachel?"

Rachel shook her head. "This is all so wrong."

Signalling to the table, Lauren nodded. "All this is wrong, yes, but what we've done isn't wrong."

Parker's tears flowed. "What did you do wrong, Aunty Lauren?"

"Buddy, you already know what happened. It was an accident."

"Wait," Trevor was frowning. "*What we've done?* You just said: *what we've done.*" He turned to Rachel. "You were involved too?"

Rachel shook her head. "I wasn't involved."

Lauren gasped. "You wrote that list!"

Rachel's voice was quiet. "You know what I mean."

"I'm not sure I do." Lauren shook her head. "Wait, you think I wanted it to happen?"

Trevor sneered. "That vile man standing in the way of your lust. Of course you did. You're happy it happened."

"What happened, Mummy?" wailed Parker.

"Oh, Rachel," sighed Rosemary.

Rachel shook her head in confusion. "I didn't want it to happen." She shook again. "I'm not happy it happened."

Lauren raised her voice. "And you think I am?"

Lifting her gaze to the photos, Rachel spoke slowly. "Aren't you?"

CHAPTER THIRTY

Two weeks later.

Standing at the back of the ceremonial hall in Farnley Castle, Lauren watched with bated breath. People seemed to be taking the seats they'd been allocated, even though it was very obvious that the old, infirm and ugly had been placed at the back and the corners, not to mention the fact that a seating plan for the actual nuptials was rather left-field, taking guests by surprise and causing the current sitting down, standing up, moving around and mumbled discussion. Nothing, however, about this day was going to be normal or usual. It had taken a manic final two weeks to get Camilla to the stage where she was fully happy with all the arrangements and prepared to walk down the aisle. Orders of service had been changed, flowers replaced and a whole new team of caterers brought in; but they were here and Camilla was happy. "You look lovely," said Lauren with as much meaning as she could muster. "I'll be sitting over there if you need me." Lauren pointed to the bench at the side of the room.

"Is Trudy there too?" asked Camilla, yanking her elderly father's arm into a different position around her own.

Lauren nodded. Trudy really had stepped up over the past couple of weeks, so much so that the brides seemed to be turning to her second-in-command as their first port of call, and while that had allowed her to skulk away from the weddings at the first possible opportunity it also further dampened her mood. On the one hand, she didn't have to see another happy couple basking in applauded contentment, but on the other hand she felt expendable and unwanted; exactly as Rachel had made her feel on that night.

Shaking herself out of her musings, Lauren moved across the back of the room, taking a seat next to Trudy. "The bride's in position."

"If we had headsets on you could have said that from over there."

Lauren felt Trudy's arm nudging her own. "What?"

"You used to laugh at my headset jokes, boss."

"Sorry."

"I know you're prepping me for partner and I'd love to tell you to go, but please, boss, don't leave me alone with Camilla today."

Lauren managed a smile. "Prepping you for partner?"

"That's my lady! Now, let's have some fun." Reaching into her bag, Trudy produced a small hip flask. "A must at every dry wedding."

"Put that away."

"You need a pick-me-up."

"I need to focus."

"You've been focusing for two weeks."

"On the wedding."

"It's all in hand."

"So I can go?"

"No!"

Lauren shook her head. "I'm not sure what's worse, seeing these two make it when I can't, or dealing with a potential gate-crashing from Sid."

"You *could* make it, boss, but you chose to walk away, and Sid's not that stupid."

"To walk away?"

"To turn up here." Trudy signalled with her thumb. "And if he does, you send him packing."

"Like I was sent packing?"

"You upped sticks all by yourself. Honestly, boss, you have to snap out of this. You're the one who walked away. You're the one who cut off all contact. You're the one who dropped her like you drop all your girlfriends. You're a pro at this, Lauren."

"At what? Salvaging what's left of my self respect?"

"Ghosting."

"What?"

"What you're doing, what you've always done. It's called ghosting. It's the practice of ending a relationship with someone by suddenly and without explanation withdrawing from all communication."

"No explanation's needed, and I'm still seeing Parker."

"You're sneaking to his school gates and watching him at lunchtime."

"He plays football, I cheer him on."

"He's your godson."

"And I'll be there for him."

"How? You're ignoring all contact with Rachel, you're placing me on look-out duty at the shop and you're making me answer all phone calls."

"People give up."

"She won't, she's not like your others."

"No, she's worse."

"Why? Because she got flustered after her son saw her face first in your fanny, then got knocked sideways by an onslaught from Trevor, then was faced with a question from her son who'd just seen her face first in your fanny, then—"

"This hasn't got anything to do with her being face first in my... You know what, Trudy? I don't even know why we're talking about this." Lauren hushed her voice. "Be quiet, they're about to begin."

"He was upset and crying. She was confused. Everyone's eyes were focused on her." Trudy glanced to the back of the hall. "Camilla will faff about for at least another five minutes yet."

"She let them think I wrote that list."

"What was she meant to do?" Trudy put on a silly voice. "Rosemary and Ken, I did love your son but I wanted to be face first in my friend's fanny for the whole time. Come on, Lauren, the pictures looked awful. She'd been accused of being a bad mother, her son was upset and she accidentally asked the wrong question."

"A question she knew the answer to, and how have you seen the photos?"

"I've heard it all a hundred times over, she won't leave me alone." Trudy paused as the wedding march began to play. "Please just give her a chance?"

"I gave her a chance when he fell out of the tree. I excused her behaviour then, but I won't do it twice."

"So that's it for you?"

"I'm fine," whispered Lauren. "I'm back in charge. I know what I'm doing with my life."

"And what's that?"

Jumping from her seat, Lauren growled. "Stopping Sid from ruining this wedding." Dashing around the area that Camilla had just vacated, Lauren reached the door at the back before it had time to swing open. She'd spotted Sid's face up at the glass, biding his time no doubt. "Don't you bloody dare," she breathed.

"But my Rig!"

"Is up there marrying Ian."

"She's not! She's paused!"

Lauren turned around to look down the aisle. Camilla was standing, hand on hip, towering over Ian's mother, Mrs Brennan, who had somehow managed to ditch her wheelchair and totter to the front at the exact moment Camilla had made her grand entrance.

"What's happening?" hissed Sid.

"Shush, that's Ian's mother."

"Why's she tapping her walking stick against the ground as if she's making a toast?"

Lauren kept her eyes on the action.

The old woman's voice was shaky but loud. "I have an announcement."

"Does she know about you two?" gasped Lauren.

"Maybe Camilla's told her? I knew my Rig wouldn't let me down."

Lauren watched on as the old lady made a cut-throat gesture to halt the music.

"That's better, am I loud enough? I know some of you are squashed in the corner. Bald Derek and Blind Nancy can you hear me?"

An apprehensive murmur rippled through the room.

"Wonderful. Camilla's father and I have an announcement."

Lauren gasped again. "Does he know too?"

Sid's smile was wide. "My Rig never does things by half."

The little old lady trilled. "We're getting married as well! Not today obviously, we'd never let anything get in the way of Camilla's big day, but we wanted to announce our official engagement!"

"Oh, Ma'mar, congratulations," gushed Ian, moving into the aisle.

Camilla threw down the arm she'd been holding. "Daddy!"

"Thank you, darling," said Camilla's father, using his new found freedom to creak onto one knee. "Mrs Brennan, would you kindly give me your hand?"

"Mother died a year ago to the day!" Camilla was pointing to the empty chair at the front of the aisle. "She's here! How could you?"

"Your mother wanted me happy." The elderly man nodded at the empty seat. "Didn't you, darling."

"She's not answering!" snapped Camilla.

"I doubt she'll eat any lunch either," added Camilla's father, "but you've got me paying for that too."

"Well, you both have my blessing," said Ian with a smile.

"Now for our tune." The old woman pulled a harmonica from her handbag. "Ask me properly then, handsome," she said, tapping her walking stick once more before blowing the first of many loud notes.

Camilla's father stayed on one knee as he started to sing. *"Daisy, Daisy, give me your answer do. I'm half crazy all for the love of you."*

Mrs Brennan continued to buzz away on her harmonica, raising her hand for the crowd to join in.

"It won't be a stylish marriage," murmured the guests.

"I can't afford a carriage," sung Camilla's father before the old woman shouted: "He can!"

"But you'll look sweet..." continued the sing-along, *"upon the seat..."*

"I have to go and save her!" gasped Sid.

Lauren reached out to stop him. "Look at her! She's moved under Ian's arm."

"Only because I'm not there!"

"She's not looked back once."

"Because she can't bear to watch the 1940s knees up!"

"Sid, you're a subplot."

"In Camilla's life? I'm not. I've come here to ask for her hand."

Lauren shook her head. "You'd never beat that *Daisy Daisy* proposal and you should never ask the question you already know the answer to."

"What?"

Lauren repeated herself. "You NEVER ask the question you already know the answer to."

"But I need to know."

"Look at her! Look at this! You do know! She chose him." Lauren nodded as the noise died down. "She's marrying him, Sid. But you knew that already, that's why you're here."

"But my Rig..."

"Has found someone who wants her," continued Lauren. "Goodness knows how and goodness knows why, but she has and they've made it. They're here. They'll get their happy ever after."

"And where does that leave me?"

"Same place as me. In that Raggy Dolls' reject bin."

"What?"

"Oh nothing. Do what you want, Sid. I'm going somewhere to think."

"But…"

Letting the door close behind her, Lauren turned and walked away from it all.

CHAPTER THIRTY ONE

Staring out across the expanse of scrubland, Lauren absorbed the vast emptiness before closing her eyes and starting to cry. She wasn't jealous or angry, just lost and alone. Lost and alone like she'd always been. Lost and alone like she'd always continue to be. Taking a deep breath, she wiped her eyes. This wasn't like her, she was strong and independent. Her head dropped again. Who was she kidding? That was just the front she presented to the world. No one really knew her, not even Rachel, because if Rachel had known her she'd have never asked that damn question.

Standing up, Lauren kicked at the boardwalk. Rachel was there. She'd seen it all happen. An outcrop of rocky boulders on one of their walks. A mutual challenge to see who could get higher. There was nothing to the story. Rachel was watching. She was cheering. A misplaced foothold halfway up and an awkward fall. Life-support turned off a week later. Lauren shook her head. How could she ask? How could she ask that ridiculous question?

"Please don't go," whispered the voice.

Lauren spun around.

"I heard you'd gone somewhere to think. And I know this is your thinking spot." Rachel signalled to one of the wooden slats. "See those marks? I've been here," the voice started to count, "sixteen, seventeen, eighteen times since that night."

Lauren shrugged. "Why?"

"Hoping to find you and this time I knew you'd be here."

"You spoke to Sid?"

"Sid? No, Trudy. I went to the wedding. I knew it was at the castle. It's in full swing by the way."

"Sid must have told Trudy."

"Sid was there?"

"Asking questions that shouldn't be asked."

"Like me you mean?"

Lauren shook her head. "Why did you do it?"

"Can we sit down?"

"I don't want to sit down."

"Okay, well nothing I say will excuse me, but I was staring at Trevor's picture of the four of us in Starbucks and I suddenly remembered you saying you could live with a secret." She paused. "And for that split second I was confused."

"You were there, Rachel!"

"I know, but I…"

"You what? You suddenly thought I swiped my foot to the side without you seeing, plunging Toby to his death?"

"Don't."

"Or you thought I was happy another human had died? He was my friend too, Rachel."

"Please, Lauren, don't."

"No, *you* don't. You don't get to do this."

"You don't get to do this either."

Lauren gasped. "Me? I haven't done anything."

"You've shut me out. You've treated me like every other meaningless girlfriend."

"It's because you mean so much that I can't live with this."

"This what?"

"This doubt."

Rachel shook her head. "There is no doubt. There's never been any doubt. I said the wrong thing. I was flustered and dazed, not to mention embarrassed; our behaviour was awful."

"It wasn't awful. It was made to look awful, just like you were made to question yourself. To question me. I want someone who'll stand up for me, Rachel."

"I told them I loved you."

"Then you asked if I killed your son's father!"

"I didn't ask that!"

"You asked if I was happy he died."

"Only because Trevor was—"

"I don't care what Trevor was doing. We fell at the first hurdle, Rachel."

"Well, I want to be the horse that staggers back to its feet."

Lauren huffed. "Even when that happens the jockey's left on the grass."

"Not always. We could be that horse that falls, but the jockey clings on and they both pull themselves up to finish." Rachel paused. "Was that a smile? You're imagining a horse on its knees with a jockey clinging onto the reins, aren't you?"

"They'd never go on to finish."

"They might."

Lauren shook her head. "I want to be left alone."

"You're done with being alone. I made a mistake and I'm sorry. I know you've been loitering around Parker's school like a weirdo."

"Says the woman who's been coming to a lonely lookout point and marking it up like a jail cell."

"You're the right to my wrong, Lauren. The plaster to my wound."

"I'm the one wounded, not you."

"You've dumped me! Royally! Your cold shoulder's like an Arctic front. I miss you and I love you and I want us to get to that finish."

"Our odds are 100-1."

"You love the outside bet."

"Stop trying to make me smile."

"I'll always make you smile. We make each other smile, that's what we do." Rachel sat down and patted the slats. "This is what happens in real relationships, Lauren. People fall out. They make mistakes. They upset each other. But guess what? That doesn't mean it ends. It means they try harder."

Lauren looked down at her friend. "But it hurts."

"And that's how we know it's real."

Lauren took a moment. It was still there, that uncontrollable pull, that desire to be close. She dropped onto her bottom, letting her feet dangle over the edge. Kicking out at a tuft of bracken, she took a deep breath. "I'm sorry if I hurt you."

"I deserved it," said Rachel, shuffling closer.

"You didn't."

"And neither did you. My silence that evening was inexcusable."

"You were shocked and confused. I should have seen that."

"I didn't know what to think. Parker was crying, Trevor was shouting, Rosemary was sighing." Rachel paused. "But I should have stayed strong."

"And I should have explained. You know I'm happy we've happened, but that doesn't mean I'm happy about what enabled us to happen."

"I know, I know, I know." Rachel shook her head. "I didn't mean to say it. I shouldn't have said it."

"And I shouldn't have left."

"I told them I wrote the list."

"The list meant nothing."

"Rosemary and Ken understand that now. They're fine with everything. In fact they've even told Trevor to stop with the photos."

"Of lost gloves?" Lauren managed a laugh.

"All of it. They apologised for his behaviour and have been desperate for me to pass their apologies on to you." Rachel smiled. "They want to see me happy, Lauren, and you make me happy. They've known that for a long time."

"So what do we do?"

"I've got a request."

"You do?"

"Stop kicking that plant and look at me." Rachel reached out and shook Lauren's leg. "Properly look at me."

Twisting around and shifting her gaze, Lauren finally focused on the beautiful woman sitting beside her. She smiled. Rachel had the sun on her shoulders and the expanse of possibilities as her backdrop. "You want me to kiss you?" she asked, feeling her hurt slowly drift away on the breeze.

Rachel laughed. "I do, but my actual request was for our next falling out not to last quite as long."

"There won't be a next falling out."

"There will. Life's not a fairytale, Lauren, but that doesn't mean it's not worth living."

"I want the dream."

"Sun, scenery, me by your side." The laugh was kind. "Pretty close isn't it?"

"I never realised I was so demanding."

"This is it, Lauren. This is our story."

Taking one final look at the emptiness around them, Lauren reached out and brought Rachel into her side. "Be the happy to my ever after?" she asked.

Rachel nodded. "My lovely, we're already there."

THE END

About the author:

Lambda Literary Award finalist, Kiki Archer is the UK-based author of eight best-selling, award-winning novels.

Her debut novel **But She Is My Student** won the UK's 2012 SoSoGay Best Book Award. Its sequel **Instigations** took just 12 hours from its release to reach the top of the Amazon lesbian fiction chart.

Binding Devotion was a finalist in the 2013 Rainbow Awards.

One Foot Onto The Ice broke into the American Amazon contemporary fiction top 100 as well as achieving the lesbian fiction number ones. The sequel **When You Know** went straight to number one on the Amazon UK, Amazon America, and Amazon Australia lesbian fiction charts, as well as number one on the iTunes, Smashwords, and Lulu Gay and Lesbian chart.

Too Late... I Love You won the National Indie Excellence Award for best LGBTQ book, the Gold Global eBook Award for best LGBT Fiction. It was a Rainbow Awards finalist and received an honourable mention.

Lost In The Starlight was a finalist in the 2017 Lambda Literary Awards best lesbian romance category and was named a 'Distinguished Favourite' in the Independent Press Awards.

Kiki was crowned the Ultimate Planet's Independent Author of the Year in 2013 and she received an honourable mention in the 2014 Author of the Year category.

She won Best Independent Author and Best Book for **Too Late... I Love You** in the 2015 Lesbian Oscars and was a finalist in the 2017 Diva250 Awards for best author.

Novels by Kiki Archer:

BUT SHE IS MY STUDENT - March 2012

INSTIGATIONS - August 2012

BINDING DEVOTION - February 2013

ONE FOOT ONTO THE ICE - September 2013

WHEN YOU KNOW - April 2014

TOO LATE... I LOVE YOU - June 2015

LOST IN THE STARLIGHT - September 2016

A FAIRYTALE OF POSSIBILITIES - June 2017

Connect with Kiki:

www.kikiarcherbooks.com
Twitter: @kikiarcherbooks
Instagram: kikiarcherbooks
www.facebook.com/kiki.archer
www.youtube.com/kikiarcherbooks

Printed in Great Britain
by Amazon